MW00572360

THE RUIN OF EROS

MAYA GRYFFIN

FIRST EDITION

For Pavol

One

The day is hot, the sun fit to split the stones, but that's not the reason for the beads of perspiration breaking out on the back of my neck.

"They're late." My father looks around impatiently, his thick soldier's hands on his hips. When he paces, it kicks up dust from the dry ground. It hasn't rained in Sikyon in many days.

"Where is Kiria Georgiou and that son of hers?"

Another bead of sweat trickles down the back of my neck. Our chariots can't take off until they arrive: Kiria Georgiou and her young son, Hector. Hector Georgiou is a vital part of today's great pageant—almost as vital as me.

Here in Sikyon we worship all the gods, like any good Greek: we place an icon of Hestia beside the fire, and one of Hephaestus outside every smithy, and pray to Eileithyia when a woman is in labor. But every town chooses one god to honor above others, one god with whom it has a special affinity, and whom it chooses to be its protector. Our town chose Eros. I think we have chosen well. Other cities may choose to worship Zeus, or the God of war, Ares, but in Sikyon we choose to worship the god of love.

Eros's temple stands above the village, high on a hill, and from the right vantage point you can see it from down in the Agora, towering golden in the sun or silver in the moonlight. On top of that, once a year we dedicate a festival to him: the *Erotidia*. This year's, though, is to be bigger, better, and grander than anything we have seen before. It marks the king's twentieth year of rule, and he's spared no expense to show his people a good time. The townsfolk are more than ready for the excuse to celebrate—it's been a hard summer with much work to be done, but the harvest is safe now and the year ahead looks prosperous. You can almost feel the exhale in the air, and the excitement of a long-promised party. I suspect many of our townspeople have been drinking since breakfast. They have a big day ahead.

Because this year, alongside the usual fare—singing, dancing, games, and sports tournaments—the king decreed a grand parade. A pageant, you could call it, to honor our patron god. As a rule, we don't pretend to be the gods, even in theater. We tell their tales, but mostly it's only the words of an old man by the fire, and only children play at reenacting them. But Sikyon will do whatever is required for the king's amusement.

Which is why right now I'm standing on the outskirts of town, breathing the hot dry air, preparing to get into a two-horse chariot and parade through the streets, dressed as Aphrodite.

Trying to convince myself that it wasn't all a terrible mistake.

Olive trees line the dirt road, drooping in the heat. It's probably just the sun that's giving me this twinge of headache and a strange sense of foreboding. I have this anxious feeling that we're playing with fire. The gods are harsh judges. Our performance had better be pleasing.

I walk to the front of the chariot and hold out a hand to the horses I am to drive. Father is a soldier, and although he is conservative about other matters, he was always keen that his daughters should know a little of the arts of war—so, unlike most of the other girls of Sikyon, I can shoot a little and ride a horse, even bareback. But I have never driven a chariot before. The Demous have loaned us two of their horses—white as shells, muscled and lean, and, hopefully, obedient.

Aphrodite, at least in theory, is only the second most important part in today's pageant. Eros, Aphrodite's son, is supposed to be the real star, and that's the part young Hector will be playing. But if we're honest, I know full well that Sikyon is more excited about seeing me in the chariot. There have been rumors swirling around about me, and I suppose everyone wants to see if they're true. What's more, it'll be the first good chance they get to gawk since my engagement to Yiannis Demou was announced a few days ago, which Father tells me has been the talk of the town. Everyone is turning out to watch the parade now, he says. The streets are empty here on the outskirts, but there'll be crowds waiting for us when we get near the center.

The blue skies seem to intensify, as though the sun is burning them to their true color. Ahead of me, the dozen chariots with other young men and girls from the town are already full: they are to play the part of Aphrodite's handmaidens and the young lord Eros's attendants. I've had enough sideways glances from them to know that most aren't best pleased at playing only handmaidens, having been passed over for the role of Aphrodite. I'd wager most of them aren't best pleased I'm engaged to marry Yiannis Demou either. As for me, I'm happy enough about the marriage. As for the role of Aphrodite…Father says it's a great honor, but the truth is, I didn't want to be chosen at all. For one thing, I've never exactly identified with Aphrodite. I prefer Demeter, the calm lady of the harvest, or in my wilder moments I might fancy myself as Artemis—fearless, barefoot, an archer running through the woods with her band of huntress maids. But I have never fancied myself an Aphrodite. The appointments were handed out by the king's council itself, though, and no one says no to the king's council, or would dream of turning down an honor conferred on them.

Across the way I spot the two figures hurrying toward us: Hector and his mother. I sigh with relief. I was beginning to think we wouldn't reach the temple before noon.

Yiannis Demou steps out of a cluster of youths nearby, ready to hand me up into the chariot.

"Steady," he says, to me or the horse, I'm not sure. His red-gold hair flashes in the sun, his tawny eyes taking me in like a meal. The chariot is high, and I'm not used to wearing such a delicate and cumbersome dress. In fact, I've never worn anything this fine in my life.

"Your mother has outdone herself with this gown," I say. Not that Kiria Demou made it herself, of course. She's far above anything like that.

"It's a shame you have to wear anything at all," Yiannis smirks. He gives me a sly smile. "Don't the legends say Aphrodite emerged naked from the sea?"

He helps me grip the bar of the chariot and arranges my stance. Then I feel his arm slide stealthily, quickly upward. His arms are long—he is Sikyon's fastest discus-thrower—and his fingers are probing the top of my thigh before I can draw breath.

"Stop it!" I say fiercely, lest anyone see him, but his hand has already disappeared again. As long as he's discreet, I don't mind too much. I would have shouted had another boy tried to do it, but Yiannis has a claim on me.

"Psyche," he murmurs, pleased with himself. The way he says my name, *sigh*-kee, sounds like a breath. The Demous are one of the wealthiest families in Sikyon, so Father is pleased. He says my looks have won the alliance. Father is a councilman. We have some status in the town, but we are not wealthy, and some people would say we have a questionable reputation. They like Father well enough, but my mother is not kindly remembered.

As for me, I am tired of the boys ogling me, tired of how they treat me like a heifer going to auction; as if my virginity is a prize they may compete for. A man's body, it seems, commands respect in this world, while a woman's may command only either lust or scorn, and I am ready to be rid of this virginity that has them all wound to such a frenzy. Once our wedding night is over, once Yiannis has claimed what is his, I know the luster will fade. They will lose interest then; I have seen it before when the girls of Sikyon become wives.

Dimitra says the ways of the flesh are only for men to enjoy. She says that a woman may use them for power, but not for pleasure. I hope she is wrong. I have heard other things, too, things whispered in undertones in the Agora, things that could never be repeated in polite company: that a woman may enjoy the bedroom just as much as men do; that there is an ecstasy in the body that can leave a woman transfixed. If there is, I should like to know it. It seems only a fair reward for the price I pay to carry this body around with me every day, for the stares, the leers, the "accidental" touches in the market-place; for the boys—and men, even acquaintances of Father's, married councilmen—that I know better than to be in a room alone with. I must watch all of them enjoy my body with their eyes every day; is it not right that I should enjoy it too?

But words like these, I would never speak aloud.

"Kiria Georgiou!" My father is calling. He waves impatiently as the harried-looking woman and her young son move toward us. Little Hector is a sweet boy, skinny-limbed and shy. Perhaps in a few years he will have grown more like the boys of Sikyon that I am more familiar with—full of cat-calls and knowing comments. But I think not.

"Here, boy, I'll help you up." My father has a limp from his fighting days in the Atlantean war, but it doesn't get in his way. He lifts Hector bodily into the seat beside me. Hector's robed for the occasion too, looking uncomfortable in his unfamiliar clothing. But he smiles at me as Father hands him up.

"You look beautiful, Psyche," he says shyly.

"So do you," I whisper, and he giggles. I catch my father's gaze then, briefly. His sun-wrinkled eyes, the quick pull of his lips to one side. I see pride there, and some sadder emotion I can't name. I wonder what he's thinking of—my mother, perhaps? He says I have a look of her. My father's olive skin bears the mark of years, but he is still a handsome man. Many women would have liked to take my mother's place after she died. It was unusual for a man like him, alone, to raise two young daughters, but he did it.

As for my sister Dimitra, she had no interest in coming to see me off. If she's here at all, she's gathered in the Agora with her friends, where the biggest crowds will be. Or maybe she's at home, ignoring all this. She doesn't like it when I get too much of the attention.

"It is very simple—see?" Yiannis holds the reins for me to watch. "Like this to go left. Like this to go right. And to slow them: so."

I glance at him, taking in his profile: strong nose, pale lashes, freckled cheekbones. He's handsome, the girls of Sikyon agree, and I like him well enough. He's better-behaved than some of the other boys in the town, the way they ogle and leer, the things they call out—Father says it's flattery, but I confess I do not feel flattered. Yiannis stares at my breasts like the rest of them but at least he pretends not to. Not like his friend Vasilis, who looks openly, lips wet, eyes like slits, small and unsatisfied. I admit, I question Yiannis's taste in friends, but I see no real badness in him.

But although I am ready to be married, I worry, still, what I will be made to let go of. In my father's house I have freedom for the most part. I love to work on the loom, but in the Demous' house only servants do such work. And at home, I still go out to the barn some days to practice with my bow and arrow, which I certainly won't have space for at the Demous'. It's just an indulgence, but I find it focuses the mind. Some days, days like this one, I wake up full of foreboding, as though some evil I've dreamed in the night might yet come to pass. It's been happening more of late. And then I go out to the barn, notch an arrow, inhale, release…it brings me peace, somehow, to see it fly true and hit its mark.

That is something I won't get to do under Kiria Demou's watchful eye. My future mother-in-law likes to have everything under her command.

There's a rustling and fluttering in the chariots ahead of us, people picking up reins, making last adjustments, waving to the family members that have come to see them off. It's time for us to begin.

"Ready, Hector? Don't fall over." I glance over at my father's proud face, and then to my left, where Yiannis is already joking with Vasilis and his other friends. Vasilis's eyes fall on me and I turn away with a shudder.

The carriage ahead of us takes off with a jerk.

"Go!" I say, and the whip cracks in my hand.

Here goes nothing.

Two

Our town must be one of the handsomest in all the Peloponnese, or at least that's what I believe. I have never gone further than Corinth and that was only once, with Father, but I think it is hard to imagine a landscape I would like better. From up here, in the mountains, sometimes it feels like you can see the whole world. The winters are harsh enough, but the summers are gentle, and in spring anemones grow everywhere in the fields. Most people with some status live in the center of the town but Father likes it further out, where we are. There, the red-gold roofs of barns and farmyards shine in the sun, and the sound of pigs and cattle and now and then a rooster pierces the air. In the early mornings all you hear are birds. At night the sky is so deep a navy it looks black, and the constellations burn.

And far down below, at what looks like the very bottom of the world, you can see the sea. Father says it is the same color as my eyes.

The streets that lead to the Agora get wider as we approach, and soon a handful of onlookers becomes dozens. The streets look different from my perch on top of this high carriage, looking down.

"Slow, you stupid beasts, *slow*," I mutter anxiously, tugging on the reins the way Yiannis showed me. Hector and I are the last carriage in the parade. Ahead of us, the others represent the sea and the heavens, the *polis* of Sikyon, and the nymphs that attend Aphrodite as handmaidens. But since we are last, I must work the hardest to keep our horses from charging forward—otherwise we will all tumble into each other like a handful of marbles.

I think how Dimitra would laugh at that.

It is only the three of us: father, Dimitra, and me. My mother died when I was born, and it was the birthing of me that killed her. She gave me my name before she died. They say it was the last word she uttered. Psycheandra: *soul warrior*. Dimitra scoffs at it. You see, my mother was not Dimitra's mother: my father has lost two wives now. The first, Dimitra's mother, was a local girl, born and bred in Sikyon as Father was. It was no great love-match, I think. He was a military man, frequently away from Sikyon on some campaign or other, and the business of finding a wife had been long postponed. When he reached the age of thirty, however, he came under pressure from his family, and Dimitra's mother was found. But then, only a year after Dimitra's birth, he returned from his latest military campaign to learn that a great sickness had come to Sikyon while he was away. Dimitra's mother was one of many to perish.

He left Dimitra with his sister, our aunt, and went back to the front to fight again. This time the war he went to was the great Atlantean war. It was supposed to be over in months but lasted two whole winters. When he returned from Atlantis, he was a decorated soldier and a married man: he'd brought an Atlantean bride home with him.

You might think that both having lost our mothers so early in life, Dimitra and I would understand each other better. You might think we'd be closer. But that's not exactly true. We *were* close, once, but no longer.

My sister was an angelic-looking child, highly praised for her prettiness since infancy. She never had an awkward stage, even in those years of puberty which afflict so many young women. Meanwhile, as a child, I was not considered noteworthy: my neck was too long, my hands and feet too big, my arms too skinny, my eyes a little too large in my childish face. But a strange thing happened the summer of my fourteenth year: I began to be beautiful. I say this not to boast—on the contrary, it worries me. They say my mother was beautiful, and because of it none of the women in the village liked her. Even the midwife was late to attend her labor. I try not to wonder whether it would have made any difference, had she been on time.

Dimitra has stayed as pretty as she ever was, but the gossip in town began to change after I became beautiful. They say I have now surpassed my sister, that I began to outshine her years ago. Dimitra knows it, and hates me for it. Meanwhile I fear the townspeople have lost the run of themselves—Sikyonians love to exaggerate—and when they have finished comparing me to Dimitra they start to compare me to others. Fairer than Persephone, goddess of spring, they say. Fairer then the goddess of dawn, Eos. Father reports the things he's heard with pride, and I worry he has become indiscreet. I worry that he's let it go to his head and boasts of it.

Gods are jealous creatures—look at what happened to Medusa. People think she was born with a head full of snakes, but that's not true. Most monsters aren't born, they're made. You'd be surprised how many of them used to be human once. Beautiful humans, most of them. But it doesn't do to be too beautiful.

The houses get grander as we make our way down the main street, toward the Agora, which is the assembly-place for the whole town. Twice a month there is a great market there, and every day it's where the men congregate to talk, drink wine, and agree on the great things they have done for the city. This long building we're passing now is where the Council sits, and behind it, raised up on a mound and decorated in blue and red and gold, is the king's palace. But that's not where we're going today.

As we move into the Agora, the murmur of the crowds becomes a roar. I don't envy the job of the first chariot in the parade, having to carve a path through them. Sikyonians get like this on festival days: transported, euphoric, over-excited. It's a combination of alcohol and hemp-flower, heat and crowds.

Fights will break out before nightfall, I'm sure of it. But right now, they're roaring with delight. Roaring for us.

"Wave, Hector," I encourage him. It's Hector, as Eros, who should be drawing the bigger cheers today. But I can see quite clearly, it's me they're looking at. Hector doesn't seem disappointed: he's a sweet boy, and looks mesmerized by the crowds. Some of them throw roses, and he reaches out to catch them.

"Careful!" I say under my breath as I wave and smile and try to keep all this pearly fabric from billowing out of the carriage and under its wheels. "Thorns, Hector."

But he's already found out his mistake, and drops the stem from his grip with a cry of disgust.

That's roses for you. No wonder they're Aphrodite's flower.

Beauty always has a sting in the tail.

"Do you hear?" Hector says, and I look down to see his eyes wide in admiration, staring at me.

"Hear what?"

"The people." He looks proudly at me. "What they're saying.

Aphrodite, I hear the crowd murmuring. The murmur grows in a wave, bigger and bigger. The children are on their fathers' shoulders, cheering. I think some of the small ones must believe I'm the real Aphrodite, their eyes are so big, their faces so dazzled and euphoric. Even some of the women look quite overcome, dabbing at their eyes; some even bow and curtsy as we pass. I had thought to face some hostility out here, families who wanted their own daughters chosen for this day or for Yiannis Demou's hand, but it seems everyone is content to stare and murmur—or cheer, or weep. I want to remind them that it's all just silly pageantry. I don't want my fellow citizens to forget, even for a moment, who I really am: just a local girl, Councilman Andreos's daughter, nothing more.

"We all knew you'd be chosen," Hector says proudly, turning my way. "More beautiful than Aphrodite herself, that's what my father says."

"Hush, Hector!" I resist the urge to clamp a hand across his mouth, and feel a cold breeze wrap around my neck. Such words are dangerous. At least Hector's were lost in the shouts of the crowd, and no one heard him but me. I just hope his father and others like him have not been too indiscreet.

I do not mean to be ungrateful, if it is as Father says and my beauty is a gift. One should be grateful for gifts. But I wonder if it is not so much a gift as a simple matter of accident. Perhaps gods scatter beauty among humans the way a handful of grain is scattered among chickens, with no meaning, no intent. Or perhaps the intent is amusement: to watch the chickens peck and fight, making chaos over what the gods have strewn.

Beauty is a currency like any other, I suppose—and for the most part, it is the only currency a woman has in our world. With it we can buy things: some security, perhaps, or a little independence. A husband; a house of our own to run. Sometimes we can buy a little respect. But sometimes it feels as though I am nothing but a face; nothing but my limbs and breasts and hair. Nothing but what they see. Whether I am good or brave, righteous or deceitful, my face can tell you nothing of that. Sometimes I feel I would like to peel back my skin and see inside of myself. Sometimes I wonder, if I were ugly, would I have figured out more about who I really am by now?

But I wave and smile, wave and smile, as we pass through the Agora. Here is where my new charioteering skills need some extra help, as we parade in a circle around the center for all the crowd to cheer. I wonder how many hundreds of people are here. Perhaps a thousand or more. It smells of sweat and scented oils, mint and oregano, and alcohol. I look for my sister's face but don't see it. The reins slip a little and burn my hand, but at least the horses don't bolt. The burn on my hand is nothing. I am a fast healer; it will be gone before tomorrow, and stings only a little. I'm more concerned about my dress, which I have to tug at to keep it inside the chariot—it's so long, I'm worried about it getting caught under the wheels and pulling me with it.

The dress *is* beautiful, though I would have preferred to be the one creating it, instead of the one wearing it. Father says my mother had a great talent at the loom, and the one she used still sits in our house, in a little room where no one hardly goes but me. I think if I'd been born a man, I should have liked to be a great artist—a potter, perhaps—but instead, as a woman, I may weave: that is *our* way of storytelling. Of creating.

The dress I'm wearing now, though, was not made by anyone in Sikyon. Yiannis's father, Kirios Demou, is a trader, and imports the most exquisite fabrics: this dress is made from the sheerest, finest linen, woven from flax imported all the way from the Egyptian lands, dyed in the most exquisite blues and golds, and fastened with gold brooches. I've never seen anything like it: so gauzy, so light, so ethereal. Surely when Aphrodite emerged from the oceans in a gown of sea foam, this is indeed how it would have appeared. Tiny pearls stitched into the gown catch the sun like beads of rolling water. No expense must have been spared.

A woman grabs my hand and kisses it. The impulse seems to start a trend as others follow suit. They mean no harm, but my skin crawls as another pair of lips presses against my hand and I hear the murmur of *Aphrodite* grow in another great wave. Surely they understand I'm only here to honor the goddess, not to be honored myself.

I see the king watching in the middle of the square, raised up on a palanquin of red silk. I can't see his face but I hope he's pleased with the spectacle. If he's not, we'll know it soon.

It's a relief when the cheers reach their peak and the parade leader gets the signal to move on. Now we must draw our chariots around in a final circle, then out of the Agora and up the mountain pass to Eros's temple. We carve our way slowly out of the square and through the last street in town, which gives over to a steep uphill path. I flick the reins now to nudge the white horses forward, following the chariots ahead of us as we slowly begin the ascent.

The white rocks kick from under the horses' feet as we climb up the steep mountainside. It's high summer, and my hands slip a little on the reins, so sticky are they with sweat. Flies buzz. Hector plucks at his outfit: they've dressed him up in a suit of gold, and it looks much heavier than my sheer frock, poor boy. The crowds are behind us now: they will follow on foot, carousing already, until they reach the temple. Instead of the awestruck murmurs of the crowds, now there is the sound of flies buzzing, and from back in the town, the yapping of dogs travels on the wind. Heat comes up from the ground, washing over us. Hector pants and wipes his brow.

"It's too hot! I need water."

I wish I had brought some for us. My headache is stronger now.

"Soon we'll be out of the sun," I promise. The crowds following us on foot won't be bringing water, though: they'll be bringing wine, barrels upon barrels of it, four men to a barrel, hauling them on stretchers to the foot of the temple. When we get there, one of the priests will call the gods' attention and dedicate the wine to them, and then our king will break the first cask and everyone will begin their merry-making.

It's going to be a long night. At least Hector and I and the other performers won't be expected to stay past the opening ceremony. Men's hands become freer the more they drink, I know that by now.

Then one of the horses stumbles, sending a rush of rocks cascading down the hillside behind us. Sweat prickles my neck as I grab the reins hard. I feel like those rocks—precarious, unbalanced, much too near to the precipice. Then the horse shies, kicking, and I fear for our chariot; it could easily lose a wheel here. We bounce hard, and Hector is flung back; I grab him by the collar, keeping the reins in one hand. A wind blows through the dusty air.

"Are you all right?"

He pants and nods, and climbs back onto his feet.

"Hurry," he says. "We'll be late."

And indeed, I can hear the crowds on foot close behind us, and ahead, the chariots are all but out of sight. I breathe deep, the hot summer air thick in my lungs, and flick the reins again. *Eros, watch over us,* I think. I'm not much given to prayer usually, but the feeling of foreboding is strong today.

And then the horses round the last bend, and the temple looms before us in all its fearful splendor, high as twenty men and brilliant in the sun. I try to shake the feeling that something in there is watching me.

Three

I don't know how many pillars make up the temple, but it is certainly more than a thousand. Perhaps many thousands. Now in the sun, it glows like fire, the most imposing thing I've ever seen. They say that some gods spend all of their time on Olympus and hardly venture into the mortal world, while others like to reside in their temples from time to time. I think that if I were Eros, I would like to live in this temple. It is a sacred place. Even on the stillest mornings they say a wind tears through here, like a herd of wild horses galloping.

"Shade at last," I say to Hector. "Perhaps the priests will have water for you."

For the priests are starting to emerge from the temple. Their gold and white robes shine in the sun, and the High Priest and High Priestess lead the way. They move easily, although both of them are blind. Whether they were born blind or suffered some childhood illness that left them so I do not know, but it has always been this way at the temple. They say it gives them better vision for the realm beyond ours. When I was little, I was friends with a girl who was blind. I am told she is one of the young priestesses here now.

The priests descend the steps slowly, a dozen of them moving in elegant formation. Our carriages are all drawn to a halt, waiting. The temple stands on the crest of the hill, ringed around by olive trees and rows of vines, its painted marble bright against the green and yellow land. It smells of rich earth here, and of wine.

The crowds behind us are close within earshot again now, laughing and ready for the party. I turn around and search the crowd, just now emerging over the rocky summit. There's the king in his red palanquin—I don't envy the servants who had to carry it up this hill. There's Yiannis and his parents, and that horrible Vasilis. Even from here I feel I can see his watery eyes on me, fixed on the parts of my body where they shouldn't be.

There's my father and, behind him, her pretty face pulled into a bored pout, Dimitra. Tall, thin, beautiful, her dark hair shining in the sun. A cheer goes up as the king reaches the foreground of the temple and joins us, and the crowd surges up behind him.

And now two priests are leading out the white bull they have readied for the sacrifice. It gleams in the sun; they have washed it and anointed it already. All the way from Crete, a gift from the Demous for the temple. After the sacrifice, the bull will be roasted and all the people of Sikyon will eat.

As the bull is led out before the crowd, the cheers intensify. The bull is held fast by a rope around its neck. I see its heaving breaths; I can feel its agitation.

The other charioteers are starting to dismount. I see some of them look back toward me—mostly the girls, mostly with dislike. They hate that I was chosen for this. But two priests are walking across the foreground toward our chariot: Hector and I have one last piece of the pageant to fulfill, now that everyone's in place.

As if by magic, Yiannis appears beside me and takes the reins.

"You were magnificent," he murmurs in my ear, his voice a purr. "Now go—your crown awaits."

This is the last piece of the pageant. Hector and I will come forward, and the priests will crown us each with a wreath of white roses. Then we'll stand with them for the sacrifice.

It's a shame to get blood all over such a dress.

My stomach roils, but I tamp the feeling down.

"Come on, Hector," I take his sweaty young palm in mine.

There's a strange energy in the crowd behind us and around us. It's the same energy that was there before, but in this holy place it feels amplified. There's a hunger in the air, a hot desire like wolves on the hunt. There's a rumbling around us, and the crowd breaks out gradually into a chant. It starts as a murmur and grows.

Aphrodite.

Aphrodite!

Aphrodite!

It is as though something has taken them over. When I glance around at them, it scares me a little. Somehow it feels as though *I* am about to be sacrificed and not the bull.

They are shouting Aphrodite's name, but it's me they're looking at—not at the temple, not at the statues and paintings that adorn it, not at the marble figure of Aphrodite placed in the olive grove next to that of Eros.

I kneel, pulling Hector down beside me. I feel the eyes of the crowd as the priestess approaches us, two crowns in her hands. I just hope they removed the thorns.

She looks to the crowd, and then down at Hector, who's beaming with anticipation. A shadow crosses over her face, and it sends a chill through me. She leans forward and places the crown gently on his head. Cheers erupt behind us. Then she turns to me.

I meet her gaze, although something in me is afraid. I don't know why. She studies me for a moment.

"So, this is the face they say is more beautiful than the goddess herself."

I do not think she is making fun of me, or even reproaching me. If anything, I hear something like regret: the voice of someone who knows it's too late to change what has already been done. She looks at the single wreath of white roses that remains in her hands, and then out toward the crowd. Then she sighs, and lowers it onto my head.

I feel it settle, but barely have the time to notice its weight, because something is happening now in the sky. That breeze I felt earlier: it's back, but now it's more than just a ribbon of cold around my neck. It's like a wall of damp, freezing air, and out of nowhere the sky has turned a roiling grey. A minute ago there was not a single cloud; now it could almost be nightfall.

The white bull paws at the ground; the horses shy and whinny. I feel a hush go over the crowd, a moment of uncertainty. The king hesitates, then steps forward. There is a script to be followed. Storm or no storm, he means to proceed.

"Great Aphrodite, Great God Eros," he intones. "In your honor we bring this snow-white bull, and the best of our season's wine…"

But his voice trails off as the wind whips louder, drowning him out. There's no doubt of it now: this is no ordinary storm. I look at the priestess, but she won't meet my eyes. The crowd's nervous murmuring breaks into shouts.

"The gods are displeased," a townsperson says.

"We must hurry the sacrifice!" calls another.

The murmuring is a rumble now. The townspeople are staring at me, but not as they stared before. The wind does not whip around *them* like this. It punishes only me.

My hair flies in wild hanks around my face and I try to claw it back from eyes, but it's entangled in the crown of roses. The wind howls once more, and then I scream in pain as the crown, with my hair still knotted in it, is wrenched from my scalp as if by a mighty hand. Beside me Hector gasps as the crown sails through the air, losing rose petals in a flurry as it wheels around, then collides furiously with the steps of the temple, falling in a heap on the dusty ground. I put a hand to my stinging scalp.

"Your daughter, Andreos!" someone shouts. "What is this? What has she done!"

And that's when lightning splits the sky.

There's a blinding light, then a high shriek, humans or animal, I can't tell. There is a terrible, searing sound, then pandemonium, and when I can see again, here is what I see:

The white bull is dead.

It lies on the ground, charred, a circle of scorched earth all around it. I'm too shocked to cry out. I stare at the circle of earth and the bull's body inside, and I know it beyond a shadow of a doubt, as everyone else must too: this is the work of the gods.

Four

Someone faints; others are shouting. In the chaos, suddenly my father is by my side.

"Psyche, come away." His voice is strained, as if he, too, has been shouting. He sounds ill.

I let him lead me through the crowd. He throws his cloak over me, but despite the chaos people spot me as he shepherds me through.

Curse is the word I hear then. *Cursed.*

For a moment I think some of the men will try to stop me, seeing the wild look in their eyes as Father steers me past, but something holds them back. They don't want to touch me.

I stumble as we reach the edge of the crowd.

"Psyche, what did you *do*?" a voice hisses.

It's Dimitra, her green eyes wide with alarm. Or is it anger?

"We're going home," my father says firmly. Small rocks skitter as we hurry down the mountainside, as if we can escape what just happened.

As if we can escape the hand of the gods.

*

I watch from upstairs as Yiannis's father, Kirios Demou, arrives to our house—no sign of his wife, though, nor of Yiannis. The look of his short, stocky frame has never inspired fear in me before.

I hear the door open, then close; from downstairs comes the sound of men's low voices, much too somber. My father and Kirios Demou are used to laughing together, patting each other on the back as successful men do. But not today.

Since we arrived home and locked the doors, Father's been

saying how it's all a great misunderstanding, how the town overreacted to what was simply a bad summer storm.

But I know it's more than that.

When I creep downstairs I hear quiet voices coming from Father's study. I move toward the door to listen, but Dimitra comes along the corridor, beating me to it.

"What's going on?" she hisses, grabbing my arm. Her hair is wet: she usually dries it out in the atrium, flung forward in the sun. It is a lengthy procedure that happens once each week, and I know she must be very concerned by Kirios Demou's visit to have abandoned it.

Father would be outraged to find us listening at the door, but everything is different now. We press our ears against it and hold our breath.

"It cannot be helped." Kirios Demou's voice is slightly muffled. "You know well, Andreos, that I have done everything to maintain my family's good standing in the eyes of the gods. We tithe our profits and our harvest. We are godly people, and Yiannis follows in our footsteps. We cannot risk everything, after decades of right-living. It is not for me to say what Psycheandra has done to so offend the Divinity, nor is it for me to judge..."

But from the smug tone of his voice, I know he *is* judging, and enjoying it.

"...Though the word is," he goes on, "she has compared herself most brazenly to Aphrodite. Parading around like that, as though she were the goddess herself and not a mere actor. I regret to say it, Andreos, but I noticed it myself, the girl's grave absence of humility." He pauses. "All I know is that we can't have our family—our only son—mixed up in it. I do regret this, Andreos. It would have been a good alliance, and she was a most pleasing girl."

Was. He speaks of me as though I were dead.

I swallow, and glance over at Dimitra's dark eyes. So my marriage to Yiannis is not to be. My brain turns around the thought like a slow carriage-wheel. No more of those bright eyes, those warm hands, that smooth, teasing voice. No more of those approving looks from Kirios and Kiria Demou when they pass me on the street; there will be no newly built home for us on the Demou land, with my own linens to choose and my own kitchen to run.

In theory I am back on the market, but who would have me now, after the Demous' rejection? Last week Father could have married me off to any family in town. Today, it seems I am a pariah.

Women who stay unmarried here may go to live in a sister's house, or a cousin's, where they have little status, helping to tend the sleepless infants and taking on the more thankless tasks, halfway between family and servant. Is that to be my life now?

There are those, too, who stay unmarried by choice. Those who have refused to play by the rules. The town has a label for each of them: witches, freaks, or whores. What they all have in common is that they are not afraid of the townsfolk; it's the town that's afraid of them.

But you have to be brave, to live that way. I doubt I am so brave.

"You must see," I hear Kirios Demou's voice again. "It cannot be helped. I only hope that the town's judgment will not be harsher."

I have not heard Father say a word this whole time, though I can picture his face—that stormy look he gives you when you're saying something he dislikes, that gets stormier and stormier until you feel you might lose your nerve completely. But then he speaks, and it shocks me. His voice is not stormy at all. There's no anger, no righteous indignation.

"Kirios Demou..." There's a tremor in his voice. Who is this man; where is my outraged father? Dimitra stares at me, her eyes wide like mine.

"...I cannot pretend this comes as a shock. I will not ask you to reconsider. But can I ask you to delay any announcement a little longer? I confess, I am fearful of what may come next." He sounds almost pleading.

"For my sake and my daughters', sir…it is important that the Council see we still have friends and allies. Just until the worst of this has blown over…"

Dimitra pulls away abruptly, the blood drained from her face. She doesn't look at me, just runs along the corridor in the direction of the kitchen. I'm torn—do I stay, and wait to hear more?

I swallow hard, and follow down the corridor after my sister. I find her in the kitchen, pacing between the empty vats and stoves like a madwoman.

"Never mind, sister. Perhaps I shall make a good spinster," I joke, or try to. I thought it might make me feel better. It doesn't, but it certainly gets Dimitra's attention. When she looks up at me her face is furious.

"You don't understand, do you?"

I stare at her, trying to figure out what she's so enraged about. *I'm* the one whose future is being ripped apart.

"The Council," she spits. "What do you think Father's so scared of? Hmm?" She drums a finger against her temple as though I'm slow-witted.

Perhaps I am. Because it's only now that I'm wondering what exactly Father meant by *what may come next.* He's afraid of something, and Dimitra is too.

"You think Father will lose his seat on the Council?"

Dimitra looks wild-eyed.

"You think *that's* the worst that can happen, Psyche? The way Father cossets you, I suppose I shouldn't be surprised you still think like a child!" She pinches the bridge of her nose, closes her eyes.

"Expulsion, Psyche," she breathes.

Banishment.

"They will turn you out upon the roads."

Five

I feel my blood run cold. Ostracism is not common, but it happens. It may be used as punishment, or to restore justice, or for protection. To end a blood-feud, for example, a town may make the sons of feuding families *ostraka,* outcasts. It is like a death, in a way: the families mourn for their *ostraka,* for they know they will never see those faces again. Towns may practice it, too, if a member of the community has badly offended the gods.

"They wouldn't do that," I say, my voice unsteady now. The truth is, I have no idea what our town would or wouldn't do. I saw how quickly their minds changed about me today, in the space of a few moments at the temple.

"Dimitra," I say. "I must find a way to appease the goddess."

Because there's no doubt in my mind which god had a hand in the events of today. The words of the priestess are seared into my mind. *So this is the face they say is more beautiful than the goddess herself.* Sikyon has boasted of me, boasted much too highly. I remember Hector reporting what his family had said. *More beautiful than Aphrodite.* They were just stupid words, but they can't be unsaid now. And though I never spoke them, it seems I'm the one being held responsible.

I'm the one who will have to appease her.

But Dimitra looks at me as though she's unsure whether to laugh or cry.

"You think you have the ear of the gods? What are you going to do to change Aphrodite's mind, little mortal girl?"

I ignore her, pacing back and forth. There must be something.

Humility.

Humiliation.

"My hair," I say slowly. My sister stares.

"Dimitra—will you shave it for me?"

She blinks. For a moment her shell cracks; I swear I see her eyes moisten.

"Your hair? Psyche..."

I know what she's thinking. In our culture, a woman's hair is her great pride. To lose it is a tragedy. Of all the things people praise me for, even above my face or figure, it's my hair. *Like a cornfield,* Father says. *Like spun gold,* Kiria Demou used to say, when we paid courtesy visits to their mansion by the Agora.

Women's heads are shaved only as a great punishment. A man may shave his wife's head, for example, if she is caught bedding another. The time it'll take to grow my hair back from bald as a chick to past my shoulders, will cement in everybody's minds that I am an outsider, unmarriageable, unlucky.

But I can't worry about that now.

"Come, Dimitra, get the shears."

*

I admit it: the shearing hurts more than I thought it would. Not physically, of course. But as Dimitra hacks through it, haphazardly as a sheep-shearer, and it falls in rough hanks around my feet, it's as though I'm saying goodbye to my childhood. The summer Dimitra took me to the river for the first time, when my hair floated around me in the water, my face upturned to the sun. It's the hair that Father braided when I was a child, and which Dimitra taught me to pin up once I was a child no longer. The hair that I am told looks so much like my mother's.

When Dimitra hands me the large bronze mirror to see her handiwork, I'm speechless. Who is this waif? My eyes look too large for my face, all hollowed out. The tufts of hair that remain here and there make me look ill, the victim of some disease. I barely recognize my own face.

And yet, there is a strange, bitter euphoria to it all. I've lost years in a matter of moments and for the first time I have an inkling of how oddly freeing it can be, to get rid of something you have loved. It's a hot, bright sort of grief that makes me feel almost powerful.

"Now the razor," I say, because bald means *bald,* not just shorn.

"Psyche..." Dimitra hesitates again, and I love her for it. But she does what I ask.

When she's done I run my hand back and forth along my scalp, watching the little flecks of hair come free like dust, falling softly, tiny gold snippets cascading to the floor. Dimitra stands with the shears still in her hand, as though afraid of her own handiwork.

"It's all right," I say. "It's what I asked for. Here, give me a scarf."

She takes the one from around her shoulders and hands it over, and I knot it under my chin. We both start at the sound of footsteps on stone, and when the door opens, we stand there like fearful children., watching Father's expression turn from heaviness to shock. His eyes roam over the floor and the hanks of hair that lie there. Kirios Demou is behind him—I had thought he would have taken his leave by now, but instead he steps closer, his eyes narrowing, curious.

"Gods' teeth," Father says quietly. "What is this?"

I feel Dimitra's hot breath beside me.

"*Kori mou,*" he turns to me. "My child...show me your head."

When I unknot the scarf and let it fall, my father clamps his hand across his mouth. Behind his hand I hear the slow exhale of breath. Even Kirios Demou makes a startled noise. I must look truly wretched.

"Daughter...what have you done?" Father turns to Dimitra.

"What have you done to your sister?"

"I asked her to do it," I say quickly. Father has always been quicker to blame Dimitra than to blame me, though I hate to admit it.

"The town says the goddess is displeased with me; they think me vain. But now they will see I am not vain. Aphrodite herself will see it. I will go to the temple and show her."

Even though it was not my transgression, I don't add. I hope Aphrodite can't see deep into my soul. She might notice that I blame the townspeople for all this far more than I blame myself.

Father closes his eyes. I can't tell whether he's upset, angry, or relieved. Then he opens them.

"Come here, child," he says, and I cross the room, feeling the hanks of fresh-cut hair under my feet. They are soft, softer than corn silk. Father draws me to him and runs a hand over my scalp. I feel the bones in my head as I have never felt them before, so close to the skin under the touch of his hand, the inside of me feels almost visible. It is as though everything I once was is burning away. The mask is gone. Maybe soon I will begin to know who I really am, without this thing the world calls beauty.

"Your eyes," he says. "They are so large, now." He pauses, identifying a spot on the top of my skull where Dimitra must have nicked me with the blade. "Here, you're bleeding."

"It will heal," I say, and take up the scarf once more. "I'm going to the temple, before it's dusk."

Father stares at me a little longer, and then slowly, turns to Kirios Demou.

"My daughter is brave. But I have a better thought. We will return with her to the temple tomorrow—the Council can accompany us. Don't you think, Kirios Demou? Then they can see in person how deep, how sincere is my daughter's humility. They will see that any..." he hesitates. "Any divine offense, is no longer."

He says nothing of my future in Sikyon: how my denuded

head means any remaining suitors will disappear too. But of course he knows it, he's known it from the moment he entered the room.

Kirios Demou runs his eyes over me again. It is a cold look.

"I will tell the Council," he says finally, and Father breathes a sigh of relief. He escorts Kirios Demou to the door, with one last look in my direction.

"Dimitra," he calls then. "Sweep up the hair."

And Dimitra grabs a broom from where it hangs on the wall, and scowls as she tosses it my way.

*

In the morning there is a freshness to the air, a smell of almond blossom on the breeze. They perfume brides with that scent, but no one will perfume me with that now.

The king himself has joined us; his carriage was waiting when we reached the council building. I don't know whether to view that as a good sign or a bad one. I suppose it confirms Dimitra's words: this is a serious matter. Father hoped yesterday to sweep it under the carpet, to attribute what happened at the temple to hysteria and weather, but if anything, today shows us just how much wishful thinking that was.

The weather is the same as yesterday's, the views as we climb toward the summit and the temple are the same, but all I can think is how different it is—no crowds, no cheering, no wine and songs. Now the people of Sikyon are holed up in their homes, passing gossip back and forth.

Gossip about me.

I saw the people on the streets as we set out this morning. They did not know who I was at first, not under the scarf, which only old women wear—but then they caught sight of Father and Dimitra, and they knew. That was when their eyes widened and they plucked at their neighbors' sleeves to whisper.

If we'd had relatives in another city, perhaps Father could have sent me there—but we don't. Father's people have been Sikyonian for generations, and my mother, from Atlantis, was an orphan. We're at the mercy of Sikyon and its king.

"Don't dawdle, child," says one of the councilmen, rousing me from my daydream.

The priests have had no word we were coming. Only one of them is out raking the olive trees, catching their fruit in a bucket. The rest must all be indoors, out of the heat, attending to their holy duties. The young priestess looks surprised when she sees us, but instead of picking up her bucket and hurrying indoors, she pauses only a little while before resuming her work.

"Kneel, *kori mou,*" Father whispers, and I do. One of the councilmen makes his way toward the priestess and speaks in a low tone with her, while she looks from one to another of our group and nods. Then she goes inside the temple, and reappears flanked by more of her kind. The High Priestess is with them, her blind eyes turning my way as if by instinct.

"So you wish to address the goddess?" she says, drawing near me. "Then speak, child." Her voice is scratchy, rasping in the deep summer air. I kneel, looking around at the councilmen and the king, unsure how to proceed. Will they kneel, too?

But instead they step backwards, leaving me alone in the center of a semi-circle. Is it my imagination, or is the air already a little cooler; are there clouds in the sky that weren't there before?

I look at the old priestess again, and summon my voice.

"Glorious Aphrodite," I say. It's not the goddess's ears I'm worried about reaching—if she's listening, she won't need me to shout. It is said the gods can hear a fieldmouse scurry in the grass. But the councilmen need to hear the sound of repentance in my voice, if all this is to work.

"Glorious Aphrodite," I repeat. "To you, none can compare. I come to humble myself before you. In the shadow of the gods, we are nothing. Now see before you my bare head, shaven of its former adornment, as I seek to atone for any vanity, any offense caused." I loosen the knot of the scarf and lift the night-cap underneath. But something doesn't feel right.

Hair, long flowing locks of it, tumbles down my back.

Six

I gasp, and I'm not the only one. I hear Dimitra's voice to my side, and my father's; even the king speaks in an angry murmur.

I shake out the nightcap as if this is some prank—as if yesterday's shorn hair could somehow have been placed inside the cap while I was sleeping—but there's no prank. I reach a trembling hand up to my head to verify what I already know. I rake my hair between my fingers, holding it in front of my eyes. If anything, it is brighter than before. It shines between my fingers like gold.

Cursed gold.

"It cannot be! I saw it myself! With my own eyes!"

"I cut it with my own hands!"

"Kirios Demou…" My father turns, appealing for another witness. But I see him, Kirios Demou, backing away slowly, his cold eyes on me.

"I demand to know the meaning of this." The king's voice is tight with anger that has not yet erupted. He won't tolerate being made a fool of, no king would.

"An outrage!" one of the councilmen says. "What do you take us for, girl?"

My thoughts are whirling too fast, like a child's spinning toy.

"I cut it off myself," Dimitra says staunchly. "It must have grown back in the night. It is the gods' will."

"Don't lie, girl," a councilman growls.

"She—she's not lying," I murmur. In the moment's silence that follows, my heart pounds.

"If it's not a lie," another of the men says, "then the girl's a witch."

Then even he stops speaking, because the birds in the trees have gone quiet, and something unearthly is in the air. The king, surrounded by his retinue, looks from one face to another as though they can give him answers. I lock eyes with Dimitra, who looks furious with me and also with everybody else.

"Renounce her."

We all turn. It's the High Priestess speaking, and yet it is not her voice. The voice that speaks from her mouth is young, not old, and it is beautiful. It's like a voice from in dreams; the moan of the wind and the rush of a river. Each of the men drops to their knees at the sound of it.

"Renounce her," the voice says again, and I feel my heart leap in fearful agony.

"Offer her to me, and I will show your people mercy."

My father stares at me, wild-eyed, then prostrates himself on the ground.

"Great Aphrodite! You would not take my daughter from me? Goddess, no offense was meant!"

But the voice is silent. The water-roar slowly fades. We are alone once more. The king's men look at each other, eyes wide.

"We must…we must seek forgiveness." My father's words fall over themselves. "Perhaps…perhaps some great tribute…"

"The time for tribute has passed." It's Kirios Demou who speaks. "The gods' will is stone. You have heard Aphrodite's will. Do not imagine that you have the power to change it."

"Get up, witch." One of the men jerks me roughly to my feet. My father's hand goes to his sword, then so do the other soldiers'.

"Peace!" the king roars. "There will be no bloodshed here." The color has flooded from his face and his voice is shaky. He looks toward the sky, then meets my eyes. I don't like what I see there.

"The goddess has been merciful," he says. "Despite great offense, she has offered us a path to atone."

"At my daughter's expense!"

"Hold your tongue, Kirios Andreos!"

The other men mumble amongst each other, and there is nothing gentle in the sound. A few steal glances at me.

"The gods do not ask your permission, Andreos, for what they choose to take." The king glances my way again. "They will have their pound of flesh either way; you will not flaunt their will or mine. You have one daughter left, old man. For her sake, do not anger me or your gods further."

A great coldness seems to have taken over my body. *Offer her to me.*

They mean to sacrifice me.

My father's voice reaches me from far away.

"There must be something we can do."

"What you can do"—Kirios Demou's voice cuts in—"what you *will* do, is what the king demands."

The king is staring up toward the temple, his eyes on its soaring columns.

"We will take her to Aphrodite's Pillow. The offering will be made at dawn."

*

Back home, Father bolts the front door and tells the servants to stand guard. My heart has not beat normally, I think, for hours. If I let myself think about what just happened, my mouth dries up so that I can barely swallow.

Offering.

Aphrodite's Pillow is a place further down the mountain, almost halfway to the sea. It is a rock formation, a sort of tabletop jutting out over the water below. They say in the olden times sacrifices were offered there, back when these lands worshipped the Titans; back when they did not only slaughter bulls and sheep for the gods, but humans, too.

I close my eyes. I have retreated upstairs, leaving Father and Dimitra to argue below. How can it all have come to this, and so fast? They say the gods are merciless, and yet I never thought to suffer like this—to suffer for something I haven't done, something that was not my fault.

How quickly Sikyon went from singing my praises to calling me a witch. But I suppose I should not be surprised. Dimitra says they called my mother a witch, too, even though she married and produced a child, did the things a woman was supposed to. Even though she wore her cloak of respectability well. She dallied with herbs and potions, I am told, and did not mix with the neighbors. Her biggest sin, though, was to marry my father when other women of Sikyon wanted him for themselves. No one objected to a soldier bedding a foreign girl when he was off at the front, but to bring her home, *marry* her? Witchcraft, they said.

And now they say it of me.

"Gather your jewels, Psyche." Father appears in the doorway to my room, his face seeming to have aged years in a couple of hours. "I have told Dimitra to do the same. I will see to our other valuables. We must take as little as possible. Only what we can easily carry."

"What are you talking about?" My voice shakes.

"Father says we are to sneak away from here in the night." Dimitra appears behind him, her voice hard as glass. "To become *ostraka* of our own making."

"To save your sister." Father turns to her. "Would you have it any other way?"

Dimitra turns away, but I know what's running through her mind. *Ostraka* are unlucky. By many, they are considered untouchable. She will lose everything. The money from our small packs of valuables will not last long. We will become vagrants.

I don't want this future for her. I don't want it for my father.

I nod.

"I will pack." But once Dimitra's withdrawn to her room

and my father's gone back to his study, I go to find him. He's hovering over a tray of valuables: a small icon made of gold; a signet ring of his father's; a knife with a jewel-encrusted handle that belonged to my mother. A strange heirloom, but the only one she had, Father says. He used to take it out and show it to me sometimes, if I begged hard enough. But he never let me touch it. *Too sharp for little fingers,* he would say. I wonder if he thinks we need weapons, now.

"What if Kirios Demou is right?" I say. "Aphrodite has issued her demand. Aren't we just trying to fool the gods by running away?"

Running away doesn't work when it's the gods who are after you. I know that much from the old stories, and Father should too. He's the one who told us the stories.

He doesn't meet my eyes, just stares down at the tray in front of him before finally shoveling everything into a satchel.

My father is wealthy because he is powerful; he is powerful because everyone here knows him. How would he manage, how would he ever support us, if we had to start from scratch somewhere new? Dimitra and I have never been taught a trade, we would be useless to him.

"*I* will run," I say. "I'll leave. Tonight. But you and Dimitra can stay here, and be safe."

"Do not ask me to give you up," he says, and his voice has a tremor in it.

"Even for my sister's sake?" I say. It is a cruel question, but I must make him see. He must protect her too. "Think of the life you will subject her to, if you force this on her."

He shakes his head fast, like a swimmer ridding his ear of water. He does not want to hear me. He does not want to see.

"We will leave together," he says. "All will be well."

I pause.

"Father…"

No one has asked me for the truth about my hair, and what happened today at the temple. Father and Dimitra both saw it for themselves. They know there was no trick to it.

"You saw what happened at the temple," I say. "It was not right."

He smiles nervously, his eyes still not meeting mine.

"It's not the time for that now. We will seek answers later."

"Father…"

"Psyche, *go*." He blinks fast, his voice tight with agitation. "Pack your things. Hide your jewels under your robes. Do as I say."

Upstairs I do as he bids me—it does not take long—and sit before the window, waiting for the dusk to turn to darkness.

I have no explanation for what happened today, but if I'm honest, it's not quite as out of the blue as it might seem. Certainly, *this* hasn't happened before. But things—other things—have happened. Like when I was fourteen and scalded myself with boiling water, but the burn was gone by morning. Or the time I fell dismounting a carriage and felt the bone go under me. Then the next day, when I could walk easily again, everyone said it must have only been a light sprain. And why not? It was the most reasonable answer. I was healthy, I was lucky, I healed a little quicker than other children. Certainly no one spoke of miracles.

But now I wonder if instead, we should have spoken of curses.

Night falls, midnight comes and goes. Father keeps us away from the windows, and warns us to be quiet, to keep our activity from the servants' notice. It's an hour before dawn when we tiptoe to the door. Father has some twine and sheets of linen; he plans to wrap the hooves of our horse, Ada, to muffle them before hitching her to the carriage. He looks at the large cowhide bag Dimitra has dragged out from her cedar chest.

"We take nothing we can't carry on foot." He takes the bag from her and leaves it by the door. I feel Dimitra fuming silently. One more indignity; one more thing I have deprived her of.

"Ready?" In the darkness, Father looks from one of us to the other, his eyes hooded by shadows. I nod. Dimitra says nothing.

"Good. Then go silently to the stable. Dimitra, you first. Then you, Psyche. I'll follow."

The night is velvet, the deep darkness of the pre-dawn hours. We step out into it, but my feet are barely on the flagstones when I hear a sound.

A clearing of the throat. Polite. Male.

I look over and there they are.

Yiannis and Vasilis.

Seven

I don't understand at first. I even take a half-step toward him. I'm thinking he's here to say goodbye, to tell me he loves me and will love me forever.

But of course that's not why Yiannis is here. Another glance at his face—afraid, unhappy—is enough to tell me that. And besides, where Vasilis goes, trouble follows.

"*Khaire,* family of Andreos," Vasilis says in smirking, formal tones. His eyes rove over me in the usual way, then he turns to my father, who's breathing hard beside me, heartbreak in each inhale.

"Kirios Andreos," Vasilis goes on, "you are early. The king bade you bring your daughter to the rock at dawn, and it is more than an hour until then." He glances smugly at Yiannis.

"He also bade us escort you, just in case you needed any…encouragement."

"Psyche—" My father's voice cracks. But he has nothing left to say.

It's Dimitra who turns and whispers, loud enough for me alone to hear.

"I can hold them off—for a little while, at least. Ada's waiting in the stable. If you move quickly—"

I place a hand on her arm. Father trained her well; her hand-to-hand combat was always better than mine, and no man of Sikyon would expect a woman to fight them. She would have the advantage—for about thirty seconds.

"It's done," I say. "We had our chance."

But we didn't. We never had a chance at all.

*

We go on foot. Father walks in the middle, Dimitra on one side and me on the other. The boys follow behind us like wolves following sheep. When the wind turns I can smell the mint pomade Yiannis uses for his hair. I don't turn to look at him. I think the sight of him now would sicken me.

The path down toward Aphrodite's Pillow is steep and curving, hugging the windward side of the mountain. The air buffets us as we walk, harder the closer we get. Eventually a smaller path splinters off to the left, leading toward a rocky cliff face that juts out high above the sea.

This part I had not expected: the people.

There are so many of them.

"She is here," a voice says, and a murmur spreads.

So many faces. I can't tell by their expressions what they're thinking, or hoping for. Do they want me to run? Do they want me to die? They are here early.

Perhaps they just wanted a front-row seat.

Some are faces that I know—the Demous; little Hector's mother; our neighbor, old Lydia; some of the girls I used to play with in the Agora when we were young. And many faces I don't know, who've come to stare, too. It feels familiar, that narrow-eyed stare that so many of them turn on me. I learned it well enough back when I was considered a beauty. Now that I'm a freak, the stare is not so different after all. I tell myself to keep my back straight, my head high. I think if my mother were here that's what she'd do.

And there's the king, in his red silk litter, with guards around him. Guards! As if *I* could harm *him*. They must really believe I am an unnatural creature.

They are afraid, I realize.

Of course they are afraid. They're caught between the gods and their own conscience.

"Psycheandra, daughter of Andreos." It's the head councilman who speaks. His voice is full of self-importance, trying to disguise any fear or doubt.

"You have come here to fulfill the will of the gods. Aphrodite has summoned you, and you have obeyed."

It's Yiannis and Vasilis who obeyed, I'd like to point out. *I* wanted to run.

I think of Prometheus, the Titan who was punished by the gods. He was chained to a rock where he was doomed to die daily, making his immortality a punishment. At least if I die today, it will only be once.

There is a metal stake driven hard into the rock—the strongest of the men must have done it—and a long chain fastened to the stake. The chain is for me.

I shiver. There will be no king's executioner today. Instead they will shackle me, and leave me here to the gods' will. But what that means in practice is that I will most likely starve to death. A king's man will be stationed here to stand guard.

The crowd leaves a great space around the stake so that the spot where I am to stand looks almost like a stage.

A stage where I am to perform—because what is all this if not a performance? A performance of power. Of strength. Of cruelty.

The *auskalos* piper has arrived. It's considered an honor to have the king's own mourning-piper, but all this theatre of grief feels like a mockery. The way all the onlookers have donned their darkest robes—it doesn't fool me. Some are here to grieve, yes, but mostly they're here for their own satisfaction. To thank their lucky stars that they're not in my shoes, I suppose; or to congratulate each other for being more virtuous than me. It must be comforting to think that all those who are punished deserve it. I suppose they may even think Aphrodite will thank them for their offering.

"Shame on you," Dimitra mutters. "Shame on all of you."

I don't tell her to forgive them. Some among this crowd suffer with us; some do not.

"It is time, Psycheandra," says the councilman. I look toward him and at the king, who has descended from the palanquin to stand behind him, but the king doesn't look me in the eyes today.

"Be well, Dimitra," I say, and squeeze her hand briefly. "We may yet meet again. Do not assume the worst."

Dimitra's face closes over. She doesn't believe it, and I don't blame her. I don't exactly believe it myself.

I turn to my father next. He shakes his head, looking at my hands as he clasps them.

"Forgive me, *kori mou.* Tell your mother to forgive me."

I see the red rims of his eyes, and the shame written there. In that moment I realize he never really expected his escape plan to work. He knew we'd end up here all along. All his packing and preparing was just something to do; a way to keep the truth from sinking in. A way to distract us all.

"Look after Dimitra," I say.

"It's time, girl," the councilman says again, growing impatient. I hear a faint hiss leave Dimitra's lips. She loves me in her way, and she loves my father and her own dignity. I can feel the fury in her, the rage at seeing our family treated with contempt.

A thickset guard moves toward me. I stare him down, and turn to the king.

"I will go of my own accord. I have no need for your show of force."

I walk across the large open space to where the stake and the shackle wait. As I go, a hand reaches out and briefly clasps mine. It's little Hector's mother. Her eyes are full of pain for me, and I almost lose my nerve. I can't allow myself to feel her sorrow now, still less my own.

"Great King." My father drops to one knee. "I beg you, show mercy to my daughter. She had no intent to offend. She is but young."

The king wets his lips. I can see the guilty conscience he carries, as surely as if it were a fog around him. But I know what he'll say before he opens his mouth.

"If it's mercy you want, Kirios Andreos, pray to the goddess."

And yet if Aphrodite had wanted to strike me down dead, or cause the earth to cave beneath my feet, she could have. She does not need my countrymen to act for her. She's just doing what gods do: testing her power, testing how afraid we mortals are. Seeing what that fear will make us do.

Well, she has her answer.

In the east, the darkness is starting to lift. Threads of grey criss-cross the sky. Far on the horizon is a sickly little hint of light. Above us, the ravens are beginning to leave their nests. They fly out from the rock face, single shapes darting out from the shadows. Ravens aren't like crows. They fly alone—solitary birds.

Wise creatures. A crowd does not protect you.

Your own tribe will not protect you.

The thickset man steps toward me, and fastens the shackle around my ankle. I feel the cold metal; I feel the click that signals no going back. He withdraws, and I try to breathe.

The councilman clears his throat.

"You make this offering, Psycheandra, daughter of Andreos, as penance for the offense to the goddess…"

Suddenly the anger is boiling in me. How dare he?

"It is *you* who did this," I say, and hear an intake of breath through the crowd. I let my eyes travel over them one by one.

"People of Sikyon, it is you who praised me, who compared me as no mortal should be compared. *You,* not I, spoke the foolish words. You made me something for the gods to destroy."

My flood of accusations surprises me almost as much as it surprises them. Until now I'd been feeling a strange sort of calm, but listening to this smug, spineless councilman has unleashed the rage of injustice.

I never tried to be more than what I was.

I told them not to speak so foolishly.

They made a god of me. And now they make a monster of me.

There is stirring and murmuring; they hear me clearly, despite the wind, and they are affronted. I am supposed to be humiliated, after all. I am supposed to be below them now.

"Disrobe her."

The councilman speaks, and I whip my head around toward him. *Disrobe*? We shear our animals when we offer them to the gods, but…

"A sacrifice must be without covering or adornment." The councilman's voice is stony. He wants to humiliate me now. This is a reward for my impertinence.

"Disrobe, unless you want my men to do it for you."

He's afraid. They have decided I'm a monster now, and monsters are reviled but also feared.

I think about refusing—I feel strangely bold now, bold enough for anything—but suddenly it doesn't matter much. What use has modesty now? It is only a custom among mortals. Something I'll soon have no more need for.

I take off my cloak, unfasten my *chiton*. A girl scurries up to me at the councilman's behest, and gathers the garments into a small pile. She looks at me with a wordless stare and backs away.

My breasts sit against my skin, and I look down at my body, the wonder of it. Is this what it takes—the brink of the unknown, the brink of death—to see ourselves this way? Suddenly I understand why the boys and men of Sikyon, and a few of the women, too, have fought like dogs over me. I understand their hunger, their need to put their hands on me. My body is beautiful—as all mortal bodies are.

I never saw it this way before.

I take a breath, and draw my head up. The waves are lashing at the base of the cliff, so very far below. Now the *auskalos* pipe is reaching a crescendo, its chilly drone seeming to grow with the wind. Or maybe it's the wind itself that's getting louder.

"The light," I hear a voice in the crowd. "See the light, how strange it is!"

They're right. There's a greenish tint to the sky, one that does not usually belong to the dawn hour. And the more I watch it, the more it seems to grow.

The wind whips the rock face and the crowd cries out, clutching their cloaks about them, clutching their children as if they might blow away.

"Is there something in the water, Mama?" one of the children is saying.

He could be right. It looks choppier than usual, and right here, below the cliffs, it seems to be turning darker.

I think about what's coming next for me.

If it's death, I have lived virtuously, no one can say otherwise. Hades may house me in a good place, and surely I will see my mother again.

The crowd is jittery now, people glancing fearfully around at each other. The piper has abandoned his song. The wind is too high; some of the children look as though they truly could get swept away. And the sky seems darker than before. The green light is still there, but it's as though the dawn has regressed: instead of rising, the sun has vanished again, as if Helios himself does not want to see what is to happen next.

"There! In the water—did you see something?"

A boy of maybe twelve moves closer to the edge, craning his neck to look down, but as he does a wave smashes against the edge of the rock. The spray hurls upwards in a great torrent, easily the height of five men; the boy's mother shrieks. Her son is on the ground now, clawing at the wet, slippery rock—just a step from the cliff face.

"Get back! Get back, everyone!"

The wind roars even louder, and people crouch down before it. Some are shouting; some screaming. Their fear breaks in a wave.

"Run!" they call.

"People of Sikyon, repair to your homes." The head councilman tries to speak, but even I can barely hear his voice, so buffeted it is by the wind. It doesn't matter. People are running anyway.

"We have honored the gods' will. We leave our daughter Psycheandra to their mercy."

No one hears his words; they're all vying to get off the rock. I feel a strange stillness inside me.

The thought comes to me that soon I will be alone, more alone than I have ever been in my life. I turn around to watch the crowds go.

I look for Father and Dimitra. There they are, being escorted into the king's own carriage. Bile turns in my stomach. It is not their fault, but the king should be ashamed of this charade—pretending that there is some honor in what has happened today, as though my father were parent to a soldier, or a martyred hero!

"Steady!" I hear someone call. The king's horses are in a frenzy—the stampeding crowd has managed to get ahead of the carriage.

My father is shaking, they have to lift him in. But even as they lift him, he doesn't look back. Dimitra does, though.

She is the last to leave, the last to see. Her face turned toward me is white in the dim, her eyes furious and bright, unblinking. Her hair bats and whips in the wind, and it is she who reminds me of a goddess now: a goddess of vengeance.

And then the carriage moves off, and they are gone.

And I am alone.

I throw a prayer up toward the dark skies. They say the shades cannot intercede for the living, but how do any of us know?

Mother, whatever is to happen, let it be quick at least.

The waves smash, the green tinge deepens.

And then a shadow falls across my vision, a shadow

darker than the darkness. A figure is walking toward me.

A stranger in a dark cloak.

A man.

Where he came from, I can't say. He has appeared, somehow, out of the storm. Despite the howling of the wind, the crashing of the waves, all I hear is silence as he moves toward me, the black hood draped over his face, falling all the way to his chin. I can see no part of him; even his sleeves fall over the place where his hands should be.

And I know exactly what he is. What he must be:
My executioner.

Eight

I catch my breath.

He is tall and shrouded in darkness, the cloak whipping around him like a storm within a storm. I feel my heart seize, and I force myself not to shy away or shut my eyes.

"She does mean to kill me, then."

The cloaked man stops in his tracks. Perhaps he had not expected me to speak; his cloaked face turns, as though surprised.

"The goddess?" he says. "Yes. She means for you to die."

His voice is deep and low. My heart pounds so hard I can't hear the ocean, or the screaming of gulls, or of the wind. It pounds so hard I feel I must bend double to keep it in my chest. Before me on the ground lies my robe, trampled and discarded. I pull it around me; I will have what dignity I can. But still when I speak, it takes everything I have.

"And you are here to do the job." At least I stand upright as I say it. I may be shackled and alone, but I will not let the gods see me cower.

The black fabric of his cloak shimmers—it moves like black light, finer than any fabric I have ever seen.

"No. I have not come to kill you, Psyche."

I stare at his hooded face.

"You know my name."

"I know many things," he says. His voice is resonant and calm. It matters little to him what becomes of me.

"You are some kind of messenger, then," I conjecture. "You are here to bring me to some worse place."

"I am not." He pauses. The hood shifts again. "What if I told you there was a way to escape this?"

I stare at him. Perhaps he is no messenger of the gods after all, and merely a fool. Some tramp or vagrant too senseless to run with the rest of the crowd.

"So, you carry the keys to this upon your person?" I say, showing him the shackle at my ankle.

He sounds impatient now.

"That is not the problem. The problem is that you have attracted the eye of Aphrodite, and the mistrust of your town. If I were to release you, where would you run? Home?"

With that, he has my attention. He's right. Even if I could escape right now, there could be no return to Sikyon. The neighbors would report me; Father and Dimitra would be punished too. *One way or another, they will have their pound of flesh.*

"And when Aphrodite hears you have run from her," the stranger continues, "do you think she will stop looking?"

I swallow.

"Once the goddess has her eyes on a mortal, there is little hope of concealing yourself from her. This darkness around us—you see it?" He gestures. "How the dawn has retreated even as the sun was due to rise? This unnatural darkness hides you from the eyes of the gods. But it will not last long."

I stare. Who is this man, and what does he know?

"While it lasts, that is our window to save you. There is a place I can take you, where you will remain sheltered from Aphrodite's sight. It is..." He hesitates, and the fabric of his cloak ripples softly in the wind. "It is a veiled place. You will be safe from her there."

I breathe shakily. He is a madman, he must be.

"I do not believe you. This *veiled place* you speak of, it does not exist." I have been taught well enough that the eyes of the gods can find us anywhere.

Beneath the hood, he stiffens.

"Do not believe me, then," he says. "It is not for me to cajole you. But I warn you—you do not have much time."

He turns toward the horizon, and I see the greenish glow

there has thickened. Churning ripples pool at the base of the cliff. I stare at them.

"Then you know what comes for me?"

"I can guess," he answers.

I force my breath steady. If this man is not to be my executioner, then surely whatever's in the water is.

"If you *could* do the things you say, sir"—I look at him, amazed at my own boldness, or stupidity—"what would you ask of me in return?"

I know perfectly well that no offer of help, particularly such miraculous help such as this, comes without strings.

The dark cloak seems to shimmer. His voice is measured, dispassionate.

"Obedience," he says.

A chill goes through me.

"This is what the women of Sikyon swear when they wed, is it not?"

I stare back at him.

"And why do you speak of weddings, sir?"

His head tips to the side, hinting at impatience.

"Aphrodite has already put her claim on you: there is but one way for me to unseat that claim. Wed me, and her claim on you must sit second to mine. That is the only way for me to offer you safe haven."

I'm speechless.

"I—I cannot *marry* you, sir!" This faceless, black-cloaked stranger!

But he sounds almost…*amused*?

"You need not be so horrified. You would offer me some companionship, that is all. I will make no demands of your body. In fact, I demand very little."

"Just my obedience," I mutter—I do not forget that word so easily.

"Your obedience," he agrees. "Though I say so myself, it is a fine offer, when you consider…" He throws a glance once more toward the cliffs, and the shadowy water. Beyond him, the sea is choppier. The light pulses.

I shake my head. This outrageous proposition...My mind flashes to the wedding I was supposed to have: riding in a carriage to Yiannis's house; feasting; my family there beside me.

"But sir...who are you? *What* are you?"

The hood shifts.

"I cannot tell you."

I stare at him, incredulous.

"What do you mean, you cannot tell me?"

"I mean it is forbidden."

"But...it is impossible." It is madness even to contemplate it. "You hide your face from me. How can I trust you?"

I feel him looking back at me from beneath his hood. He shrugs.

"How can you not?" he counters. "It cannot be helped. The bargain must be made. If you wish me to take you from here, it must be so. Decide, Psyche. Your time has all but elapsed."

As he says it, something lashes out of the water, something otherworldly. A tentacle of sorts—but far too big to belong to any octopus. I smother a cry of horror. When I recover enough to look back, the stranger's head is inclined to one side. Studying me.

Waiting.

"This...this marriage, then." The very word seems unreal. "It would not be...physical?" My whole body seems to flush as I say it.

"Nothing will be forced upon you."

"And what... tasks would you have me perform?" I can't help thinking back to that word, *obedience*. It's true, it's in our vows back home; I would have had to swear as much to Yiannis. Only now do I realize how sinister such a vow can be.

"Very few," he says dryly. "I do not seek a servant."

"So what, then, would you have me obey?"

"The rules of my home," he says, impatience clipping the edges of his words now. "Designed to protect us both."

No: I must be mad. The very thought of it—yoking myself to this stranger who comes from the darkness…

"Even if I were to accept," I say boldly, "there could be no true marriage. There is no temple here, there would be none of the holy rituals." In our land, marriage requires many things. Without these things no union can be sealed; nothing would hold either in the eyes of the gods or of the people.

He waves a hand. "We have no need of those things. Do you know so little of the Old Laws?"

I don't know why, but at those words another shiver passes through me.

"I have never heard of the Old Laws."

"So much is forgotten," he says, as if to himself. Then he turns back to me. "There are laws which are older even than the gods, Psyche. Laws which even the gods themselves must yield to. All we need do," he says, "is bind your words."

My words. I look back down at the sea, at its churning green. The tentacled thing is submerged again, but I'm not fool enough to believe it has gone. As for the man who stands in front of me…no honest man need hide his face. My words, it seems to me, are the only thing I have left.

But what choice do I have?

"Very well," I say. "Bind them."

He doesn't hesitate. He steps toward me…and then away. He's walking to the path that led me here, toward the scrub and vegetation that grow scantily on this forsaken spot, a little ways from the cliff edge. When he comes back to stand before me, he's closer than he was before. He's taller than I had realized. There is a scent of him: of incense, of the woods at night. And there's something in his hand—a peach. One of those shriveled, wild peaches that grow here by the rocks, stunted and dry.

Involuntarily I take a step back.

He holds out the fruit to me, a shriveled, salty thing. His

hand is the first part of him I have seen uncovered. It consoles me a little to see that there is nothing fearful in it. On the contrary: it is bronze in color, large and strong, not monstrous.

"Take it," he says. "Eat it."

I stare at the withered little fruit in the center of his palm.

"Your time is almost over. I will not wait for you, once the beast comes." He plucks the peach from his palm and holds it up for me to see.

"Under the Old Laws, I must make you a gift of food. In offering it, I bind myself to you. In accepting it, you bind yourself to me."

He drops it into my palm and from sheer instinct my hand tightens around it. It's warm from his hand.

Could it be poisoned? Or perhaps one bite will trick me into something worse—will fasten me to some more dreadful fate than any I have yet imagined.

"Isn't there some other way?"

He folds his arms, not deigning to answer. The rock beneath me shakes as something—something I dare not imagine—smacks the side of the cliff with its mighty limb. My hands shake; the peach slips. I fumble and catch it before it hits the ground, and down in the water I see another flick of a scaled, greyish tentacle.

I raise the peach to my lips, thinking of all the reasons I should not bite into it. One above all stands out. *No honest man hides his face*.

I bite the peach.

*

An explosion of gold floods my eyes. My knees buckle. This sensation…I cannot call it taste. I feel it everywhere, my mouth, my throat, then flashing through my blood, to every thread of my being. It is exquisite and voracious. It is a tortuous kind of hunger.

More, I think blindly.

The euphoria spreads through me, feeding its own desire like a snake eating its own tail. I feel it in the tips of my fingers, the soles of my feet; down my spine, tingling in the pit of my stomach.

I open my eyes, breathing hard.

More.

I raise the peach to my mouth for another taste, but a hand closes around my wrist.

"That's enough."

I wrench at my hand, trying to free it. "Another bite!"

But he lifts the peach from my fingers and smoothly tosses it toward the cliff. I bolt, my whole body yearning after it, but the chains yank at my ankle and pain rips through me. The force pulls me to the ground. I wheeze with the impact as a few feet away, the peach rolls over the edge of the cliff.

If I hadn't been chained down, I might have thrown myself into the sea after it.

"It was enough." He speaks from behind me.

My breathing starts to quiet.

"What was that?" I pant from the ground. "And why could I not have more?"

"Come," he says. "It is done. The bond is sealed."

He reaches toward my ankle and, as if the metal is mere clay, he breaks the shackle open. Then he lifts me to my feet. I feel weak, but whether from the cold, from fear, or from that bewitched fruit, I can't say. It takes me a moment to realize that I am free.

"I wouldn't try to run," he says, as though reading my thoughts. "You would regret it."

Then black shadows are quivering at his back, taking shape. It takes me a moment to understand what's happening.

They're wings.

Great dark wings like a dragon's, unfolding from his back.

This is no man.

"No," I breathe. "Get back. Get away from me."

A warm hand grips me.

"Foolish girl. Don't you see where you're stepping?"

I look down. I've backed up almost to the cliff's edge. My heart leaps, staring down at the vertiginous drop, the choppy white spray.

The black-winged creature closes the gap between us, then lifts me into his arms, the way I have seen brides in our town carried over the threshold of their new husbands' homes.

Bride.

What have I done?

And then, before I have time to weigh all my terrible mistakes, we're airborne. I would shriek, but no sound leaves my mouth. I picture myself plummeting, like Icarus. There's nothing around us but empty air. Nothing but his grip keeping me from dropping down that ever-increasing distance into the inky sea.

"Breathe," he says, and I realize I have not been.

"You are...you are a demon," I say at last. The words are flat. It is not a question.

I almost think I hear a smile in his voice.

"But not so bad as the other."

The other.

The sea is already far below, but not so far that I can't see a flash of green; a long, scaled tentacle thrashing against the rock face. Not so far that I can't hear a howl of its inhuman, disappointed rage.

"Where are you taking me, demon?" I whisper.

And then he murmurs a word—*skotos,* "darkness"—and that's the last thing I hear before a great fog overtakes me, and everything turns to black.

Nine

I force my eyes open and blink—it's like swimming out of a drugged sleep. But once I can focus again, I can't stop staring.

I've never seen so much gold in one place. I'm gazing up at a ceiling that feels as tall as a temple. The walls are marble, inlaid everywhere with gold. The draperies are silk. When I turn my head I see shimmering fabrics laid across the floor, nothing like the hide or woven rugs we had at home.

Home.

Father. Dimitra.

Do they think me dead?

Am I dead?

I always pictured the Realm of Shades being a little…greyer.

My gaze shifts to the window. No, this cannot be the Underworld—there is a blue sky outside, and a blue sea. The water is still, utterly motionless. But it's nothing I recognize. Wherever I am, it must be far from Sikyon.

I raise myself up a little and examine my surroundings. I'm in a bed, one that must surely be finer than the one even the King of Sikyon sleeps in. There are objects of luxury everywhere around me: marble and onyx statuettes, bouquets of flowers made of molten gold, and golden vines that climb the walls and twist their way to the towering ceiling. No mortal smith could create anything so fine. I sit up in bed, and the heavy feeling starts to lift. How long have I slept for—hours? Days? I frown, looking around me at this stately bed. It comes to me that this is not an ordinary bed. It is a marriage bed.

And this silk garment I'm wearing, where did that come from? It's finer than any *chiton* I've ever worn—these seams, the curve of them, they fit my body like a glove, with no need for brooches or pins. But it's paper-thin, and evidently not meant to be day-clothing, for there is a fine gown laid out on the chair in front of me, together with the most luxurious undergarments I've ever seen.

What is all this? What place is this? How did I get here? I touch the back of my skull. I remember the cliff, the peach, and then…nothing.

I raise my hand to my face to brush back the loose hair matted against my forehead, and stop. That smell. Woodsy, like incense. I smell of him.

I look around me at the rumpled sheets, the wide marriage bed. Why can I remember nothing of last night? Nothing from when the demon lifted me into his arms, and I looked down into the water—after that, everything is blank.

As I draw in a breath, the scent of him hits me again. I shiver, then pull back the sheets and place a tentative foot on the floor. These floor coverings…the softness is extraordinary. It's as if all my senses are waking up, or maybe it's just that everything here is incomparably finer and more luxurious than anything I've felt before.

The bedroom's gilded door opens noiselessly, and I find myself staring into a room that at first my mind cannot fully absorb. It makes the bedroom look humble by contrast. Here, there are murals on every wall that put the first craftsmen of Sikyon to shame. And the room is so enormous! It must have taken years to paint it all. The furnishings are lavish, too, and none more so than the tremendous dining table at one end of the room which looks as though it could host a king's gathering. The table is heaped with food—figs, almonds, dates, yogurt, honey, bread with split seams of warm crust—and involuntarily, my stomach cramps and growls. How long since I've eaten; how long was I asleep? It seems like days that I've eaten nothing but that peach…

That peach.

Next to the dishes of honey sits a single peach, sliced open on a golden platter.

I want to approach the table. I want to devour everything I see there. But I would be a fool to do it: the last bite I took, took me here.

A door swings open across the room and I step back quickly, almost tripping over a lushly embroidered footstool. My breath hitches, but it's not him—it's an old woman. Her hair is bone-white, thin as spun sugar. Her face is deeply lined, her eyes black and beady.

She doesn't look surprised to see me.

"Grandmother," I address her as I would back home. "Please, tell me where I am."

She says nothing, just looks at me with those birdlike black eyes.

I bow my head, then try again.

"Forgive me. I am a stranger here. Where is"—*what to call him?*—"where is the one who brought me here?"

But she remains silent—watchful, and silent.

Has she been instructed not to answer? Or perhaps she doesn't speak the Hellenic tongue. She may be from one of the neighboring countries. A slave, perhaps?

I place a hand to my chest.

"I am Psyche. What is your name, Grandmother?"

Nothing. After a few moments, she turns and disappears back through the doorway.

He told her not to speak to me, no doubt. A wave of foreboding goes through me. Those last memories are becoming clearer the longer I'm awake; the details sharpen. I see it in my mind again, those great dragon-wings, black as oil, unsheathing from his back.

I shiver. Everything here is so beautiful. But demons may be rich, I suppose, and enjoy fine things as much as any king.

I scan the enormous room again: there is the door beside the dining table, where the old woman came from. The bedroom door where I stand now. And on the opposite side of the room, another door. That is the one I make for.

If the old woman will not give me answers, then I must gather them for myself. I will find out what this place is.

And I will find *him*.

The door leads to a corridor with a high, vaulted ceiling, lit with torches in sconces—when I looked out the bedroom window it was daytime, but there are no windows here. The corridor seems to go on for a very long way, with doors leading off to left and right. There were slippers by the bed but I did not put them on, and now my feet pad on marble cool to the touch.

I come to the next door and pause. There might be hundreds of rooms in this place, for all I know. It all seems like a dream.

I remember how I thought he was lying when he told me of an enchanted place, one that could shield me from the eyes of the gods. But it is no great stretch to see that this place must be enchanted: at the very least, it was not made by mortals.

So the black-winged creature is no madman. But he might be something much more dangerous than that.

I hesitate, then push open the door beside me.

An empty room—beautiful, grand, and bare. I stand there a moment, then let the door close again and move on. The next room is empty too. I start to open the doors of each room I pass. Some are bare, some are not. One is a music room, but giant in size, with harps and lyres that appear to be made of solid gold, and pipes and flutes and bells, and stringed instruments of every kind. Another room is some kind of library, housing hundreds—perhaps thousands—of papyrus scrolls. Some scrolls hang on the wall, where the writing glows like jewels. Others are tied with silken ribbons and housed in long cabinets that run the length of the room. I've never heard of anyone, even the king, owning more than one or two such scrolls. Such work must take years—decades—to produce.

Gently, I close the door again and move along to the next

room. No one has forbidden me from exploring, but I probably wasn't supposed to venture this far.

Then I open the next door, and gasp.

In the center of the room is a white cage many times my height, and so wide it would surely take some time to walk its diameter. And inside it, birds: cawing, clicking, chirruping. A riot of noise and color. I stare. Birds such as these don't exist where I come from, nor have I ever heard stories of such creatures. Their feathers are yellow, or red, or sea-colored; some are small as gemstones, others as big as a man. They are beautiful, exquisite and strange. And noisy.

After the silence of the corridor, the sound of them is overwhelming.

The noise seems to intensify as I watch them—I think they see I'm here, and are calling to me. Suddenly my breath catches in my chest and I step back, closing the door roughly. I don't want to look at them anymore, all that beauty in a cage. I move fast down the corridor, which seems more claustrophobic now than before. Doors and more doors! Where is the end of all this?

I go left, then right, wherever turns present themselves. My footsteps echo and ring out. I feel tight-chested, breathless. I need air.

The things I don't want to think about are piling into my mind now. The rocky ledge in the green dawn; the black-winged stranger and his unholy bargain. The peach. The *binding*, as he called it. The way I smelled of him when I awoke.

I am his wife now.

The words don't seem real. They're fantastical, absurd. It's as though I dreamed the whole thing, and perhaps I did—after all, where is he now, the cloaked stranger? There's no one here but me and that old woman.

At last there's an end to the corridor, and a door in it. My breath fights in my chest as I burst through it and find myself outdoors, with sky above me. I gulp down air. I'm in a yard, with what looks like a horse stable to my right. The sky is full of scudding clouds, and in front of me there's an enormous double gate, black metal, intricately formed. There are no gaps in it, no way to see what lies beyond. The rest of the yard is enclosed by high walls. What's outside those gates? What strange land houses this place? I go to the gate but when I push, it doesn't budge at all, not a hair's breadth. I wonder whether it's a locking mechanism, or something more. An enchantment, perhaps.

I turn, hearing a noise from the stables. The stamp of a hoof, then a whinny and snort, and a horse's black muzzle nudges its way over the top of the stable door. I don't know that I've ever seen such a majestic creature. Its coat gleams like black silk, and its eyes are golden, like clear honey.

For a moment we stare at each other.

Then it whinnies again, and three companions come to their stable doors too, snorting softly in answer. One's a chestnut, one a roan, the last a shell-white. I think they might be the most beautiful animals I've ever seen. In Sikyon, horses are rare and valuable beasts. Our horse Ada is a stocky workhorse, old and tired, nothing like these exquisite animals—and yet we were thought rich to have her.

Poor old Ada. My eyes tear up despite myself.

Dimitra always loved horses. When we were children, a wealthy family nearby had a few horses, and Dimitra used to make me go with her to visit them. They would always be there behind the stone wall, as if waiting for her, ready to nuzzle her palm and collect whatever treats she'd brought. I was always afraid they would bite her, but Dimitra was fearless. She was so tender with them—tender in a way she never was with me. She'd stroke their foreheads, whispering.

"Were you hungry? Were you lonely? Hush, I'm here now."

As if they were the motherless ones, not us.

Oh, Dimitra.

I close my eyes. My sister. My father. What are they doing

now?

The door back into the great palace opens, and there's the old woman in the doorway, frowning at me. She still doesn't speak, but the look on her face confirms my suspicion that I'm not supposed to be here. She just lifts her hand and gestures, beckoning me.

I hesitate, then step her way. Where else is there to go?

Once I'm in front of her, she holds out something for me. A piece of fabric—black, shimmering. It reminds me of that cloak—the cloak *he* wore last night.

"What is it?" I ask.

She scowls deeper, then shuts her eyes, miming something: a ribbon being drawn across them.

A *blindfold*? She stands in front of me, waiting. I shake my head. Why she wants me to blindfold myself, I'd prefer not to guess. But I know one thing, and she might as well know it too.

"I will not be putting that on."

Then from behind me, I hear a noise: the clanging of a metal gate.

"And what"—a voice, *his* voice, travels toward us—"seems to be the problem here?

Ten

My stomach flips over. I turn and there he is: tall, cloaked, striding toward me. Daylight doesn't make him look any less intimidating.

You did not dream him after all.

But I rather wish I had.

"Well, Psyche." He comes to a halt before me, a faceless figure in black. "You are up and dressed. That is well." The hood swings as he looks between the old woman and me. "But what is the problem; has Aletheia not made herself understood?"

The old woman looks at me, her eyes narrowed. I indicate the piece of fabric.

"She seemed to wish me to wear *that,* across my eyes."

He pauses a moment.

"That is correct. In my own house I claim the privilege of shedding this cloak—which means you must be the one to wear a covering."

I stare at him, at the darkness where a face should be.

"What do you mean, sir?"

"I mean," he says, "that you are not to look upon my face. And since humans are deplorable at keeping their eyes closed unless they are asleep, a blindfold, regrettably, is necessary."

I can only stare. I had thought his strategy in concealing himself last night was all just a part of coaxing me into making this bargain. But I had been expecting—expecting with some dread—that today he would show his true self to me, whatever terrible face accompanies those demon wings.

"You mean I am not to see your face, even now?"

The black hood shifts.

"You are not to see my face—now, or ever."

I stare. I do not wish to be blindfolded. Besides, however bad it is, whatever's under that cape, it would be better to know than live with horrible imaginings.

"And why should that be?" I challenge. "Are you Medusa's counterpart, then? Is your head made of snakes? I hear no hissing."

He sighs, as though addressing a child.

"No, Psyche. I am no Gorgon, as you surely know."

"Then why may I not look upon your face?" I demand. I knew it: he keeps me from seeing him, not for my protection, but for his own vanity. For power. He does not want me to know how ugly he is.

He does not hurry to answer.

"Think of it as a test," he says finally.

"A test of what?"

"Obedience." It seems to me there is a touch of humor in his tone, but I see nothing funny here. Nothing funny in being bound to an oath I never wished to swear. My throat feels dry.

"But how am I to live here…and never see you?"

"You must," he says simply. "I will not risk anything else."

My thoughts spin. Is this really to be my life? To live with a faceless host, and spend my days blindfolded? And what risk can he mean? There is nothing *he* can fear from *me*.

"It is only for the evenings," he says lightly, as if it's no imposition at all. "During the day I will be absent and you may do as you please."

"But…" I step backwards. "I can go to another room while you are here. You will have your privacy…"

"No. I request your company at my dinner table." His tongue lingers on the word *request*, as if I could doubt that this were anything but an order.

"Aletheia?" he says.

The old woman hands over the black cloth.

"Hold still," he commands. I want to argue, but I'm too disoriented by all he has just said. What is it he doesn't want me to see? Why go to such lengths to hide it?

The black silk slides down my face, settling over my eyes, blocking out the world. My eyes fight against the darkness, straining for light, and my mind fights too, like an animal refusing to be caged.

I will myself not to panic, then gasp involuntarily as the blindfold tightens, pulling hard against my eyes as he fastens the knot. Perhaps the blindfold is enchanted, too: the darkness is absolute, denser than the darkest night. And something tells me that if I tried to slip the knot myself, I would find it as stubborn as that iron gate.

"Breathe," he tells me.

He said that before. Memories rear up in my mind again, as if the darkness sharpens them. I remember his black wings, the rush of air on my bare skin—and that voice, telling me to breathe.

I grimace.

I breathe, but not at your command.

"Good. Now Aletheia will give you her arm. She will lead you upstairs."

I feel her bony grip on my arm—not hard, but not gentle—and then she moves away, pulling me with her. I have the terrible sense of stepping off a ledge, as though the next time I place my foot down it won't find the marble floor, but a void to plummet into. A memory rushes up of Dimitra and me as children, playing at leading each other blindfolded around the house. It always gave me vertigo. Father had an explanation.

It's not the threat of falling which makes us afraid, he said. *It's fear of the unknown.*

Dimitra had pulled a face at that.

I'm *not afraid of the unknown,* she'd said. She was right.

The fear was always mine.

*

We make left turns, and right turns, and go up a flight of stairs—though I remember no stairs from my wanderings—before Aletheia lets me pause. This blindness—this forced blindness—is exhausting. My mind feels too alert, like an animal that senses something is amiss. I hear a door open, and then close once I'm ushered through.

His voice speaks from behind me.

"We are back in the great-room, Psyche. Come—there is something I wish to show you."

The great-room: I suppose he means that enormous, muraled room that my bedroom opened onto.

I feel his presence draw nearer and he takes my forearm, quite gently. A strange feeling floods through me. I remember once again the ride through the air from Sikyon, the few moments of it before I lost consciousness. I felt it then, too, where his skin touched mine—this sensation, as if I could feel the life in his veins, the same way that when dipping one's hand in a moving stream, one feels its current. It seems to sing out under his skin, the song of his life force, coursing and rippling.

Are demons immortal, I wonder. Perhaps this is what it feels like to touch an immortal.

He leads me a few paces forward, and stops.

"Careful. This stone is uneven."

I hesitate, then feel it out with my foot. One wide, square stone, raised higher than the rest.

"This is the Hearthstone," he says. "The heart of this palace. The oath-binder."

Beneath the black silk, I blink.

"And why do you speak of oaths?" I fold my arms across my chest. "Have you not taken all the pledges you needed from me already?"

He sighs, as though I require some great patience from him.

"Psyche, I wish you to speak it here, on the Hearthstone: that you will never look upon my face."

I don't know why I hesitate. Why would I even wish to see his demon face? It is the other faces I'm thinking of now. The other faces so far away from me, which I love and cannot look upon.

"Very well," I say. "I will never look upon your face."

Not that I can imagine having the opportunity, given the lengths he's going to prevent it. But my words seem to hang in the air, strangely final. Then he clears his throat, and the moment passes.

"Aletheia, we will eat now. Please prepare the lady Psyche for our meal."

I feel Aletheia's bony grip close over my arm again, and she tugs me away, into what I realize—once she shuts the door, and loosens the blindfold—is my bedroom. But out the window I'm greeted by the strangest sight. The view has changed: it is no longer of an endless, tranquil sea, but instead, seems to look out over a thick forest. I stare, then close my eyes and open them again. But the sea does not reappear.

Am I to believe this palace is…*moving*, somehow?

Aletheia makes an impatient noise in her throat, and indicates the divan where a new change of clothes has already been laid out.

"I am to wear these?"

I wait for Aletheia to turn her face to the wall while I change. My old nurse helped me dress often enough, but I do not wish to be naked under those scornful, beady eyes.

When I've finished, she gestures to a chair and table with a large mirror on it. I hesitate, then take a seat. She takes a comb from the desk and begins to run it through my hair, none too gently.

"Ow!" I protest. "You might go a little slower."

She doesn't listen, but proceeds to fasten my hair with surprisingly nimble fingers.

Since our nurse left, Dimitra is the only one who has dressed my hair—we used to dress each other's. But that stopped some years ago, around the time people started to call me beautiful. Which was also around the time Dimitra began to dislike me.

Aletheia's hands do not shake at all; they are precise and deliberate. Her movements do not match her age, I have noticed. Her walk, too, is the sprightly, powerful walk of someone much younger. But as I watch her gnarled old hands secure my hair in braids and pins, I can't help but cringe. Despite her deftness, she is too old to labor over me like this, doing something I could certainly do myself. It makes me uncomfortable for another reason, too: I do not wish her to beautify me for *him*. But when she has finished, I must admit she has some special gift. My hair has never looked so elegant, and she has brushed it to a fine radiance, so that now it seems to catch the light strand by strand.

Then she holds up the strip of black silk once more. I feel my jaw lock. I want to protest. Perhaps I *should* protest. But what are the chances of me getting my way?

"All right," I sigh. "Put it on."

She does, and I try not to think of a lamb being led to the slaughter.

*

When Aletheia leads me through the doorway, I don't need to see the table to know a feast lies there. The smells are mouthwatering, to the point that I have to keep swallowing the saliva that pools under my tongue. Grilled meats—something rich, like venison, and the briny smell of roasted fish; there's the earthy tang of rosemary, oregano and thyme…stewed berries and jellies, I can smell them all.

Is it the blindfold, enhancing the senses that must substitute for sight? Or is it possible that my senses really are getting sharper in this place? Everything seems so…heightened.

I swallow, feeling the desperate growling in my stomach the nearer we get to the food. Aletheia stops, and I stop abruptly with her. She lets go of my arm and I hear the squeal of a chair being dragged out. She nudges me toward it; I feel for it, then sit.

There's the sound of another chair sliding out.

"Well, good evening, wife."

The voice sounds almost amused again, delivering the word *wife* like it's a joke. It *is* a joke, I suppose—just not an amusing one.

"Your hair looks very well."

"Aletheia did it. I had no say in the matter."

"Hm," he says. There is the sound of wine being poured, and the heady smell of it wafts toward me. My stomach rumbles again. How long since I last ate?

"Here," he says, and I feel a glass next to my hand. I shake my head.

"No wine? You are sure?"

"I am sure," I say, because although every fiber of my being wants to reach out and grab at whatever heaven-scented food and drink lies before me, I don't trust myself to let any of it pass my lips. It might undo me completely; unravel me, like the peach did before. I don't know what enchantments, what spells of seduction, exist in this place. There is no telling what they might do to me.

"I am not hungry, either."

There's a pause.

"Not hungry?" I hear him sip the wine. I swallow; my throat longs for a taste.

"You think my food is drugged," he says. "I suppose to a mortal it may seem so. Things are different here. You will notice your senses become more heightened, pleasure and pain are amplified." He pauses. "After dinner I will show you the gardens. You will see where some of our food comes from. You will see there is nothing sinister in it."

Gardens? I had thought to find only walls and doors in this place.

"Nevertheless," I lie through my teeth, "I am not hungry."

"Very well." His voice is unconcerned. "Suit yourself."

He thinks I am being pettish, perhaps; that I am sulking for attention. Well, let him think it.

He carves something on his plate. I hear the sound of his lips parting, the sound of chewing, swallowing. I can almost feel the pleasure he takes in it.

"So," he says after a while. "You explored my palace while I was gone. What do you think of it?"

I keep my hands folded in front of me. My belly growls, tormenting me. There is no need for me to answer his question. He knows well enough how astounding a place like this must be to my eyes. It would be extraordinary even to a king.

"You are blindfolded, not gagged," he comments after a while. "I believe you still have the use of your tongue."

"Where are we?" I say finally. "Where is this place?"

There is the sound of him chewing quietly. He does not hurry to swallow.

"I do not think my answer will satisfy you. In your world, you speak of the thin places—places where borders between the realms are more permeable."

I've heard that. At home, they say there are parts of the forest—deep caves, or deeper lakes—where we may glimpse the Underworld.

"We are no longer in the mortal realm, Psyche. This is an enchanted place. A protected place."

My throat dries up.

"We've left the mortal world?"

He pauses. "We are not outside it, but beyond it. The mortal world overlaps with us, as two footprints might overlap each other in the sand."

I frown, struggling to understand the analogy, and what it

means for me. "But you—you can move freely between them?"

"*I* can. Mortals cannot."

His voice is easy, its timbre rich and low. It is not how the voice of a demon should be. It is the kind of voice Father used to adopt when he would tell us stories, back when Dimitra and I were small children and sat at his knee. A voice for heroes and their great deeds.

But those days are long gone. I'm no longer a child, and I know that voices lie, just as faces do.

"I don't remember getting here," I blurt. "I remember the peach"—I blush, just thinking of it—"and then nothing. You lifted me from the cliff, and then…everything is blank."

"Yes," he says. "I did not wish you to see which way we flew. So I bade you sleep." I remember the single word he intoned, and the darkness that came over my senses then.

"You magicked me, you mean." An angry shiver goes through me. "You put a spell on me."

And if he can do that, what else can he do? Can he command anything he likes? If he wished to, could he command now that I eat, and my hand would take the food and my mouth would open for it, against my will?

"I do not force mortals to act against their desires," he says quietly.

I don't let him see me scoff, but it is as though he hears my thoughts.

"Not," he amends, "unless it is absolutely necessary."

His confession only reminds me of what I already know: I must not trust this man. Although he is not a *man* at all, is he?

"What happened when you took me here?" I say. "I woke up in that bed wearing strange clothes, that's all I know. What happened before that?"

He stops chewing.

"It is a short story. You were asleep. I told Aletheia to find you a sleeping-gown, and some clothing for the morning, and to put you to bed." He takes another sip of wine; I hear the swish of liquid and the deep swallow.

"That is all?" I say, forcing my voice to be steady; remembering the rumpled sheets, the scent on my skin.

"That is all," he confirms.

"Your smell was there," I flush. "When I woke."

There's amusement in his voice.

"I carried you here in my arms, Psyche. If my smell on your skin offends you, there is a remedy for that. Or don't they bathe in Sikyon?"

To my horror, I feel a rush of heat gathering suddenly behind my eyes. I will it back down. I will not rise to his bait.

"I have already told you, Psyche," he goes on, when I say nothing, "I will take nothing from you that you do not freely give."

Except for my obedience. My obedience, in exchange for his help. That was no small bargain.

"So what does it mean, then," I keep my voice in check. "That we are…bound, this way?" What *can* this senseless "marriage" mean to him? It certainly does not seem to mean what it means in my world. He does not intend to make a slave of me, nor a courtesan.

"What," I say slowly, "do *you* get out of it?"

Eleven

There's a long pause.

I hear him swallow more wine, and then the abrupt sound of his seat being pushed back.

"Come," he says abruptly. "Seeing as you are not hungry, there is no need for us to linger."

I hesitate, then feel his hand under my arm, and push back my chair. His hands are stronger than Aletheia's, much stronger, as he helps me to my feet. So close, the scent of him washes over me again: pine and cedar and myrrh; forests under the moonlight.

He leads me across the room, but not in the direction of my bedroom.

"Where are we going?"

"I told you I would take you to the gardens, did I not?"

There's a rustling, silken sound.

"You may remove the blindfold now," he says, his voice a shade more muffled than before, and I realize he's donned his cloak again. But instead of ripping the blindfold from my eyes, I move nervously. To my surprise, the piece of silk unknots with perfect ease, dropping freely into my hand. Was I right to believe it was enchanted?

I blink around at where we are. The torches in the corridor are brighter now, and seem to flicker harder as he passes underneath them. Shadows dance along the walls. His stride is long and he makes no efforts to modify it for me.

"Tell me something," I pant, keeping pace beside him. "The window in my bedroom. When I woke today it showed a sea—then earlier, a forest. I don't understand."

His hood flicks briefly toward me, but his pace doesn't slow.

"The windows are not real windows. What you see through them is an artifice—like a mural. You can conjure other images, if you wish."

Illusions. I suppose I should not be surprised.

I follow his fast step down the corridor; his black cape makes me feel I am chasing shadows. As he swings along one turn and then another I try to memorize the way. *Are* the doors in different places than they were before? I can't tell, but it seems to me I did not come this way before. Finally we come to the end of a corridor and a great double-door. He unbolts it and swings both panels wide, and a soft twilight floods in, turning the marble walls of the corridor a glowing lilac shade. He steps out, beckoning me to follow.

I do, and my mouth drops open.

It *is* a garden—but the word *garden* seems ludicrous to describe this place. For one thing, it's enormous. The grounds seem to roll out in a lush infinity, and if there are walls at the far end of this exquisite land, I don't see them. I see trees, pathways, vines and flowerbeds, profusion everywhere, all under a soft evening sky streaked with pink. In the middle-distance a crystalline pond reflects the sky, waterlilies shifting gently on its surface.

"How far does it go?" I say, my eyes still on the horizon.

"Far. But you need not worry—all of it is my domain, shielded from the eyes of the gods. You may wander here at will."

He makes it sound so exposed, as if in the mortal world, the gods are watching our every move. Can they really care that much about us? Will Aphrodite really be looking for me even now?

"Come." He leads me along the nearest pathway, and the wonders of the garden only increase as we walk. The leaves on the trees glisten like jewels; on many of them, blossoms and ripe fruit bloom together.

"You like it?" he says. He's watching me, I can tell. The

black cloth shimmers slightly as he moves. I think I am starting to be able to decipher the language of his body, even despite the cloak—I can read the movements in his shoulders, the tilt of his head. And I can tell that he's looking at me, and that this time, it's not with mockery. He's curious, perhaps, to see the effect of this place. He probably doesn't remember what it felt like to walk these fields for the first time.

"It's beautiful," I admit. "I thought only the gods lived like this."

If I had imagined Mount Olympus in my dreams, it might have looked this way. Perhaps there are plants here that bloom with the nectar of the gods; perhaps there are rivers that flow with ambrosia.

"Aletheia tends it now," he says. "But she is growing old. Perhaps you can care for it. Would you like that?"

"Does such a garden even need tending?" It seems to me its growth must be enchanted. The plants are too perfect, nothing is amiss or decaying. In my world, it would surely take an army to maintain such a place.

He turns his head.

"I suppose it does not need it, exactly," he admits. "But it welcomes it. Every living thing responds to every other living thing. The earth will welcome your touch, Psyche."

I frown.

"And the birds? Does Aletheia feed them too, or are they an enchantment, like the windows?"

He turns my way; I feel his curious glance.

"Aletheia feeds them," he says. "Though she says she does not much care for winged creatures."

A joke, perhaps? I remember those terrible dark wings, opening above me like a bird of prey.

Then up ahead something moves in the pond ahead, disrupting the water. Something strange-looking. I almost think…

"What was that?"

"That," he says, "will be the nymphs."

Nymphs?

"I should think they are curious about you."

He leads me past one of the flower-beds, then crouches down beside the plants. I think at first he's checking them for pests, but then I realize he's just admiring them. I watch his hands, golden-skinned and dexterous, the nimble fingers turning the leaves gently this way and that. Beautiful hands.

And yet, what is beneath the hood must be hideous.

Even so, I would prefer to see it. To know would still be better than not knowing. At least, I think it would.

He rises to his feet again.

"I do not know what to call you," I blurt. *Demon* will not do: not to his face, even if it is what I call him in my private thoughts.

He half-turns; I think he is amused.

"Why, call me *sýzygos*—husband." He is teasing me, and I flush.

"Have you no name, then?" I say, more sharply.

He straightens beneath the dark robe.

"I have more names than you could imagine," he says. "But I do not wish you to know me by them."

"Why not?"

He looks at me; I feel the burn of it even from beneath the cloak. But he does not answer me. He merely moves along to another bed of plants, stoops, and examines them as he examined the ones before.

"Do you recognize these?"

His change of subject is pointed. I'd like to press the point but I'm not a fool: he has great power, and I have none. What he will not tell me, I will not wring from him by force. Maybe if I'm clever, I'll win what I wish to know some other way.

I look where he's crouched, next to a plant with small white buds. It is exquisite—and not at all familiar.

"We did not have such flowers in my land," I say, with a

sudden, sharp pang of homesickness.

"Well, perhaps you will recognize some of them by name." He points: "Orphine. Bettany. Celandine." He moves to the next furrow, indicating them one by one. "Mandrake. Artemisia. Thousand-seal. Moonflower. And here: wolfsbane, amaranth, and herb of Lethe."

I stare.

"The garden is all witching-herbs, you mean?"

He laughs a little.

"If that is what you wish to call them."

The names he speaks are ones that, for the most part, I've heard spoken only in whispers: herbs and plants with strange properties, some which I believed to be purely mythical.

He bends down to another plant, and crushes a leaf between his fingers, then holds his hand out for me to smell. I inhale cautiously. There's the smell of *him*—that cool, dark forest smell—and something else.

"Rosemary?" I frown. Surely *that* is not magical.

"Deep magic does not come from any one root, Psyche." It sounds like an admonishment. "The true potency is in the combinations. Very little is magical on its own."

"So is this—is this where your powers come from?" The words escape me before I decide to speak them. But he just laughs.

"These herbs? The source of my power? You will ask me next whether it is your little mortal king that powers the sun."

I hate when he speaks in this mocking, teasing way. For a brief moment, I had forgotten to be on my guard.

"What is it, then?" I say staunchly. "What *is* the source of your power?" He may call me ignorant and provincial if he wishes, what do I care?

I can feel him regarding me from beneath the cloak.

"You ask a lot of questions, don't you?" He plucks the stalk of rosemary, grinds it beneath his fingers.

"Do you think you can find your way back to these

gardens?" he says.

I'm reluctant to answer since he refuses to answer *my* questions, but I nod anyway.

"Good. Perhaps you can help Aletheia gather some herbs tomorrow. Harvest season will soon be upon us."

And with that he has moved on, his long stride already pacing ahead of me down the path.

*

Back in the palace, our footsteps echo down the corridors. His pace has slowed, and as we walk together, something occurs to me.

"Aletheia…she wears no face covering before you. *She* may look upon you. Why is that?"

I hear the shrug in his voice.

"Aletheia? She is not an ordinary mortal."

"Not a mortal?" I frown. "What is she, then?"

"She is a god-child. Her father was mortal. Her mother was not."

A god-child. Like Heracles and Perseus, and the other great heroes of myth.

"But she is old, like a mortal."

"There are holes in your knowledge, wife." When he says the word *wife* his voice is wry, and my cheeks warm once more.

"God-children are still mortal; all of them age. Aletheia, however, is gifted with more longevity than most."

I lift my head.

"How old is she, then?"

"She was born before your great-great-grandfather."

That silences me for a moment. In Sikyon, the elderly are given great respect. But "elderly" does not begin to describe a person of Aletheia's years. She must be over a hundred years old.

I narrow my eyes at him.

"And how is it that you have a god-child who keeps house for you; is this common practice among your kind?"

I feel his gaze shift; his voice travels more sharply.

"My *kind*?" he says. "What kind is that?"

"Demons," I say.

I hear the irritation he's trying to tamp down.

"You don't think much of us, do you?" He pauses. "But I suppose you think mortals are very fine. You should ask Aletheia what she endured among your kind."

"*Endured?* God-children are worshiped in our lands."

Beneath the cloak, he shakes his head.

"Oh, you like to tell their stories. But if such a creature is born among you, in your own town? It upsets the order of things. Any king would fear such an imbalance of power."

I had not thought of it that way.

"Aletheia's mother," he says, "was a farmer's wife. And one day she was accosted by the god Pan. You've heard tell of him, I suppose?"

He's being ironic, no doubt. Of course I know of Pan, every girl in Sikyon is taught his name. We are taught to avoid walking the mountain passes alone for fear of him.

"Well, Pan had his way with her, and then, when her husband found out, he took her to trial before the village elders. They agreed the woman was impure—they said she had sought out the god's advances, and was to be stoned."

The skin on my neck prickles. I would like to say such injustice belongs to the past, to my great-great-grandfather's time and not ours. But I know better. Blame is a cursed arrow, burying its target in those who least deserve it.

"Then," he continues, "when they realized Aletheia's mother was with child, the village delayed its sentence. Not out of mercy, but because they feared Pan's wrath if they destroyed his child." His voice hardens. "So they waited until she had delivered herself of the child, and *then* put her to death. As for the child—Aletheia—they took her away, and kept her locked up as if she were an animal."

"Why?" I feel sickened.

"She was a god-child. They feared that she would learn to use her powers and turn against them."

I sit with the terrible story for a while. It makes me ashamed of my own kind, of the things we are capable of.

"That's…so horrible."

"It is," he says simply.

"Is that…" I hesitate. "Is that why she's mute?"

There's a surprised silence..

"Mute?" I hear the twist of his mouth. "Aletheia is not mute, Psyche."

I blink. So she is simply choosing not to speak to me. She really does despise me. Perhaps it's how she feels about all mortals. I flush, and feel his gaze pouring into me.

"You see? Your kind, Psyche, is as capable of evil as my own. Alone, you wield little power, and yet you band together to do great harm."

It is true, I know it. And yet I know the opposite to be true, too. There is good, great good, among my kind.

When it's not being smothered by other, darker things.

I am expecting him to bid me goodnight and disappear down one of the corridors, but it seems he intends to walk me all the way back to the great-room. The table has been cleared now of its half-eaten feast. The room is empty and quiet; only the Hearthstone seems to shimmer in the dim light. We're halfway to my door, and still he walks with me. I slow my pace, my heart battering in my ribcage. We reach the door of my bedroom. He is still at my side, making no signs to leave. *Call me husband,* he mocked me earlier. Does he plan to claim his prize tonight, then, after all?

"I shall leave you here."

I exhale so hard my knees tremble a little. I will sleep alone after all. He must see the relief flooding through me.

"I told you that I would ask nothing of you, other than

obedience." He pauses. "The latter, I'll grant you, needs some work." He mocks me again. "But understand, Psyche, I will take nothing from you by force. I have never entered a woman's bed I was not invited into. I will not enter yours without your invitation."

I'm almost as breathless now as I was before. My *invitation*? Can he really think I'll ever invite him to share my bed, of my own volition?

He laughs quietly.

"Are you so revolted? I should have thought I was rather pleasing—for a demon."

His footsteps echo as he moves toward the door, and the wood-scent of him dwindles.

"Good night, Psyche. Rest well."

Twelve

My sleep is troubled and fitful; all night I toss and turn as though on a boat. And when I wake my stomach grumbles fiercely. I think if I were to see that peach on the table this morning, I would take it. I know I cannot keep this fasting up forever. Sooner or later, I will have to eat.

I wince, and roll over to the sight of a new landscape outside the window: a wide meadow, dotted with black opium-poppies under a wind-tossed sky.

The sound of voices in the room outside rouses me from bed, and takes me to the doorway. I open it just a crack, enough to peer through. They are speaking in low voices, the demon and Aletheia, over by what I take to be the kitchen door. Or at least, *he* is speaking, his black cloak shimmering around him as before, while Aletheia listens, looking nonplussed. Then her gaze turns, and although my door is only the minutest bit ajar, her dark eyes fix on me, I am sure of it. I tell myself that I will not be the first to look away, but her gaze burns hot, and I drop my eyes.

"Psyche, will you not join us?"

He turns around, the hood low over his face, and it occurs to me that if he has bothered with the cloak at all, it is because he suspected I would spy on them like this.

I clear my throat, and inch out of the bedroom.

"I trust you slept well?"

"I slept," I say shortly. "But not well."

He inclines his head.

"That is regrettable."

His words suggest sympathy, but his tone does not. I can't help thinking back to last night, and my unanswered questions. Why *did* he save me from that monster; what's in this for him?

No mortal bridegroom would have waited an hour before taking his new wife to the bedchamber. I wonder suddenly if demons find mortals repellent, as well as the other way around. Perhaps everything about me that the boys of Sikyon found so appealing, he can barely stand.

If so, that is my good fortune. I clear my throat.

"I thought you said you were absent from this place during the day?"

"And so I am. Only this morning, I had some instructions for Aletheia."

"About me?" I say, guarded.

The black cloth shimmers slightly as he nods. The fabric seems to hold the light, even though it's the color of midnight. There's something mesmerizing about it, and the small movements beneath its surface.

Aletheia shoots a last glance my way before disappearing through the kitchen door.

"I said to let you roam as you wished until I arrive home," the demon says. "And to prepare you a lunch at noon."

I'm about to tell him I have no need of it, even though my stomach growls at the very prospect, but I hold my tongue. I don't want to antagonize him: I have a question I want answered instead. I keep my gaze on the black hood, holding steady.

"Have there been others?" I say. "Have other mortals come here before me?"

He doesn't answer at first; I have the sense he doesn't wish to.

"You are the first."

I turn it over in my mind.

"No other mortals have seen this place? At all?"

He sounds irritated.

"I have explained it to you, have I not? No mortal can find this place alone. None may enter unless I myself carry them over the threshold."

"But you could," I say. An idea is coming to me slowly. "You *could* bring any mortal here that you chose, and then return them to their realm. You could, for example, carry my father and sister here. To visit me."

"No."

"*No*?" I repeat. He expects that one word to satisfy me?

"I do not wish to, and besides that, I do not trust them."

"Trust them?" I stare at him. "What do you mean?"

His voice is taut, prickling with irritation.

"Aphrodite does not know where you are—yet. But if tongues begin to wag…"

"My family," I say hotly, "would not betray me."

He is quiet for a moment.

"Psyche, they already have."

"That's not fair." I feel the tears squeezing against my throat, and push them down. "My family had no choice." But even as I say it, I know it's not true.

There is always a choice, however poor, however small.

I remember how my father could not meet my eyes that morning, as the king's men locked me in irons. How he got into the king's carriage without looking back.

And yet, perhaps he did the best he could.

"If you will not have them visit," I say, "you must get word to them, at least. You can tell them that I am alive, that I will see them again."

There's a pause.

"I cannot," he says.

I turn angrily.

"I cannot allow you to make such promises…"

"But…"

He cuts me off. "…when it would be a lie."

Dread pools in my stomach.

"What are you talking about?"

"Psyche." He says my name as though I am a child, a fool. "What did you think would happen? That you would roam freely between the mortal realm and mine? That you would have a palace as your home, yet keep all the freedom you once had?" His cape seems to shimmer with dark color, as though his emotions are visible there.

"Don't you understand? We have gone against *Aphrodite*. The goddess was angry at you before; only think how enraged she would be now, discovering you have thwarted her. Did you think that you would spend a few months here, a year, and then all would be forgotten? You should already know how quick the gods are to anger, and how slow to forget. You think this will simply *blow over*?" He scoffs. "Your lifetime—yours, and your father's, and your father's father's—is nothing to her!

The words move through the air like shards of glass. Small, light, deadly.

"Inside these walls," his voice continues, drumming the words into me, "you are protected. Outside them, you will perish, and painfully. This is your home now, and you will not travel outside it."

I stand very still. I ball my hands at my sides, trying to keep them from shaking.

"I cannot stay here forever." My voice comes out small and sharp. "With no friends, no purpose, no *life*. I…I cannot. It does not matter how grand your palace is, how vast your gardens. They're like your windows, that show whatever you want and none of it real. It's meaningless." I take a breath, clench my fists tight.

"You will take me back."

"Little fool," he says coolly. "Did you not see the sea-monster? Have you so soon forgotten?"

"At least a sea-monster wouldn't have locked me in a cage and blindfolded me!" I snap. "You call this a palace, but what it really is is a prison."

"Ungrateful mortal!" His voice is hot with anger now. "You are like the worm who complains it does not like the earth, when above ground the eagle's beak is waiting."

I raise my chin.

"I'll take my chances," I say.

He smacks his fist against the dining table.

"You will *not*. You will not expose yourself to Aphrodite's vengeance, and you will not expose me to it!"

My anger is a wave, bitter and sharp.

"So you mean to be my jailer, then," I say.

"Your *jailer*? When this palace is a hundred times your former home and more? Tell me," his voice sharpens dangerously. "That mortal boy you were to marry. What great independence would you have reveled in under his roof? What heady freedoms do you think you would have enjoyed *there*?"

I stare at him. He knows about Yiannis?

But of course he does. He knows everything, I realize: he knows exactly what happened to me at the feast-day, and what Aphrodite commanded afterwards. How would he know any of it, unless he had been observing our every move?

Until now, I'd had the half-formed idea that he just showed up that morning by accident—that he was drawn to the cliffside, perhaps, by the crowds or the chaos. That he intervened according to some whim. But now I realize how very calculated it was. He knew every part of my story.

So he knew how desperate I was.

"You say you, too, fear Aphrodite's wrath." I hear the shake in my voice. "But if you fear her, why defy her at all? Why step in to rescue me?"

The silence sparks, grows. From across the room I can feel his look of disdain.

"*I* know why. Because you saw a girl there who would agree to any devil's bargain: I was easy pickings." I turn on him. "You said you were *saving* me. You did not say you planned to lock me up for the rest of my mortal life!"

"You came of your own free will," he snaps. "You needn't act as though I forced it from you."

"I had no free will!" I yell. "You knew that when you had

me come with you!"

"I made you a sacred promise, and I have not broken it," he thunders. "Do not insult my honor!"

"*Honor*! What honor has a demon?"

I feel the fury building underneath the black cloak. He cannot hide what he is.

"What mistake did I make, bringing you here." His voice snaps like an angry wind. He draws the cloak about him.

"But it's too late now, mortal. The sooner you become used to it, the better."

And he turns from me, and storms from the room.

Thirteen

I'm on my bed, eyes shut tight, but the hot tears I was waiting for don't come. Now that I'm alone, in the privacy of this strange bedroom, I can't cry. My body has forgotten how.

What do Father and Dimitra think; do they think me dead? Does anyone know the truth of what happened to me that night?

Even I *don't know the truth.*

I stare up at the window, now showing a blue sky and a calm sea again.

Lies, lies, lies. I sit up in bed, take off one of my silk slippers and hurl it at the picture.

"Leave me *alone*!"

To my surprise, the window goes black. Did it obey me, or did I somehow break it?

I turn away and collapse once more on the bed. My whole being smarts with betrayal—but who is it who has betrayed me? My town, my family, or myself? Was *I* the fool, agreeing to this devil-bargain? Or just a woman with no choice left to make?

I don't know which answer is worse.

Hours pass, and when a knock sounds at the door, I ignore it.

"Go away," I say when it comes again.

But it persists, crisp and insistent.

Finally I go to the door and fling it open. It's Aletheia. She stands a few feet back, gazing her impassive gaze at me. I had thought to feel more sympathy for her, knowing what I now know of her past, but all I can see is the stony dislike in her eyes. I've done nothing, and yet she hates me. Is it to be my fault, that I'm a prisoner of this place?

She takes another step back, and I see the dining table is laid again—it must be lunch hour. My stomach does something at the sight of the food, but all I feel is a bitter knot where hunger ought to be.

I shake my head.

"No." I make to close the door again, but she reaches out and stops its path. She's stronger than her old body looks. She nods her head toward the table and the message is clear: *Sit. Eat.*

I scowl at her. "I said, I don't want any."

She says nothing, only walks to the table and waits, her eyes fixed on me.

"You needn't pretend you don't understand me," I snap. Now that I know her silence is intended merely to snub me, it's driving me to the edge. She may hate mortals, but she *is* part-mortal. She ought not to treat me as though I am less than a beetle.

But now my eyes can't help straying to the table, stacked with persimmons and pomegranates, dates and figs; cheeses and yogurts and sweet curd and all manner of confections baked in honey. There are foods there I haven't yet learned to name, foods no one in the Hellenic lands has seen. A surge of hunger roars through me.

"I don't *want* it, damn you!"

A pang of guilt shoots through me for swearing at her, but the look on her face when I say it—the way her scorn only deepens—makes me push the guilt away, and want to do worse.

Something is bubbling through me, a kind of rage I haven't felt in a very long time. It pushes me forward to where Aletheia stands smirking, her arms folded in a sardonic stance. The words burst out of me before I know they're there.

"I'm a *person*, damn you! And I don't want to be here—do you understand? *I don't want to be here.*"

And I push the table as hard as I can.

It doesn't tip, but it rocks—and piled as high as it is, rocking is enough. One tureen crashes into another; platters slide toward the floor, the weight of them tugging the table-covering with them, and the goblets follow. Dishes careen to the floor and shatter. Glass smashes. Fruit splatters ripe against the marble tile, or rolls across the floor; yoghurt and honey pool and drip.

I stare at it all, feeling dazed. Did I really do this? I feel the tingling under my skin turn electric, then fizzle. Once I'm no longer angry, I'm ashamed.

Aletheia is down on her hands and knees, slowly picking things up from the ground. She still doesn't speak, doesn't reproach me, doesn't show any emotion at all. Just a methodical crouching and lifting as she bends her old knees down to the ground, straightens, and replaces a piece of broken earthenware on the table, and then another.

I can't bear the sight of it—her old body, her age-spotted hands, bending and stooping.

"Leave it!" The words choke themselves out of me. "Aletheia, please."

But she doesn't leave it. She doesn't look at me.

"Please, Aletheia. I'll do it."

She stoops again. She has taken a rag from her pocket, and is swabbing at the floor. Shame drives into me like a knife.

"I said *leave it*!" It comes out as a scream, and we both stop dead. I have shocked her as much as I've shocked myself. The shriek of my voice still rings in my ears.

She drops the cloth and disappears through the door without turning back.

My limbs are shaking. I stand for a while, panting. The silence of the room seems to have a life of its own—as though it is watching me. Eventually I turn and go back to my bedroom, and lie on my bed in the tangle of sheets.

What's happening to me? I should never have spoken that way to an old woman, friend or enemy. Shame washes over me.

Is this who I will become, if I remain here—someone cruel, violent? I turn in the unmade bed; it seems every part of me aches.

I don't know how long I've been lying there when a voice—*his* voice—sounds on the other side of the door.

"Psyche—are you listening?" He doesn't wait for me to answer. "I have made accommodations for your sullen ways. But it will not continue. You'll treat Aletheia with respect, and my home the same way."

He stops. He's waiting for me to retort, but I say nothing.

"It's dinner-time now," he says. "I won't ask you to join me, though I think you must be hungry." He pauses again, and after a while I hear him take a step back from the door.

"Starve yourself to death if you like," he says finally. "But I don't think you have the will for it, mortal."

His footsteps retreat and I roll onto my back, blinking up at the ceiling.

Courage, Psyche.

I can cling to one thing: I will not let this place change me. I will not lose sight of who I am.

For the rest of the night I push down the hunger pangs when they scrabble for purchase in my belly. I think of baby birds, their mouths stretched open, pushing each other aside, demanding to be fed. I can hear him out there, the scrape of his chair as he sits down, the sound of a flagon of wine pouring into a glass. I can smell everything out there, the honey-roast smell of browned meat; the sharp scent of lemons and of mint; the waft of bread warm from the oven.

After a little longer of this, I'm light headed. I can't think of anything else but my body.

He's right, I am weak.

But not that weak.

I curl into a ball on my bed, and wait for sleep.

*

When I wake, the window in my room shows a view of a field of emmer wheat under the morning sun.

The light is thin, still early. But I push myself from the bed and begin to dress.

I see now how it has to be. I will have to be strategic. Patient. I cannot live inside a cage—however gilded it may be—but if *he* will not release me from here by choice, then I will find another way. Every prison has its window. Every cage has its crack.

I will get to work on finding mine.

When I nudge open the bedroom door, I find a note.

Aletheia requires your help in the gardens today.

So he wishes me to go back to the gardens? Well, I have other plans. My intention is to find my way back toward the yard with the stable and the high gate. I know it is the way in and out of this place. All I need is to figure out how it unlocks.

But though I try to find my way through the corridors as before, somehow the correct turns elude me. I reverse back from dead end after dead end until I'm hot and frustrated. I was sure I was on the right path this time. Before, I found it quite by accident, but now it seems almost to avoid me.

I turn on my heel, and go in the opposite direction, and after a while come to a door that is familiar. My heart leaps, but then I recognize it. It's not the door to the stable-yard at all, but the door out to the gardens.

I grit my teeth. *Of course* this would be the one door I can find. Again I find myself wondering if these corridors have a will of their own.

Well, I suppose it won't hurt to have another look at the garden, since I'm here.

As I push open the doors into the golden light, I have to stop to catch my breath. If anything, it's more beautiful now than it was at twilight. Despite everything, the sight of it sends a ripple of peace through me. I step out into the light, so bright

I almost have to shield my eyes.

The land I grew up in is beautiful, to be sure: I love its black soil and sun-bleached skies, its hillsides of white chalk, where donkeys pull their loads up steep paths. But this? This is beauty of a kind I'd never dreamt of. The grass is long and wet, with winding pathways between flower-beds that stretch in every direction, and fruit-trees that overhang the meandering paths, all of it seeming to go on forever. The pond in the middle is a glassy mirror of the sky. And all around it, herbs and flowering plants in row after row, leaves and petals of all colors and shapes, glowing faintly as though underwater.

I have the sense of being watched, and look up in time to see a flicker of movement in the pond, and a splash.

Nymphs, he said. Did I imagine the faint, silvery sound, like a distant laugh? I start to move toward it, where telltale ripples are spreading. But then a sound from right behind me stops me in my tracks.

"Where are you going?" a voice rasps, and I spin around.

Fourteen

Aletheia—she's speaking to me. I'm not sure it's much of an improvement though. I'm certain she made me jump on purpose.

"I—I didn't know you were there."

Her eyes travel over me, sharp and quick, and I wonder what information she's taking in.

"There is much you don't know," she says.

I don't argue. She's right.

I clear my throat. "Aletheia, I want to apologize. The way I behaved yesterday, it was very wrong. I should never have spoken to you like that."

She says nothing, just continues looking me over with those birdlike eyes.

"I've known worse," she says finally, and turns from me. "Come this way."

She has no interest in my apologies, I suppose, no interest in my words at all, and why should she? Disoriented, I follow her—she steps nimbly for an old woman, over tree roots and fallen fruit as if they're nothing, and she moves fast. After a while, she comes to an abrupt stop, and turns to point out a plant with bright yellow buds. "We harvest this today."

She's holding two baskets, and hands me one.

"Flower is delicate," she says. "If we don't harvest right, pods will break. If you cut stem too low, plant will die."

She's speaking an older Greek than I am used to. The words are the same, more or less, and yet it's different. But it's no wonder, if she was born more than three generations ago, that our dialect is no longer quite the same.

She demonstrates to me how the harvesting should be done: where to cut, and how to hold the plant as she makes the incision. Then she drops it gently in her cupped palm and holds it in front of me.

"Later, dry the pod and harvest seeds. I show you."

There's nothing friendly in her tone, and yet when she says *I show you* it occurs to me she does not hate me, perhaps, so much as I had thought.

She hands me a small knife then, to see if I can harvest as she showed me. I take it with some trepidation. I hadn't planned to be out here at all today, being Aletheia's garden assistant. I'd planned to be devising some kind of way out of this place. But then it occurs to me that this garden might help me with that, too. It is a garden full of witching-herbs, after all. Surely some of them can be useful to me. So for now I take Aletheia's hand-knife and try to repeat what she showed me, but she interrupts, shaking her head.

"Stem is too young. Needs more growing. You try this one."

We continue like this for a while, me attempting and her correcting me. Finally, I seem to be doing a passable enough job and she moves off to another corner and busies herself with the plants there—when I look up I see she's moving through them at least five times faster than me, wielding her small knife with quiet efficiency, almost like a dance. Her basket fills quickly, though mine only has a thin covering of herbs across the bottom. I take advantage of her intent focus to scan the plants for ones I recognize.

The sun beats down on me but with none of the harshness of Sikyonian sun. I move through rows of strange and beautiful plants—I think I remember some of the names he told me: bettany, herb of Lethe—but not their functions. It's with surprise then that I stumble on a bed of garden peas beside them. But the demon did say that not everything growing here is magical. The garden supplies the palace and its dining table; demons must eat, too, it appears.

I stare at the rows of pea-pods, inhaling the green scent of them in the sun. They look so delicious. When I run a finger over the pods I can feel the plump peas inside, ready to burst out. The hunger is tormenting me. They are only garden peas, I tell myself: what harm could they do?

I pop a few pods and tip them into my mouth. The taste courses through me like emotion. This is not the way taste used to feel. I move the peas around my mouth, tasting the seasons, tasting spring; honey-water, crisp as dew. I open my eyes, breathing fast. I throw the empty pods on the ground. Taste is not just a sense anymore, it's something more than that.

Senses become more heightened here, he said.

Having eased the roiling in my belly now, I feel more clear-headed than I have for days. And so I go back to harvesting Aletheia's plants, working my way back to where she stands. *She* clearly knows much about this garden. Why not start here, to learn its secrets?

We harvest a little longer in silence before I turn to her.

"What is it this plant does? Once it is dried and prepared."

She glances at me.

"First we take seeds, crush them, mix with celandine oil. Leave one moon cycle. Then it is poison."

The basket almost drops from my hands.

"Poison? But…why would we make such a thing?"

"For his arrows."

Poison-tipped arrows. So the demon is a hunter.

"And what does he hunt?" My voice trembles a little despite myself. "Animals or men?"

"You speak as though men do not kill their own kind," she scoffs. "He does not *hunt* men. But as one man may kill another, he may end a life, if it must be done."

And who decides, I wonder, if such a thing *must* be done?

"Show me your basket," Aletheia gestures, already bored with my questions. She inspects what I've picked so far.

"You are slow, mortal girl. Not even enough for one arrow. You must work harder. Try that bush, there." She directs me to a patch of the garden further away from her—too far for more questions. I do as she says, but my mind is turning fast.

There are powerful things in this garden, indeed. And though I do not seek to poison him, surely there are other things in this garden that I can use. I know the gods have often gifted mortals with magic herbs to help achieve superhuman things. What if, even for an hour or for a few minutes, I could acquire the strength of some great hero? Or better yet, a glamor of invisibility. I could creep out to the stables unnoticed, then, and wait for the demon to open the gate himself.

I could follow him when he retires at night. I could see his uncloaked face.

I could—

"Psyche!"

At the sound of my name I whip around. The black cloak moves in the breeze around the shape of a man, cool-looking in the heat, as though shade follows where he goes. How does he manage to sneak up on me like that?

Beneath the cloak I can see he's looking at me. Then he turns aside.

"Aletheia—you have gathered amply for today. Will you take these inside—the lady Psyche's basket, too?"

Aletheia gives the merest nod, and takes the basket from me without a word. I watch her spry figure make its way back toward the palace walls. It's easier than looking at him.

Whatever he's kept me behind to say, I doubt I want to hear it. More insults? More patronizing rationales for why I should not only accept captivity but be grateful for it?

"Walk with me."

He moves off down the path, pomegranate trees making a dappled light over him as he goes. I stay rooted where I am, and then I remember I have a goal. A goal that might mean humoring him for a while. Let him think me a tamer creature than I am, if it keeps me the freedom to go where I wish around the palace and its grounds. I follow him down the path.

After a few paces he speaks again. His voice is stiff and oddly formal.

"I wish to apologize. I fear I have not been mindful of just how great a transition this has been for you. What's worse, I failed to control my temper." The hood shifts in my direction. "It is a foul temper, I am sorry to say. I have been told that before." He clears his throat. "I do not wish for you to feel yourself imprisoned here, Psyche. I think perhaps, once you are here a little while, you might see that it is not the prison you imagine." He slows his pace a little, noticing I'm lagging, and gestures to the vast space around us.

"There is more to these gardens than you've seen. Orchards and vineyards and wide open fields. I can bring one of the horses for you if you like; you can learn to ride."

I don't tell him that my father taught my sister and me to ride years ago—though on a short-legged old workhorse, not on one of *these* majestic creatures.

"And you will not be without companions," the demon goes on. "There are nymphs in these gardens; dryads too. They are merry, social creatures." He hesitates. "I can understand how my company and Aletheia's alone might not feel sufficient for a young woman."

I walk alongside him, silent and confused. His tone is cold, but it seems he wishes me to be persuaded. And yet what need has he to make his case? I'm here whether I wish to be or not. I can't fathom this. Yesterday he called me a worm; today he courts my favor.

Perhaps he just wants me to see him as my benefactor. He wishes to win my gratitude so that he can boast he rescued me as he rescued Aletheia. He wishes me to overlook that he lied to me, entrapped me, and now refuses to let me leave. I feel his sidelong glance again.

"I do not think it impossible," he says, his voice as stiff as before, "that you could be happy here."

I look over. "And do you care, if I am happy or

otherwise?"

"I am not indifferent," he says shortly.

Not indifferent—how flattering. A sharp laugh bubbles up in me, but suddenly I find myself wondering: who exactly *has* cared whether I was happy or not?

My father wished me to be safe and healthy. He wished me to marry well and make him proud. But did he ever question whether I was *happy*?

Perhaps *I* never questioned whether I was happy.

As for Yiannis, he always liked to see me smile, but not, I think, because he longed for my happiness. If he had, he wouldn't have commanded my smiles to suit his pleasure.

Without my noticing it, somehow, we have made our way back to the palace door. Now the demon opens it—one broad, bronzed hand against the dark metal—and steps back.

"Come inside," he says. "There is a room I wish to show you."

Fifteen

He stops at a turn in the corridor and opens a door, gesturing me to step inside. I hesitate, but once I see what's through the doorway, I gasp.

A loom. But it's the largest I've ever seen, larger than I knew a loom could be. Its wood gleams like some magnificent instrument, its shafts and beams and heddles so intricately connected I feel dazed just looking at it. This whole vast room is dedicated solely to the loom and to its craft: over on the far wall are skeins upon skeins of spun silk, of more colors than I ever knew existed, all neatly spooled, waiting there for their beauty to be put to use.

"Whose…whose room is this?" Somehow I already know it's not Aletheia's.

He turns a little; the hood shivers.

"It is here for you. I guarantee you will make no tapestry more beautiful than any you weave on it. It is made from the trees of the forest of Foloi."

The forests of Foloi. It's where the centaurs are said to roam.

"But…it's extraordinary…" I stare at the length of it, enough to fill many times over the room I slept in in Sikyon. I don't know if I *could* use a loom so grand; if I would even know how.

"It looks more fit for the Moriae than for mortal use."

I'm speaking more to myself than to him, but the black hood shifts sharply.

"The Fates—you believe in them?"

I flush. I wish my cheeks did not redden so easily. I wish my voice did not give everything away. It is unfair that I should be so transparent to him, while he has the advantage of his cloak.

"Everyone believes in the Fates," I say. The Moriae, the Fates, the Three Sisters—people have different names for them but everyone knows who they are. They measure out a person's life. The youngest sister spins the thread, the middle sister weaves it, and the eldest sister holds the shears. When she decides your time is through, it's through.

"Not *everyone.*" His voice is crisp. "Faith and ritual are two different things, Psyche. Anyone may follow a ritual, but not everyone believes. Besides," he says, "I asked whether *you* believed in them."

I'm silent for a moment then.

When I was a child I believed every story my father told me: of great heroes, powerful immortals, celestial battles through the ages. No detail was too extraordinary to be believed. But as we age, our minds change. And yet…

"I do believe in them," I say quietly.

My mother died the hour I was born. They say she only held me long enough to speak my name. And perhaps that is the reason I believe. It seems to me there must have been some reason for it. Not a kind reason, or even a fair one—no one ever said the gods were merciful. But I have to believe there is some order by which they weave and cull our lives. Otherwise it's just chaos. No rhyme or reason. And it seems to me I can't believe in that.

"And this?" He lifts a small medallion at my throat and I swallow, feeling his hand so near me. I can smell the cedarwood scent of him. The medallion bears the figure of the god Eros—my father gave it to me when I was a child, to ward off harm. Although perhaps of late it has not done its job very well.

"You have a particular devotion to Eros?" I am sure I hear a smirk in his voice. I know what he's thinking. Eros is the god of Love, but the god of more bodily pleasures too.

"He is the patron of my city," I snap. "And I gladly give him my allegiance."

"Then tell me—" He drops the medallion back against my throat. "What would you say is the difference, exactly, between demons and gods?"

I eye him sidelong. I have no interest in his trick questions.

"Seeing as you despise demons so much, and yet worship your gods so ardently. What's the difference between them?"

Something about the way he asks the question makes me feel stupid—makes my father, and Dimitra, and all of Sikyon, *sound* stupid—and I resent him for it.

"Demons sow confusion," I say boldly. "Anarchy. Brutality and war."

"And what of Eris?" he counters. "What of Ares? Of Deimos and Phobos?"

I know the gods he's naming: the goddess of discord, the god of war. And Ares's twin sons, young gods of terror who go with him to the battlefield.

I set my jaw. I feel he's tricking me, and yet I can't find a winning answer. The gods he names may wreak havoc, yes, but they are part of the great balance of all things. They, too, must have their place in the pantheon. I frown. But then, if we were to call a demon by a god's name…

I can feel his eyes on me, enjoying my confusion.

"Perhaps gods and demons, Psyche, are all in the eye of the beholder." I hear the satisfaction in his voice. "Perhaps all either of them do is bring man's true nature to the surface."

*

I follow him back along the corridors, until we near the door to the great-room. And then he takes a familiar strip of silk from his cloak and beckons me to turn around. I hesitate.

"Psyche, there's no need to make this difficult."

Reluctantly I turn and feel the blindfold slip over my eyes. The touch of his hands is a shock again. His skin feels no different than a human's, but something very different throbs below its surface—the immortal part of him, the life force, more silent than a heartbeat but alive as a hummingbird's wing.

"Very good."

I hear the door open, and he puts an arm under mine to guide me. Such a strange feeling. It's almost....

No matter. I dismiss the thought as we advance into the room, and the delicious smells fill me with desire and dread.

"I know you have been reluctant to dine here." His voice seems very near. "But you must eat. You are mortal: we both know what must happen if you continue to refuse my food."

The few shelled peas from the garden have long since ceased to quiet my appetite.

"Maybe…just some bread and water…"

"Sit," he says, and guides me to a chair. If he senses the desperate grumbling from my stomach, he makes no comment on it. There is something strangely intimate about his voice when I am blindfolded—as though he speaks directly inside my head, to my inmost thoughts.

"I recognize you are at a disadvantage: I have desired you to eat with me, but you cannot see all the dishes laid before you." He clears his throat. "Perhaps I can describe them to you. I will fill a platter with whatever you desire."

I say nothing. If his gallantry surprises me—which it does—then I don't let it move me. Gallantry is easy when you're the one in charge. I'm not so cheap a plaything that he can sway me with some handsome words. But it galls me, how my skin responds to his voice.

"Rolled lamb," he begins. "Stuffed with mint and dates. Skewers of fish with lemon and tarragon. Sliced pomegranate. Aloe with shaved ice. Braised eel, sturgeon roe; asparagus broth…" He goes on, naming delicacies I could imagine only on a king's table.

I shake my head slightly.

"Psyche, you must stop this. Do you think I will send you home if you do not eat? I will not."

"It's not that," I say faintly, although perhaps part of me *had* been thinking that. But I don't think it any longer.

I don't know if it's fear or hunger that makes me tremble; my hand smacks into something, and I hear the sound of a glass topple and roll. The smell that wafts my way tells me it was wine.

"Never mind," he says. Then he takes my hand in his, and places a fresh glass in it. "Have mine."

I pull away, but he's already let go and I don't want to spill a second glass.

"It's good," he says. "Trust me."

But I can't trust you.

I can feel him watching me, even if I can't see it. Slowly, I take the glass to my lips, and take the smallest sip. It floods me—the most miraculous feeling. It's like jumping into the sea and feeling all the blood in your body cry out with cold, but instead of cold, it's joy. It's as though I can feel all the pathways of my body at once, all lit up like a bright torch.

I put down the wine and let out a small gasp.

"You like it?" he says, a smile in his voice. Unless it's a smirk. Beneath the blindfold, I can't quite be sure.

Then a plate lands in front of me, very gently placed. I hear it, but mainly I smell it, the wonderful aromas drifting toward me.

And I cannot hold out forever, he is right. Even if *he* were not determined that I eat, I know I can't keep going like this. If I am to break free of this place, then I must live; I must keep my body strong.

"Will it be like before?" I say. "Will I…lose myself?"

He is quiet.

"I cannot say," he admits finally. "It is different for everyone."

I turn my face toward his voice.

"What do you mean? Different for whom?"

"Those I feed," he says simply, "all feel it. But what each

feels, tastes, that is different for everyone. It is about you, Psyche, as much as it is about me."

I think of Persephone, condemned to the Underworld because of one bite of Hades' fruit. But this creature is no god, and I am no goddess.

Falteringly, I move my hand. On the right is the lamb, he said. I move my hand a little to the side, and my pinkie finger nudges the warm bread. I tear a piece, then use it to scoop up some of the lamb. My mouth is watering uncontrollably; my stomach is growling. But still I cannot seem to put it in my mouth. The sip of wine, small as it was, was enough to remind me of the magic of this place; of how intoxicating any morsel on this table can be. I don't know if I can bring myself to eat in front of him. I lost myself once before, with that peach—I would surely have dived off the cliff for one more bite, had I not still been in chains.

I swallow.

"My hand shakes too much. I cannot see what is on my plate. Let me take it into my room, and eat there, without the blindfold."

There's a pause.

"I have not asked to share your bed, but I ask that you share my table." He pauses. "Here. I will help you."

I hear movement; new wafts of deliciousness. Then a shock of nearness: I don't know how I know exactly, but I sense him here, quite close to my face. I smell, underneath the smells of food, that particular scent of his: myrrh and honey, cedar and pine.

"A morsel of lamb," he says. "With rosemary, thyme, lemon. On a piece of bread, with olive paste."

I sit frozen. He's holding it in front of my mouth. He is proposing to…feed me?

"I…"

I sit back into my chair. This is how infants look, I suppose, resisting attempts to make them eat.

"Psyche, come." His voice is reasonable, even amused. "You cannot starve."

I'm trying to resist, but all I can smell is the mouthful of food hovering just before my nostrils. My stomach feels like there is some wild creature inside, hurling itself at the walls. I am so empty inside, I could faint.

"Psyche?"

The meat smells of open fires, of red wine on winter nights; of butter pooling in a hot pan; of juniper and the deep woods.

"Just one bite."

I'm hungrier than I knew a person could be. Every fiber of my being calls out for it and I can already all but taste it, the crisp charred edges of the lamb, the melting center, the juices flowing down my throat.

I don't think I even decide to open my mouth, it just happens. And then I'm tasting it, and it's like nothing I can describe. The meat slides onto my tongue, the richness of the herbs, the bright glow of salt, all of it unfolding in my mouth like a gift, touching all the corners of my tongue at once. And then the taste spreads beyond my tongue—to my throat, and up into my skull, and down to my belly, where a hot glow begins to spread.

Yes, I remember this feeling. This euphoria that stokes the very hunger it satisfies.

"Not so bad, see?" I can hear the smile in his voice. The myrrh-and-honey smell wafts my way again.

My hands are still trembling, but it's a different kind of trembling now.

"More?" he says.

I nod, and when he puts another mouthful in front of me I don't even need his voice to guide me—I can tell by my quivering nostrils, and I open my mouth again.

It is as though my blood has turned to gold; it is as though all my veins are singing. My head is swimming, my body is aflame. It is almost a trance; I suppose that I could move if I wanted to, but I don't have to. All I need do is sit here, and open my mouth like a baby bird.

Like a bird.

The images flash into my mind, jarring and sharp: the birds squawking in their aviary, their white palace. Their cage.

Birds that never see the sky.

His fingers brush against my lips. Fingers that smell of every delicious thing—of spices and butter and smoke and berries and warmth—and that beneath it, smell of him.

Suddenly my stomach turns. I push my chair back as hard as I can.

"Get away from me!"

On my feet now, I bump against the chair and feel it topple. I find my bedroom door blindly, and scrabble inside. I lean against the wall, rip the tie from across my eyes, and stare at the ceiling, my breath heaving.

"Psyche…"

When he calls out, his voice is distant; he has not followed me to my door.

"Leave me alone, *demon,*" I spit back.

There's a pause. When he speaks, his voice has turned from impatient to something colder.

"I would advise you, mortal, to have more care with how you talk to me."

I hear the squeal of a chair then, and the slam of a door. I don't have to peer out to know the room is empty once more.

*

I go to bed in my clothes; I don't want to see my body or its bare skin. I am ashamed of it tonight, of how it betrayed me in so short a time. I pace the room to the point of exhaustion before collapsing on the bed, and when I sleep, dreams plague me. Inconvenient dreams, dreams I do not wish to acknowledge.

In the morning when I wake, my heart is beating fast. It's as if the memories of last night have struck fresh. My cheeks burn.

What was I thinking?

I *wasn't* thinking. I am a mortal; mortal temptation, I could resist. But this…it was not the stuff I was made for.

I hate him. I hate him, this dark shadow of a creature. *Aprósopos,* the Faceless One. I sit on the side of the bed, and feel a dullness in the pit of my stomach. I don't want to face him tonight. He enjoyed it, I am sure, seeing me suddenly so in thrall. How he must have smirked. I set my jaw. His demon foodstuffs cast some spell I cannot help. What I felt last night, for those few moments…it was some bewitchment, some entrapment. Nothing more.

I will refuse to join his table tonight. He can threaten me however he likes.

It's barely light when I hear a noise in the room outside. *Him?*

But when I peer through the crack, it's not him, but Aletheia. And she's carrying something.

A key.

My heart beats faster. *A key.* Keys are rare things in Sikyon, but I am sure that's what that metal object is. And I think I know what this key is for: there is only one place in this palace that I have found locked, and I know that gate leads to the outside world.

I watch the door fall closed behind Aletheia, then take a breath, and slip from my room.

Sixteen

I dart to the door, leaving my slippers behind—these corridors echo, and the slightest tap or scuff would be amplified. Every moment I think she will turn around, but she does not. Instead she moves, surefooted, through the corridors, and it's clear that she knows this path as well as a person can, that she travels it often. As we walk I'm more and more certain that I was right: these are the turns I could not find before. And finally we round another corner and there it is: the door that leads to the stable-yard. Aletheia disappears through it.

I wait a moment, then proceed on tiptoe and crack open the door. The yard bakes under the sun. Aletheia is in the stables, I can see her shadow in the doorway and hear the horses snorting. Eventually she comes out leading two horses—her thin old frame looks odd next to these tremendous beasts, which seem almost twice her height. She leaves them in the center of the yard, flicking their tails and pricking their ears in anticipation, while she goes back for the other two. Then, finally, she takes out the key and goes to the gate. I hear the great clank of a bolt sliding, the sigh of the gates as they open. I crane my head, but the angle is wrong and the gates open inward: I still can't see what lands await outside them.

Aletheia comes back into the center of the yard, and leans up to one of the horses, seeming to whisper something in its ear.

"Go!" She smacks it on the rump then, and it shoots through the gate into whatever lies beyond. I stare as it bolts, riderless, into the unknown.

She repeats it for the other horses, and finally for the black stallion with the golden eyes. When they have gone, the yard is strangely quiet. Are they coming back? I suppose she must expect it. I wait for Aletheia to do something, but she just sits down on the rim of a stone trough and pulls a pipe from her pocket. She lights it and begins to smoke, blowing a soft blue ring into the air. After a while—I don't know how long we sit there, Aletheia watching the gate, and me watching her—there is a pounding of hooves and the horses return, one by one, galloping through the gate and slowing just enough to canter round the yard, then ease at last to a shivering, snorting halt.

Aletheia pats each one, then leads it back into its stable.

This is one of her duties, I suppose—to exercise these great beasts. Does she do it every day? I'll have to rise early to find out. Once I know the rhythm, I can make use of it. All I need is to get through that gate, and it will be easier to slip past Aletheia's watch, at any rate, than the demon's.

For now, I don't let myself think too hard about what lies outside those gates—what strange land I'll be in, or how long it may take me to reach anywhere close enough to get a message to Sikyon. I just have to do it.

When Aletheia rises from her sitting-place I start backwards. Hopefully she doesn't notice the door's ajar, I have no time to close it. I race back along the corridors, praying I make each turn fast enough before she rounds the bend and sees me.

Back in my room, I breathe fast, pacing up and down in front of the illusion-window, which today shows a mountain ridge covered in thick olive trees. If I get through those gates, it will not be a return to my old life. That life, and the life I thought I was meant to have, are gone forever. But all I know is that I can't grow old in a gilded cage.

As to Aphrodite…if I let myself think it, the thought of her chills my blood, but how do I know the demon isn't lying to me? A god's anger may find a new victim from one day to the next. Perhaps it's just arrogance to believe she's still looking for me.

I suppose there's only one way to find out.

*

Later in the day I practice for myself, to see if I can find the door to the stables again. This time I close my eyes once in the corridor—there is something to be said, after all, for depriving oneself of sight. I have spent a good amount of time without it, these last days, and I believe it has begun to sharpen some other skills. Memory, for one. Now with my eyes closed I can see Aletheia's bony frame hurrying down these halls, and I follow in my mind's eye, taking the turns exactly as I remember them, opening my eyes only when I must. And to my surprise it takes no more than five minutes.

I've made it. I'm smiling widely as I step outside. The yard is quiet, and I go to the great gate and study it again. Now that I study it more closely, I can see it, disguised almost perfectly by the filigree design: the slot where the key must fit. I reach out, half-expecting it to burn me, but nothing happens.

All well and good—but how to get the key?

I must be patient. Inspiration will come, I tell myself. I sigh and turn, leaning my back against the door to my prison. Over in the stables, the black horse puts its face over the half-door and studies me, unperturbed. Truly, he is a noble creature.

I walk over, but don't quite dare to stroke his muzzle. Instead, I open the door and peek inside the stable. Four stalls, one for each horse, and here by the door, hanging from a hook on the wall, a quiver of arrows. The poisoned arrows, no doubt. I shiver, and the black horse watches me closely. He stamps a foot and scuffs it backwards, tossing some hay from the floor, and his horse-shoes flash gold.

"Do you hunt with him, then?" I murmur. "Do you see all his dark deeds? It is not right: you are too noble a creature to serve one such as him."

Then I hear movement from outside. The gates are moving, their great black mass swinging inward. He has returned already!

I want so badly to see what lies beyond those gates, but my fear of being seen is greater. I shrink further back into the stall, the stallion's black tail flicking softly beside me. I hear the demon's treat in the yard and know he's approaching the stables. The horses whinny in anticipation, and he greets them, one by one:

"Good evening, Ajax." That's the black horse. Then he moves along the row, further away from me. "Good evening, Velos; Tharros; Anemos."

I hold my breath. I hear him move toward the palace door, and through the stable's doorway I glance out, confirming that his back is to me. I wonder if I will see him remove his cloak now: he says he does not like to wear it in his home, and he will think me upstairs, safe from view. But then, with one foot on the step, he pauses.

"Psyche," he says.

My heart skips a beat. *How does he know?*

"I suggest you come out of there, and go upstairs. It is evening already."

My heart has resumed its work, but badly—now it beats twice as hard as before. I feel a wave of boldness run through me. I step forward, out of the stables. Beneath the black hood, I feel him look at me.

"I will not dine with you tonight," I say. "I will have no more of your demon food."

He moves his foot back from the doorway and turns fully to face me then. He is quiet for a while.

"I can see you fear what happened last night." He stops, as though considering his words. "For a mortal to find pleasure in this place—that is neither fearful nor shameful. But if you don't want it to happen again, it will not." The hood shifts a little.

"I hope in time you shall accustom yourself to the pleasures of this realm, but in the meantime, if you wish to subsist on bread and water, it shall be so. I have asked Aletheia to prepare some for you tonight."

I fold my arms. I suppose he means to trick me with that, too.

"And you will not go blindfolded," he adds then, and I stare.

So he means to show me his face, after all?

"I will keep myself cloaked while you eat."

This is almost as surprising. Why make such a concession? Why have me sit with him at all? We have surely proved by now that we do not make for good companions.

"Come," he says, his voice commanding, and opens the door.

I suppose I could refuse. I could dig my heels in and sleep in the stables all night. But for whatever reason, he seems prepared to offer concessions today, and those may prove useful to me. The great generals agree, it is wise to pick one's battles.

Slowly, I walk toward the door.

*

It is a strange experience, sitting at the table with no blindfold. Seeing everything. Seeing *him*. I cannot help but flash back to last night, and I hope he does not see me flush. He sits in shadow, and all I see of him are his hands, golden-skinned, folded on the table before him. He looks so calm, so assured. The lord of his kingdom, who believes that everything in this room belongs to him—even Aletheia. Even me. I want to ask him what he does all day. Where he goes. What has earned him the right to return to this table at night with such a self-satisfied air, as though he's been laboring in the fields all day, when surely he is up to much darker work than that.

The table is set, as before, with a variety of sumptuous food. Platters with crisp-skinned meat, oil-glazed vegetables, soups and ices; fruits and cheeses and fritters that smell of herbs. I try not to move too much. If I stay quite still, maybe I'll avoid all those exquisite food smells wafting toward me, assaulting me with every turn of my head. Then Aletheia emerges from the doorway with a plate of bread, and drops it brusquely on the table before me.

A few crusts of bread, dry as wafers. I exhale.

"Well? Eat," he says, once Aletheia has left us again.

Slowly I raise one to my mouth and take a small nibble. The taste is recognizable—better, richer, far more delicious than mere bread-crusts should be, but nothing too ecstatic. Nothing I can't manage. I breathe more freely, and take a small sip of water. Even the water tastes like sunshine, like the freshest spring from the deepest forest—but it does not disturb my peace too much. It does not leave me breathless.

"Better?" the demon says, and I nod.

I remind myself that he is not solicitous for my well-being, even if he sometimes appears it. I remind myself of the secrets he keeps from me, and the freedom he denies me. I must not let his small courtesies tame me—I may only let him *think* that they do.

"I think that you are lonely here," he says.

I drop the crust back on my plate and look at him. The dark hood shimmers; I see his head move to one side, as though waiting for an answer.

I try not to let the tears well behind my eyes. *Lonely.* I had not realized until he said the word, how true it was.

It occurs to me then that loneliness is the fate of many women in my land. Overnight, they are removed from their families and placed in a new household, expected to be the dutiful and submissive daughter their husband's parents expect. She must give up her old home, her old friends. She must give herself over to a man she knows only a little, and a family that is not her own.

And yet nobody ever talked—at least not in my hearing—about how painful it all must be. Perhaps the world does not wish for it to be talked of. Perhaps they know that women will be more pliant, more willing to please, when they feel all alone.

Easier to control.

And what happens to them, finally? They survive, I suppose. They grow to like their new worlds, or they don't. And either way, life goes on.

The demon clears his throat.

"I have been thinking," he says abruptly. "Although I make no promise of success, I can try to deliver a message to your family as you asked."

I look up at him. He means it?

"You must not say too much. But they need not think you dead, and grieve you." He pauses. "You have writing knowledge, I suppose?"

I nod.

"Very good. Aletheia will leave some papyrus in your room." He glances over. "I cannot guarantee that I can deliver it, but I shall try."

I sit very still. Images of my family burst into my mind. My father sitting by the fire in winter, telling us stories. Dimitra with her hair flung forward, drying it in the sun.

"You must warn them," he says quietly, "to keep the knowledge of your true fate to themselves."

A lump forms in my throat. At least they will know I am safe. And yet…somehow it seems more like a goodbye than ever.

*

In the morning, I rise early, waiting for the sound of Aletheia's tread in the great-room. When I crack the door open I see she has the key in hand again. Once more, I follow her down the passageways—I am beginning to find my way with ease, now—and spy on her as she lets the horses out for their run, cantering into the great unknown. I envy them: how I would like to have their freedom!

Although they, too, must come back here after their run is over, to be locked up inside the gates once more. Perhaps we are not so very different after all, the horses and I.

Wife. He calls me that, but I am no wife. I have not the duties of one, nor the freedoms. At home a married woman may be happy or unhappy, she may have many burdens to bear, some worse than others. She must prepare her husband's meals and please him in the bedroom and bear his children. But for a few hours each day he is gone and she is free: free to walk in town and see her friends; to laugh and move in the open air. This "husband" treats me elegantly enough—courtly, courteous, he has never laid a hand where he should not, or trespassed upon my body except with those occasional lingering stares I feel from beneath his cloak. But though he gives me finery to wear and a palace to walk in, I cannot roam and chatter in the Agora with others, as even the unhappiest women of Sikyon may do.

I set my jaw and go back to watching Aletheia. I'm looking for signs of distraction. I think perhaps that while she waits for the horses, she may sleep a little, or wander. But she stays where she stayed yesterday, perched on the stone trough, her eyes gazing toward the open gate and whatever lies beyond. It is disheartening. I cannot see how I am to get past her, unless I slip her a sleep-potion or somehow overpower her. But there is bound to be a way.

Back in the great-room, by my bedroom door, I find a scroll of papyrus laid out for me, and ink. It is as he promised—I am to write a letter to my family, and he will deliver it.

I can write well enough, though Father dismissed our tutor when I was ten—Dimitra and I had enough book-learning for two girls, he said, and indeed probably more than Sikyon thought good for us. But when I sit down at the table, my mind goes blank. It seems an impossible feat. What can I say to Father or Dimitra that they will possibly understand? While they know nothing, they can at least hope for the best. Once they see a letter written in my hand, they must face some reality or other—a reality that I decide. If I tell the truth, they will hardly believe me. If I tell them "I am alive but not to see you again," is that even worse than imagining me dead? If I tell them I am married and living in a distant land, they will wonder how such a thing came to pass—and they will want to visit, they will seek me out...

I am not fool enough to think the demon will not read the letter himself. Which means I cannot comfort them with the truth—that I plan to leave here, and find my way to them again.

Dear Father and Dimitra, I begin, and then sit staring at the page.

Finally I put down the stylus. It is too much. Too many thoughts roaring at me, each one wanting to be heard. Too much weight upon my shoulders. I pace the room a while, then peer out the door, checking if there's anyone outside. There isn't, and I let my steps carry me into the corridors again, along the twists and turns until I open a door into fresh air and sunshine. The reprieve I needed, though even now I'm still not quite prepared for the garden's strikingly perfect beauty. It catches my breath every time.

It's not yet noon and the trees wave gently in the breeze, casting dappled shadows along the paths. But as my eyes adjust to the brightness I see movement where I did not expect it.

The pond is busy with life, and not fish or birds: creatures, lithe and silver-haired, splashing and laughing together. As I stare, I sense movement beside me and look around to find one of them close by. She is beautiful: taller than me, sharp-chinned, her hair a shimmering mass like a silver sea.

"*Khaire,*" she hails me in the formal way. Her voice matches her skin and hair—it shimmers, yet there is something hard in it.

"You must be the lady Psyche."

Seventeen

"We have heard much about you." She laughs a see-sawing laugh; if I closed my eyes, I would think it was no more than tree boughs moving in the wind. "You must join our little party—we have brought music. And wine."

What power nymphs wield, and whether they are easily offended, I have no idea. I dare not refuse her. She leads me toward the pond, which close up is bigger than I realized, and busy with a whole host of her kind. I see that not all of the nymphs are women: some of them are young men—boys, really. One or two look to be only little Hector Georgiou's age, and look at me curiously—perhaps they have not seen a human before, just as I have not seen a nymph.

Most of the younger ones glance up briefly, then go back to splashing in the water. But I see our appearance has caught some interest. A smaller group of nymphs that look closer to my companion's age move nimbly out of the water and draw near. One smiles, some of the others eye me coolly.

"I am the nymph Eido," says the one who brought me here. "These are my kin. Well, let us not stand on ceremony." She flashes her teeth at me and waves some of her companions forward.

They usher me to the bank of the water and make space to sit down in the sweet-smelling grass. The wine is opened, glasses poured.

"We drink to your health." Eido glances at the others, then back at me. "Our lord's new bride."

Bride. My stomach twists nervously. And *lord*. The demon is more powerful than I knew—I have not yet heard of one who holds dominion over a host of nymphs.

"A rare choice, certainly."

One of them giggles. Another edges closer to me, then holds my hair back from my face, inspecting me. Her hands brush my ear, soft and silken, but there's no mistaking the way she's appraising me. Part of me expects her to pull back my lips and check my teeth, the way Father would with a new cow. What does she see me as? A prisoner? A strange trophy?

I do not like that all of them know *him*: they are on the demon's side. No doubt they laugh and sport with him, whereas I am left in the dark, wedded to a creature who will not tell me his true name, nor what sort of life he has outside these walls. *Nor even show me his face.*

One of the smaller nymphs paddles over then. She is little, just a child.

"She is very fair, is she not?" she pipes.

"Indeed." The dryad next to me flashes a cool smile. "Very fair—for a mortal."

"You're jealous, Khelone," another butts in. "*You* would covet her space in his bed, wouldn't you?"

"Hush, Klaia," the one called Eido says. It's clear she's the one in charge.

I wonder what they would say if I told them we shared no bed at all? But the trading of insults and innuendo continues, until finally one of the nymphs pushes another into the water. Most of the others seem to have forgotten me by now, delighted by this new drama. But the small girl has padded over as her older companions snipe and curse each other in the water.

"Are you *really* a mortal?" she says, and I nod. Her eyes widen.

"Does it hurt?"

The question should make me laugh perhaps, but instead it gives me a strange pang.

"Sometimes," I say. *But not in the way you think, little one.*

"I like mortals," the child says. "They're shiny." And she puts her hand on my hair, patting it gently, like a dog.

I decide I might as well capitalize on this show of loyalty.

"What do you know, little one," I say, "about the lord they call my husband?"

She stops petting me; her eyes widen again, growing cautious.

"He has a name among mortals, does he not? Do you know what it is?"

"Phoebe!" one of the older dryads calls sharply now from the water, and the little one starts and puts her hands behind her back.

"Don't get the child in trouble." The one they call Klaia walks toward me. She drops down on the damp bank beside me and pushes a cup of wine into my hands. "You look far too serious, you know."

She hesitates a moment.

"We call him Lord Aetos."

Aetos: we know that bird throughout the Hellenic lands. A great, majestic hunter, with a wingspan as long as I am tall.

"It is just a nickname. I believe you mortals have a different name for him." Her gaze is direct. "He prefers you not to know it, because if you know it, you will see him differently. You will believe what the stories say, instead of learning him as he is."

I scowl.

"And what does it matter, whether I believe the stories or not?"

The nymph looks at me. There is something serious for a moment behind those color-shifting, mischievous eyes.

"I suppose, because he wishes you to love him."

It's a good thing I haven't been drinking the wine, because if I had been, I'd have spat it out on the ground. Surely she has it wrong. And besides—

"He doesn't need me to love him," I say. "I've sworn a vow. He can have what he wants from me, whether I wish to give it or not."

Klaia shakes her head.

"Lord Aetos isn't like that. He claims from pleasure only, not from obligation."

I reach for my wine, take a shaky sip. The brightness courses through me, dazzling my tastebuds, but I'm so distracted now, the effect passes quickly.

Perhaps she's making trouble for reasons of her own, or it's a mistranslation. The nymphs may not use words in the same way mortals do. Whatever he wants from me, it can't be the thing *I* call love.

She shrugs her sleek shoulders. "We were surprised by it too. For most of us, you see, mortals are seen as rather…coarse. No offense intended."

I'm flushed to my roots, now, but she takes a long swig of wine.

Over her shoulder, I see two of the young boy-nymphs tiptoeing toward us, giggling softly. They may not be mortal boys but I've seen that sly, mischievous look a hundred times before on the youths of Sikyon, and I know they're up to something. One of them sees me watching, and puts a finger to his lips. One step further, and together they drop a small, brown toad right onto Klaia's lap.

The commotion is a relief. In seconds Klaia's up and shrieking, chasing the boys back to the water with wild threats, giving me the chance to slip away unnoticed.

*

Back in my room, though my mind teems with thoughts, I force myself to finish the letter.

Dear Father and Dimitra

I trust this letter reaches you securely. It is my first chance to send word and may be my last for some time. I need you to know that I am well, that I am safe. Fate intervened that day on the cliffs, and I was delivered from that danger.

More than that: my rescuer has taken me as his wife. Alas, his homeland is very distant, but know that it is the dearest wish of my heart to see you again, and I hope it may yet come to pass.

For now, I send you my love. Do not grieve me.

I add some words about not letting others in our town know the truth. It will only cause trouble, if the king should get wind that his plan for me was foiled.

I roll the letter back into a scroll and seal it. I glance out the window, which shows the sea again. By the light it is already evening. Is he back yet? Some part of me fears he will have changed his mind now, and not take the letter after all.

I open the door to the great-room, and stop in my tracks. He is back, and he stands before the window—but tonight, the window does not show any view I could expect. Its image is nothing I've ever seen before. A dark landscape, mountainous, stormy—and at the peak of one of the mountains, a city built up high. I say a city, but truthfully I have seen no city like it in my life. It shines like marble, all peaks and spires. The sight of it stops me where I stand. I'd like to think it is a sight from the Outer Lands, from Persia or Aethiopia perhaps. But a cold feeling under my skin tells me this is no mortal place.

Then, just as fast, the picture disappears. Quickly, the demon withdraws his hand back inside his cloak, and there is something of regret in the gesture.

"Psyche," he says, without turning. Once more, he has sensed me without seeing me.

"What was that?" I say. "That place…was it real?"

"Real enough." Something in his voice signals he will not speak further of this to me. I am learning to read him better than would seem possible, for one whose face I can never hope to see. I put the strange vision from my mind, and walk toward him, scroll in hand.

"The letter is written."

He nods, and takes it wordlessly from me. So close, I breathe the scent of him again. The fabric of his cloak is the color of midnight, yet despite that it seems to hold the light.

Aletheia comes into the room then, bearing bread and water, and he gestures me toward the table.

"Sit. Tell me of your day."

I scoff inwardly. Who asks such a thing of a prisoner? And yet truth be told, my day was eventful enough. Klaia's unnerving comment lingers in my head.

"I met some of your nymphs," I say.

He nods.

"And did they amuse you?"

I think of the giggles and stares, the comments. The one they call Klaia was friendly enough, I suppose, but…

"Not much." Why should he expect me to like such creatures? "They're…so *purposeless.* Do they really live whole aeons like this, just gossiping and sniping and tending to their beauty?"

"Well," he seems to consider the question. "Sometimes they swim."

I glare. He thinks everything I say is so *amusing*.

"I wouldn't expect you to understand," I snap. "What has an immortal to do with time except waste it? I can see it is quite foreign to you, the idea that a person should *use* their time. That there is more to life than disporting oneself. That in the time we have, we might want to do something *real*."

I feel him looking at me. I hear the smarting anger in my voice.

"You may think it is a petty thing, a mortal life. A *woman's* life. But it is what I have."

What I had.

"This again?" He sounds disgusted. "You ride a high horse, *wife*. You wish me to congratulate you on being mortal; on being a member of such a miserable, murderous race? Very well: I congratulate you." His chair screeches as he pushes it back from the table, and in a few sweeping strides, black cloak flowing behind him, he's gone from the room.

And my letter remains on the table.

Eighteen

"Hello, pretty ones," I say softly.

I have found my way back to the bird-room today. They are extraordinary creatures, and the longer I watch them, the more I marvel at them. Some have long legs that fold up underneath them like dancers; others, enormous bills that drape down toward the ground; others still, extraordinary tails that unfurl like wings as I watch.

They do not seem unhappy here. Green shrubs fill the corners of the room, tricking my eye into imagining I'm outdoors, and perhaps it tricks the birds, too. And yet…one yellow-breasted bird cocks its head at me, looking at me with bright black eyes that remind me of Dimitra. They are intelligent creatures—intelligent enough, I believe, to know they are captives. They may seem tame, but I believe the instinct to be a wild thing lives inside us all. I think even if I lived in this palace for a thousand years, I would still have that instinct etched deep in my soul, the knowledge of what it is to live free. And deep down, I feel sure these birds are the same.

I woke today to find my letter gone from the table. The demon had taken it after all. Whether he means to deliver it or not, I cannot say.

The yellow bird hops over to the side of the cage and tilts its head at me, looking at me with curious black eyes. I smile at it, but I don't reach out to it.

Pretty things can bite you.

What you trust can turn on you.

I know that now.

I curl my hands into fists, then uncurl them. Perhaps Father and Dimitra are reading my letter even now. Was I right to send it? Should I have tried to tell them more of the truth?

Do not give me up for lost, I think, as if my thoughts could travel to them and speak themselves aloud.

I wander like a shade around the palace for the rest of the day, impatient for the demon to return. Eventually I retire to my bedroom and gaze out of the window—today it shows a lush forest—and wait for the sound of his footstep. When it comes at last, I hurry though the door.

"Psyche." He greets me with surprise, and I flush.

"You took the letter," I say. And then, though it sticks in my throat a little: "Thank you."

But even as I say it, I observe his air of heaviness, of distraction. The way he stands by that chair, his hand clenching the back of it.

"I was not able to deliver it," he says curtly. "I am sorry."

I stare at him.

"Not able? For what reason?"

Distrust surges in me. Perhaps he didn't even try to deliver it; perhaps he never intended to.

"Your family—they are no longer in Sikyon," he says. My ears ring. Does he think me a fool, that I cannot hear the hesitation in his words?

"What are you keeping from me?" My voice is hot.

There's a pause.

"It is as I have said. They are gone from Sikyon."

I sink into a chair.

Can it be true?

"Banished?" I say. "Or of their own accord?" Aletheia's plate of dry crusts lies before me, incongruous and strange. What use have I for food, now?

"I have no further details." His voice is cool. Curt, even. He does not care. He is not sorry.

I turn away. My family. *Gone*. What does it mean? Gone *where*?

A panicked feeling rises inside me. No escape plan will serve me now. There is no one to go home to. Not until I find them again. And how am I to do that?

I swallow down the thickness in my throat. "You probably never intended to deliver the letter at all."

My voice is as sour as my stomach; even my blood feels sour. The demon does not like the sound of it.

"Do not lever your accusations at me."

"You are lying to me, I hear it in your voice," I retort. "You think you can blindfold me with your words, too."

His voice rises. It seems I have touched him where it hurts—his pride.

"I'm telling you the truth. They're gone from Sikyon. More, I cannot say."

His cloaked form looks as ghoulish now as it did the night of our first encounter. How could I have placed any trust in this creature?

"You don't care," I say. "And why should you? My loss means nothing to you. You know nothing of family, or the bonds of love."

The folds of his cloak seemed to stiffen.

"And what of you?" he says, his voice like steel.

I look up. What does he accuse *me* of? I am the one bereft, orphaned.

He is the one devoid of feeling. But he's clenching the chair-back harder now. I see the veins rise up on the back of his hand.

"*You,*" he says, "are so determined to be dissatisfied, you turn away from every opportunity. You snub every attempt to please you."

Snub? Please? I can only stare.

"You say you are lonely, but do you make any effort with those who would befriend you? No: you have treated all of us here to your scorn.

"You have access to a greater library," he continues, "than any of your poets could dream of, and could spend hours immersed in any subject you cared to know—yet you have not once ventured through those doors, though I have ensured that all of them remain open to you.

"You have a thousand instruments here, any of which you could teach yourself now to play. You have a garden you could tend, but that does not interest you either. You belittle the nymphs for not living more…*creatively,* but though you have a more exquisite loom at your disposal than any mortal has known, and the talent to use it, have you so much as raised a finger to it?"

"I…"

But he goes on.

"You have endless opportunities here for your own betterment, but do any of them earn a moment of your interest? No: you are too busy locking yourself away in your room, preferring to fantasize about a future you pretend would have made you happy." He scoffs. "That mortal boy, how would your fate have fared with him? How would he have liked you, once you had been married a year? What freedoms would you have had under your mother-in-law's wing? We both know you would have been little more than a breeding-mate, used to produce strong heirs and pretty daughters, and nothing more." He thumps the table. "Why, it is not only the sea monster you should be thanking me for saving you from: it is your whole life!"

I stare at him, speechless, too astounded for anger.

"You know nothing of mortal life," I say at last, my heart pounding in my chest. "Nothing of what it means to be *alive!* Nothing of real feeling! Nothing of anything worth knowing!"

I shove my plate across the table, hoping it smashes, and knock over the water glass while I'm at it. The cold water splashes against his cloak and puddles quickly on the table. And I run from the table, and slam my bedroom door behind me.

*

I stare out my bedroom window as dusk sets.

Father. Dimitra.

Unless the demon is lying, they are gone from our home. But why?

They thought me dead. It was too painful, perhaps, to remain in our home after what happened there. But could they afford to leave? Corinth is the nearest great city, but would it care for two Sikyonian migrants? Corinth has not always had warm relations with us. Perhaps they have set out for Caphyae, then, or Argos…

I shake my head. How am I to guess at their path? And what am I to do now, when I break free of this place; where do I run to?

If only I had got the letter to them sooner.

But now my family are gone: sand through my fingers. I lie on the bed and stare at the darkness over the forest, and if tears come instead of sleep, I let them.

My dreams, when they come, are cruel. I see my father as an old man, walking on a high mountain pass as the wind batters and wrenches at him and he falls to his knees. I see our old horse, Ada, struggling through a great flood, her legs pushing gamely even as she sinks, while Dimitra calls hopelessly to her from the shore. I see fire and ash, and terrible things.

When I wake, I don't leave my bed. I watch the sun get higher, and then, finally, lower. When a knock comes at my door I ignore it. But the door opens anyway. I turn quickly, but it's only Aletheia. She carries a tray, with a platter of bread and a pitcher of water.

Quietly, she places it on a side table. I look at her; she looks back at me.

"He is not here tonight," she says, as though I had asked. But I didn't. I refuse to.

"He said to tell you, he still searches."

I stare at her then.

He still searches?

The message is clear enough. And am I to believe it—that after last night, he still looks for my father and sister?

"He told you that?"

She nods, her dark eyes roving over me. I think of what the demon said last night. Does Aletheia think I scorn her? Since the first, I thought that beady gaze was full of hate for me. Is it possible I was wrong?

I hesitate.

"Thank you for the bread and water."

She betrays no sign of having heard my words at first. She ignores me, I think. But then she taps a knuckle against her chest—a small, brief gesture that I recognize. It is a sign my people make to invoke courage. *Strong heart*, it means.

A sign of encouragement? Of…sympathy?

But she is already gone, leaving only the tray of bread and water, and my startled gaze on the closed door.

*

The demon does not return the next day, nor the day after that. I eat alone, in my room. During the days I roam the palace, learning every twist and turn of its hallways. He has taken the horses for his carriage, it seems: all four are gone from their stalls now. Which means Aletheia does not take the key downstairs in the mornings. Where she hides it, I don't know.

In the mornings she leaves some bread and water in the great-room for me, and in the evenings, the same on a tray in my room. During the days I sometimes go to the gardens, but I do not see the nymphs again—whether by coincidence or because they avoid me, I can't tell.

I explore another place, too.

When I open the door to the weaving-room, awe hits me afresh. The loom is as tall as a statue and delicate as a lyre—truly an object fit for the gods. Sunlight streams in and turns the veined wood gold in parts.

I am not so haughty as the demon thinks. I do not scorn this place—its rooms of libraries, dazzling gardens, or magnificent loom. How could I? But it's true, I have not let myself touch anything, or enjoy the slightest of its offerings, as if to do so would be a concession. As if I would be submitting to my fate here.

Now, if I am to believe what Aletheia says, the demon may bring word for me soon of my family's whereabouts, but how soon, I cannot guess. It strikes me that, since I may be here a while, it would be no bad thing to practice my arts a little, if I can. If the time must pass, it had better pass well than badly. Besides, if—*when*—I do escape this place, I will be alone in the world, at least for the start of my journey. I will have to live on my skills. So why not practice them?

I go and stand in front of the loom. I am almost afraid to touch it. Almost, but not quite. When I run my fingers over the wood, it is as if I hear music.

I go to the back of the room, where spools upon spools of silk lie waiting. I select my colors one by one. The gold, for how it glints and shimmers. And the red—an irresistible, luscious shade. And white—I have never seen weaving-silk of such a pure, alabaster white. I tease out a thread and run it between my fingers.

Then I thread the loom carefully, and begin.

Nineteen

The easy motions are so familiar, I could be at home in that little upstairs room once more. It is like a dance I learned in childhood, and my limbs move back into it as easily as breathing. Except that this loom is more powerful, more sure, more effortless, than any instrument I have known. My fingers feel graceful, and my movements sure.

It was Old Lydia, our neighbor, who first taught Dimitra and me to weave when we were young girls. I was fascinated from the first—the movement of the threads, the way the pattern slowly emerged like a shape rising from the sand. I remember Lydia's calloused hands on mine as she showed me the rhythms of it. *Warp, and weft. Warp, and weft. Gently, Psyche. Use patience.*

Patience was something Dimitra did not have. She found it tedious, this women's work. And true, the carding, the spinning, all that is slow and dull enough. But once the thread is on the loom—to me, that is where the magic begins: where a story knots itself to life. It is only fabric, it may not last as long as the glazed pots and ewers that our menfolk get to make, but once those threads knot into place, it feels to me as if nothing can ever truly unknot them. No matter if the fabric is reduced to ash or rot in the years yet to come. Whenever we make something truly beautiful, its story lives forever.

Or at least that's what I think.

Even so, it surprises me, how *right* it feels, to be weaving again—despite all that has happened to me. Everything certain has crumbled. Everything I knew is upended. But *this,* this simple movement, feels like one true thing. I watch my hands move, shift, adjust, as if of their own accord. Without anxiety, without doubt. And for the first time in days, I allow myself to exhale.

I don't know how much time passes.

I stop with a jolt when I notice the thread is gone, and I have to return to the wall for another spool. Then I begin again, the tray of the loom sighing gently with each warp and weft, moving with the lightest touch, following the pressure of my hand like some great beast trained to the subtlest command.

When I look up again it's past dusk.

I stand back from my handiwork and look at it properly for the first time. It's beautiful—without a doubt the most beautiful thing I have made—but it unnerves me, too.

Sometimes it is like this when I weave. Images come to me, pictures in my head that have no home in my waking hours. Perhaps they are things I dreamed once, I cannot say.

Here I have woven a gold background, overlaid with white feathers. But the feathers do not float gently through the design, the way I had imagined—instead the pattern is turbulent and chaotic, as if it were the result of some terrible skirmish. Except that they are white, they remind me of *his* feathers, those great and terrible wings.

And the ribbons of red which I'd woven through the design…they are beautiful, like a river of rubies glinting against the gold…but even more than rubies, it makes me think of blood.

I take another step back. The tapestry shimmers, glints. It is beautiful…but part of me is glad to turn away from it.

I close the door with a last look back, and move swiftly down the corridors. It is dinner-hour—but when I enter the great-room, it's empty and silent. No fire burns in the hearth. I retreat to my bedroom, where I find the bread and water on a tray. I eat it steadily, and try to ignore the unnerving feeling of disappointment. It is not *him* I wished to see, I remind myself. It is only his news I am hungry for.

My dreams that night are feverish and strange. First I dream of Sikyon, and in the dream the streets are covered in smoke, and I glimpse the agora through a canopy of flame. Then when I finally fall back asleep, I dream of something else entirely. I hesitate to admit it.

I dream of him.

I dream that he steps toward me and waits, and in the dream I know exactly what he's waiting for. And so I reach for the black hood that shrouds him, gathering up a silken handful. I can feel it already, that song of life-blood when my skin meets his. And then I lift the hood back, and—

I wake up.

A moment more, just one moment more, and I would have seen his face.

And it troubles me, just how much I wanted to.

*

The next day I return to the loom again. It's strange, but it calls to me. I want to feel the silk thread running through my fingers; I want to close my eyes and follow this call that summons me, creating patterns that don't belong to my waking thoughts. It feels as though I shed the most burdened part of myself, and instead, some great, deep magic is called up from a hidden place inside me. The act of creation brings me release. Relief. *Purpose*. It gives me a place to live for a few hours where I don't have to think about Father and Dimitra, and if they're all right.

Where I don't have to think about *him.*

But when my fingers are stiff and the light's growing dim, I stop. I feel a strange fluttering in my chest as I walk along the corridors, and push open the door to the great-room, but once again the room is dark, the table bare.

In my room, I toy with the crusts on my plate. The truth is, they taste less appealing as the days go by—more and more like mortal food. I wonder if I'm getting used to this place, after all. If I might be getting stronger, better able to resist it.

I dream the same dreams as the night before. This time he turns his face from me just as I am about to see it. And when I wake, it's not like awakening from the Sikyon nightmare. There's no horror, just a strange ache. An ache I'd rather not think about.

An ache that is much to inconvenient to admit.

*

In the weaving-room, these strange and beautiful visions continue to pour out of me—images of spires and temples I've never seen; a whole blue-green city submerged under the water. Perhaps they are childhood fantasies I've forgotten, places spoken of in myth that took root in my imaginings. Wherever they're from, it is a release to me to give them voice here. I am in no danger of running out of silk; there seems to be an endless amount.

On the third day, as I ready my tired limbs to return to the great-room and its silence, I hear a sound in the corridor.

Echoing footsteps, firm and sharp.

I wait by the doorway as he rounds the corner. He pauses, as though startled by the sight of me. Then he bows stiffly, just a small dip of his head, like the gentlemen of Sikyon do to the women of high rank.

"You are returned," I say.

"As you see."

I have heard that in some distant lands the women are cloaked from head to toe, their faces veiled and bodies covered as if by a shroud. Perhaps in those lands they have learned to read each other's forms the way I have learned to read his. It feels as if I know his every movement now: the way the back of his neck lifts in surprise when I startle him, or how those broad shoulders straighten from behind when he hears me enter a room. The slightest drum of his hand on the dinner table, or how he presses the pads of his fingers thoughtfully against the wood before he speaks. Now, what I notice is the stiff way he holds his hands at his sides. I read reluctance there.

"You have news?" I say.

"I regret to say…" He clears his throat. "I have discovered nothing yet."

I drop my eyes. Travel can be dangerous in these lands. My father's fighting days are behind him, and though Dimitra has skill enough with a weapon, I do not think the two of them alone could fight off many men.

But I must ward off thoughts like these. I must keep my heart strong.

"Thank you." I stumble over the words. "For continuing to search."

His head dips low.

"They are beloved to you." He pauses. "And you to them."

"Yes," I say finally. Before, it seemed he only wanted to remind me of their abandonment. Now he offers me sympathy. Is he the one who has changed so much…or am I?

He draws closer to the doorway where I stand. It does not escape him, I'm sure, that he has found me in the weaving-room. I wonder if he is remembering the last conversation—argument—we had, before he left. I see him shift his gaze: he's no longer looking at me but over my shoulder, toward the loom.

"This is your work?"

I flush. In Sikyon I was always praised for my handiwork. But perhaps to him, it is clumsy and…what was the word Klaia used? *Coarse.*

"I am out of practice," I say stiffly, touching my warm cheeks, wishing they would cool before he returns his glance to me.

"But this is no traditional design." He sounds puzzled. Displeased, even.

He's right, of course. All our art-making follows strict patterns. The potters make only certain shapes of vases. The vase-painters only paint certain kinds of scenes. It is the same for weavers: we weave the patterns we have been taught. Some are geometric, following a strict order and color. Some are scenes from popular stories, showing patron gods or goddesses. But never anything like this.

The white feathers float in the air, disconnected and without meaning. The blood-red ribbon weaves through it. It looks like what it is: a strange dream.

"I don't know why I made it," I admit. "It just happened. I think perhaps I saw it in a dream once."

He steps past me, his back to me now, and touches the fabric.

"And do you have many such dreams?" I can't quite identify what I'm hearing in his voice. Not anger, nor disapproval, but a kind of urgency, it seems. But perhaps I have imagined it.

"Not many," I say. "Not that I remember. I rarely remember dreams."

"I see. And do you remember what you dreamed of last night?"

I flush deeper, and shake my head. I do, but I'm not about to tell him.

We are silent for a moment, then.

"Aletheia will be waiting," he says, and proceeds down the corridor.

He does not eat tonight, only sits at the table while Aletheia brings bread and water.

"Tell me about them," he says. "About your family."

I look at him, not knowing what to say.

"My mother died when I was born," I say at last. "I have a father and a sister."

He nods. *He knows this,* I think. He knew my life before he took me from it.

"You are the younger sister?"

I nod. I'm off-balance in this conversation, which feels so natural, so calm.

"Dimitra is my half-sister, in fact. Her mother is dead, just as mine is." I pause. "We were close as children. But"—I wonder how my tongue runs so loose, tonight—"my father showed me too much favor, and it came between us."

It is something I have always been ashamed to admit. It is not until tonight that it occurs to me to question why *I* should carry the shame. I never asked for, nor wanted, such inequality.

"He favored you," the demon murmurs. "And yet he let the king appoint your death."

The comment does not offend me now as it would have before. It's simply true.

"My father is a brave man," I say. "A soldier. But he is not a rebel by nature."

"Not like you?" There's a touch of amusement in his voice which I recognize from before, but it doesn't seem mocking now. *Was* it mockery, before? Was it always so unkind as I believed?

"I am no natural born rebel, either." I look up. "If I am one now, it is through my situation and not by birth."

He refrains from disagreeing. I toy with another crust on my plate. Eventually he speaks.

"You think I understand nothing of your life. And yet, I do. I had a family too—and they, too, are lost to me."

I stare at him. A family! And yet, why should a demon not come from somewhere?

"I was born one of three brothers," he goes on. "As children we were always together. But as we grew, we became divided. I had my mother's favor, which made them dislike me." He taps the table gently with his fingers. "Such favor is not always a gift, is it?" He pauses again. "They have abandoned me, now."

I frown. Until now, he has cloaked every detail of himself—even more effectively than he has hidden his face. I do not even know what name he goes by, in my world. Now, this fragment of information seems to change him.

"Do you miss your brothers?" I say. I don't know why. The words just spill from me. The black hood shifts; his head tilts to one side, considering.

"We are very different," he says shortly. "And besides, they have each other."

The strangest impulse comes over me then. His hand rests on the table, and my own is only inches away. If I wanted, I could reach out and cover his hand with mine.

But I don't.

Because that would be madness.

"Why can I not see your face?" I blurt out.

He turns; I feel the stare.

"I know I cannot, but *why* can I not?"

He is quiet for a while. When he speaks, it's not an answer to my question.

"Does it matter so very much?" His hands lie on the table in front of him, each knuckle smooth and well-defined in the candlelight.

"The eyes," he says quietly, "are only one-fifth of the mortal senses."

Why must you cling to this one thing? he means. I look toward my plate.

"But it's not that I *cannot* see you," I say. "It's that I *may* not. There is a difference."

"Yes," he says at last, and there's a sigh in his voice. "There is."

If I had been born blind, I wonder suddenly, would I, could I, feel like a true wife to him?

Senseless thought. I am a wife in nothing but name. *Wife* is what I might have been to any human man. But this…this is just a bizarre and temporary alliance.

Temporary. That is key.

That is the part I must not forget.

"I am sorry, Psyche." He touches my arm, only a brief touch, but I jerk back as though from a hot spark. It was not painful—quite the contrary—but the warmth of it lingers, just above my elbow. A glow, as if I had been standing in the sun.

He clears his throat.

"I—I am tired," I say. "I will take my leave now."

He says nothing as I push back my chair. The cool air of my bedroom is a relief against my hot cheeks. I go to the window and stare out at the unmoving sea.

I can surely diagnose what is wrong with me. I have been torn away from those I love; from everything I know. After so much loss so fast, I am not myself. The madness will surely pass. It is some symptom of my unfortunate situation, that I should be developing this…this grotesque preoccupation, I must call it, with the creature who brought me here. I suppose any wind-tossed, dizzy sparrow might cling to a wildcat's back in a storm.

But I am no sparrow. I am a woman, with a woman's courage, and a woman's sense. And however wind-tossed my mind, I know what I may and may not cling to.

I wish I could go home, just for a moment. The pang comes over me as I stand here. The thought of sitting, just for a moment, in our courtyard again, hearing the soft splash of a fish in its shallow pond…of walking the road to the agora, with all its familiar sights, the trees and houses and stalls and merchants…

I wish I could see it all, just for a moment. It would be such a comfort.

And as I stare out the illusion-window, the thought comes to me. *Think of it as a mural,* he said. He told me I could conjure other images if I wished. What if that means real places, as well as imagined ones? When I saw *him* conjuring that tremendous citadel, before, didn't he as much as admit it?

I stand in front of the window and clear my throat.

"Show me Sikyon," I say aloud. Nothing happens. I take a

breath, and place my fingers against the gypsum. My heart seems to constrict for a moment.

Sikyon, I think, closing my eyes. *Show me Sikyon. Please.*

And when I open my eyes, the seascape has disappeared into darkness. Slowly, haltingly, a new image floods in.

And when it does, a wave of horror floods me.

Twenty

This can't be real.

What I'm seeing isn't the town I know. It's a town destroyed. Buried alive. As though there was some sort of avalanche, as though the mountain itself gave way.

It can't be real. The enchantments on this place have a life of their own; they're playing some cruel joke. I push the back of my hand against my mouth to stop the bile from surging upward.

I fling open the bedroom door, feeling only the pounding through my body, seeing only darkness. He's not here. The room is empty. I hurtle through it, into the corridors.

I don't know where he goes at night, where he sleeps, if he sleeps. I move blindly, without instinct.

"Demon!" I shout, but my voice comes out strangled. "Where are you? Answer me!"

He knows what happened. He must know.

It's not real, I tell myself. And yet another voice, deeper inside, disagrees.

It's real. All too real.

He said he searched for my family. He said they were not in Sikyon. That they were gone.

"Are they dead?" I hurl the words into the darkness. I don't stop moving, I can't. "Answer me: *are they dead?*"

I take each turn at a run, the thin torch-flames my only light. It doesn't matter: I see nothing but the visions in my mind.

"You will not hide from me!" My voice rises and cracks, hardly human. "Answer me, what has become of my home!"

And then, there he is. A dark form in the darkness.

"Psyche..."

"I saw it. I saw Sikyon. In the window." I sag like a reed. My face is wet. My voice is pleading now, as though he can save me from what I've just seen, but beneath it I feel rage, readying the next wave.

My voice shudders no matter how I try to control it.

"Why didn't you tell me?"

"How could I tell you such a thing?" His tone is steady, abominably so. How can he address me so evenly, even now!

"How could you *not* tell me?" I shout.

"Listen to me," he says. "I did not see them among the dead. There was a quake in the earth, as you have been shown: the mountain fell. When I went to seek out your people, I found a scene of devastation there. But more fled the town than were killed, Psyche. That is what I am trying to tell you."

I stare at him.

"What are you saying? They are alive?"

"I'm saying I did not see your father or sister among the bodies, or hear word of their death."

I slam my hand against the wall.

"In other words, you offer me nothing! My family may be dead, may be alive! They lie buried under all that rubble, for all you know!"

"There is very little in life that is certain," he says, carefully. "I am telling you what I know. The rest we must wait for."

His voice is cool, logical. Free of all emotion. But images flash through my mind: limbs, helpless outstretched hands, dusty and lifeless under fallen stone. Sounds of wailing and keening that echo through ruined streets. How can he speak this way! How can he try to—to *philosophize* about such horror?

And then I realize something else.

Aphrodite's husband is Hephaestus: the blacksmith of the gods, the one whose flaming forges lie below our mountains, ever-ready to erupt. The one whose hammer and anvil rattle the bones of the earth. But they have never rattled Sikyon before.

"This isn't coincidence, is it?" My voice shakes.

The demon told me before now: if Aphrodite heard she'd been thwarted, things would go badly for us. They say Hephaestus is devoted to her. That he does anything she asks.

"It's retribution, isn't it? It's because of me."

He is silent. I want him to tell me I'm claiming too much, that it's arrogance to imagine I'm the reason for all this. But he doesn't say that.

"How could you keep this from me?" I whisper. *This whole time.* This whole time, I knew nothing.

"It was better that you did not know," he says stiffly.

The audacity of his words!

"Better! According to *your* judgement? Better that I know nothing of the death—the *murder*—of my townspeople? That I know nothing of my family's suffering?" My breath is shallow; my legs feel unsteady.

Father, Dimitra...did they flee with the survivors? Or are they in Hades' realm now, after all? And what of the others? Too many faces flash through my mind. Neighbors, friends, merchants we've frequented for years. What about the Georgioues? What about Yiannis?

"What would it have achieved?" Something else has crept into his voice now, something that shores up any crack where guilt or remorse might have settled. And when I look up, everything about him is as blank as that stupid cloak, that faceless face.

"How many dead?" I whisper.

Silence answers me.

"How many?"

He lifts one shoulder, minutely.

"They are mortals," he says then. "Their deaths would have come anyway, whether today or tomorrow."

"I'm a mortal!" I slam a fist against the wall. "Death may mean nothing to you, but it is everything for us!" My head throbs. "You have no soul. You are a scourge, a disease. You may live forever, demon, but you will bring no goodness to this

world."

He says nothing. No angry retorts or shallow self-defense. He doesn't even move. But I can't look at him any longer. I turn on my heel and go back to my room, to stare through the night at the ruins of my home.

And then, by morning, I have a plan.

*

I wait for the first rays of light. I know the rhythms of this house by now. Soon Aletheia will come out of the kitchen with the key, and go down to let the horses out. But not this morning: this morning will be different.

I've been a fool, waiting here for the demon to return with news of my family. Thinking he would help me find them. Thinking he was my ally. All he offers me is lies.

I slink into the corridors and along to the door I know so well.

The birds chirrup and flutter—the smaller ones, at least, those clustered in the cage next to where I'm standing. They think I am here to feed them.

"Not food, little friends," I say. "Something better than that."

And I take the small, golden latch and slide it across. I pull back the panel and stand back, leaving the large square opening in the aviary wall, and I wait.

For the first few moments nothing changes, and my stomach rolls over. Don't they understand? Have these creatures lost themselves so far, that they cannot recognize freedom when they see it?

But then one little red bird twitters, and takes a curious hop toward the opening, and hops again, out of the cage. It flies dizzily for a moment, circling left, then right, disoriented. Finally it lands on the doorframe, perches there, and begins to sing.

As if drawn by the tune, a couple more birds fly out, and then a few more. And then more, faster now, and it seems to me the dam is breaking. Soon there is a steady stream of them, and the ones in the cage are growing agitated. They paid little attention to that first bird, or the first ten or twenty, but now that their brethren are freeing themselves by the dozen, the rest are clamoring and protesting. Everyone wants out.

The chaos intensifies, rising toward a fever pitch, and for a while I'm worried they'll destroy each other. The birds still in the cage are in a frenzy now: the entrance is too small for many of them to escape at once. Some are pecking at each other in between trills and shrieks. One is bashing itself against the cage in its fever to be released.

"Hush," I try to coax them. "You'll all have your turn." But soon I have to step back from the cage as the birds come racing out, filling the room, a jumble of feathers and color and sound, beating wings everywhere, squawks and deafening calls. They seem to take up more space outside the cage than in, and they just seem to keep coming.

But this is what I wanted.

I fight my way through the maelstrom of birds toward the door, and manage to fling it open. I stumble into the corridor and the birds burst out behind me, like some kind of stampede, cawing and shrieking. It occurs to me that perhaps the cage, too, was enchanted—that it contained more birds than even its tremendous size should have allowed, because there seems now to be no end of these birds, flooding out of the room in such chaos.

But can I control the chaos?

Ducking, I run forward at a crouch, trying to avoid the swoosh of beaks and feathers and talons. I scurry toward the front of the cloud. Will they follow me? They only have two choices, backwards or forwards. I run as fast as I can. Some flap and swoop behind me, while others are already ahead of me, swarming the corridor to the limit of my sight. I worry for a moment I'll lose my bearings and forget which turns are the ones to take, so camouflaged is everything by the frenzy of birds. But I race on. There are so many of them! If only a fraction took this path with me, it would still be enough.

It is a mad sort of plan, I realize. But here is what I know:

That I cannot wait another day to free myself from this place.

That Aletheia will be making her way down these corridors any moment now.

That she will be carrying the key I need to escape.

The demon said she had some fear of birds, and this wild cloud of beaks and talons would frighten anyone, I think.

But as we race along them, the corridors are all empty. Aletheia is late. Why is she late?

When I reach the door of the great-room I fling it open, and the birds flood in. I watch, mouth agape. For how enormous the room is, I can't believe how they fill it. Feathers that were shed in skirmishes flutter to the ground everywhere, all the colors of the rainbow; suddenly there are droppings, too, on the rugs and the divans. And the noise…

I don't know if it's the noise that summons her, but it seems only moments before the door across the room opens. I'm afraid she'll retreat then, but it's too late: the birds have crowded her already, and the door has closed behind her. I hear her shriek and see her crouch, covering her head. I hold my breath, watching from the doorway, although in this vortex of color and noise she'll never see me.

She's carrying my morning bread-and-water, and it's the bread that interests the birds: they duck and dive, squawking louder, their calls vying with Aletheia's screams. Though they're not attacking her, I suppose it feels like they are.

The bread and water are not all that have tumbled to the ground: I heard the clang of the key fall from her grip. My mad escape plan just might work. I dart as silently as I can across the room—Aletheia is shielding her head, shouting, and does not see me—and in a moment I'm grasping the cold metal in my hand.

There'll be little enough time. Aletheia's shrieking will alert him soon. No doubt he'll quiet the birds with a word or two of enchantment, and they'll notice the key is gone, and come for me.

I run back through the corridors, on and on until I reach the yard, my chest pumping in the cool dawn air. I find the lock, jiggle the key. It takes a few tries, but then I feel the release of the bolt and the gate clanks ajar. I swallow hard. I want to push it back, all the way back, and see whatever's out there. But I need one more thing first.

I hurry across the yard and into the stables. This part may be madder than the last—but my escape has been noisy and unsubtle, not the stealthy kind I had earlier hoped to devise. I have a head-start of a few minutes at best: if I leave on foot, he will catch me.

All or nothing. I must try.

I take a breath, and push open the door to the first stall. There he is, the black stallion, the one I heard the demon name as Ajax. He is taller, even, than I remembered. For a moment I almost lose my nerve. Then I glance back toward the palace door, and remind myself that any moment now, he will be coming for me.

And that my family needs me.

"Hush, it's all right."

I try to fit the bridle over the stallion's ears; he whinnies, shying back away from me, his enormous hooves stamping the ground. Perhaps he reads my own anxiety. I pat his side, hoping to convince him.

"It's all right. We're going to get out of here, you and I."

I stroke his mane and then bury my hand in it, trying to secure a good grip—there are no stirrups to hoist me up, so I'll have to throw myself onto him. *Dimitra could do this,* I tell myself.

But the attempt takes me only halfway. I land with just my arm splayed across the stallion's back, the rest of me dangling. He grunts, steps back quickly, dislodging me with a thump to the ground.

"Come on, boy. Come on," I murmur. This time I take a running leap. I hold my breath, I am determined—and somehow I make it onto his back. I scramble for purchase, burying my hands in the mane, tugging myself toward a sitting position.

But now he's spooked. He bumps the walls of the stall, whinnying, and then while I'm still struggling for my grip, he rears up. I feel my neck snap back, my body sailing through the air.

The ground is hard as slate. The breath is gone from my body. The stallion's whinnying, stomping. Then he's rearing again, his great hind legs much too near me. I need to move my leg but my mind can't seem to command my limbs. He's going to trample me. He's going to trample me, and then it will all be over.

The great hind legs come down. I hear someone scream, and the world goes white.

Twenty-one

There's movement beside me, and light in the darkness, and someone moves the cool rag from across my eyes. I gasp, the light is so bright.

"Psyche."

His voice. And it comes back to me then: the rearing horse, that moment of blinding pain. A shudder goes through my body.

It didn't work.

I close my eyes again. Trapped. And worse than before, now. Will he lock me in my room after this? I'll never get another chance.

He dabs the cold compress across my forehead again, then drops it in a pail by his feet.

"Ajax is a strong creature. Your injury is serious."

I try to turn away, but a shriek of pain races up my right side.

"Be still," he urges. "Psyche, did you hear what I said? Your injuries are...considerable."

Even blinking hurts.

"How bad?" I say finally.

"Your right leg and arm were crushed. Some bone fragments, I fear, may be too small to heal fully. Your organs, at least, were spared. The damage to tendons, ligaments, I have not counted."

The recitation is a grim one, and I can tell by the flatness of his voice that he knows it. He doesn't sound angry: he sounds cold and emotionless, which I suppose I should be used to by now. Perhaps the anger will come later.

"I will bring whatever remedies my garden has to offer,"

he says. "But nonetheless, you are mortal."

I look away.

"If you mean I'm to die from this, then say it."

He sighs.

"No, but as to whether you will walk again, I will not venture. It may be a slow process, and the healing will be painful." He sits back. "But you will have my care and Aletheia's, day or night."

I close my eyes tight. To never walk again...I try to picture such an altered life. After all that has already happened, perhaps such a change should feel small. But now it strikes me that I should have taken up the demon's offers when I had the chance: I should have run through those endless gardens and felt the scented grass crush under my feet, exploring as far as my legs would take me; I should have swum with the nymphs in that crystalline water.

"I had to get to Sikyon," I say. "My family..."

But the act of speaking hurts, and I stop.

"I should have guessed you would attempt something like this," he sighs. I look up at the cloaked face. From here, I see the merest trace of his shadowed jaw.

"You think Aphrodite's eye does not search for you out there? It is foolish of you not to believe me."

"Believe you?" I wheeze. "You wonder that I do not trust your words? Think of what you concealed from me." Although the pain is shattering, I turn my head to look at him directly.

He bows his head just a fraction.

"I should not have concealed Sikyon's fate from you. And yet I spoke the truth about your family. I believe they are yet alive, and thought perhaps in time I would be able to bring you good news. I did not wish to torment you with the knowledge of a tragedy you could not change. What is done now, is done. Neither of us can undo it."

"You spoke so carelessly of them," I murmur. "You told me their lives did not matter. As if what had happened was nothing."

The black hood bows further.

"I did not mean to sound so callous. I merely meant...Psyche, I knew you would hold yourself responsible. As I held myself responsible: I should have predicted there would be some such retribution. I should have predicted it, but I did not." He pauses. "I don't regret saving you that day—I cannot regret it—but I blame myself for not foreseeing what would happen, for not being able to warn or save your people. When I spoke harshly last night, I was trying to ease that guilt. It is true that to my kind, all mortal life seems brief—sooner or later, all of you will enter Hades' realm. But that does not mean your lives aboveground do not matter. I will carry Sikyon's tragedy with me."

Something floods me with his words, and I close my eyes. I cannot help it: I picture the children of the village, the small ones playing with marbles in the agora. And the youths I knew and the girls my age, recently married or about to wed. The elderly, the infirm, the frail. Which of them made it out of there?

"If you had left me on that rock…" The words tumble out, bitter. "If we had let the goddess have her way, they would all still be alive."

He sits silent for a while.

"Lives are not coins, Psyche," he says at last. "They cannot be so easily traded, one for another. Justice has a price of its own, and your death would have been a great injustice. I cannot regret my actions there—only that I could not avert that which came after."

I say nothing to that. What's to say? What does it matter to me, what he regrets or doesn't?

"I will never know what happened to my family," I say finally. "And they will never know what happened to me." I feel my voice growing fainter, and greyness starts to cloud my vision.

"For now, Psyche, you must rest," the demon's voice says. "Your body needs it. Rest, and I will be here when you wake."

The last words are all but lost. They float as if on grey mist, and I fall into a dreamless sleep.

*

I wake and sleep many times, and whenever I wake either he or Aletheia is there. Mostly, though, it is him. They feed me broth, and some sort of nectar, and there is always some new poultice or compress, the smell of strange herbs and ointments.

"Drink this," they say, and I do. Whether it is days or hours or weeks that pass, I could not say.

And then I wake, and the room seems brighter than before. Sunlight is streaming through the windows, and this time it does not hurt my eyes. I am alone, but only for a short while. The door soon opens, and when he sees me awake, he hurries in, his black cloak swirling around him like water.

"How do you feel?"

I hesitate, making a quick inventory of my limbs.

"Tired, but there is only a little pain."

"Indeed? Our remedies may be helping more than I expected." I see his hood shift toward the window.

"You have slept for a day and a half."

Is that all? He could have told me years.

The demon leans forward, and I shiver as he unwraps the bandages. I stare at his hands, the wiry golden hairs on the backs of them. His bronze skin seems to cut the air with light, and his grip is strong and sure. One palm cradles my leg as the other hand unwinds the bandage, and I feel the warmth of him, the weight of my limb suspended in his grip. I can feel each of his fingertips and the skin of his palm, and smell his wood-and-honey scent.

I think a sigh escapes my lips, and I clamp my mouth shut.

"I will check the bones." He clears his throat. "If you do

not object."

I hesitate, then nod, though I'm not sure what he means. Gently he pushes my sleeve back to my shoulder, then moves a hand slowly down my arm, as though his skin is listening to mine. I stare at him.

"You can…feel, what's inside?"

He ignores me. He seems distracted: I think at first he is about to deliver some ill news, but I can read him better than that now. It's not dismay I'm witnessing, but surprise.

"What is it?" I say.

He doesn't answer, just moves his palm to my leg.

"May I?"

When he skims his hand along the skin I bite down, because although the sensation that shoots through me is not pain, it's just as vivid. A shiver so keen and bright, it's *like* pain.

He sits back then, and I can feel his stare.

"Your bones," he says slowly, "are healing extraordinarily well. Or at least, extraordinarily fast." He pauses. "If you continue like this, perhaps in a few days you could be walking again."

I stare at him. In my fever, did I misremember? I thought he told me I might never walk again; that if I did, it would likely be a long road.

"A few *days*?" I say. "That is all?"

His voice is halting.

"I admit, I am also surprised. Though I suppose…" He seems on firmer ground now. "My garden may have even greater healing powers than I realized. And Aletheia, too, is a talented nurse."

"It was you who nursed me," I say, and then regret it. I see how still he grows at those words.

"I will let her know of your progress." He stands from the bed. "She will be glad to hear."

I watch him stride from the room. I am not so sure that Aletheia cares very much about my recovery. I think, perhaps, he just wanted to get out of here as fast as he could.

When he is gone I stare at the wall, thinking. Nothing is as I expected. I will not be bed-bound for weeks or months, or the rest of my life. And the demon…I had thought he would be angry, full of rebukes and punishment. But it is not like that at all. There is a heaviness in him, a strange air of resignation which I do not understand.

Am I a fool, not to listen to him? Not to believe that Aphrodite's wrath will find me once I am outside these gates?

I suppose I am a fool. But even a fool may do what is right.

Later he comes to my room again with a vase of fresh flowers and places them by the window.

"I thought you should like to look at these."

"Thank you," I say, surprised.

The sunlight streams in. He hesitates, then takes a seat by the bedside. Neither of us speaks for a while.

"I know you think," he says at last, "that I came for you that morning on the cliffs because you were desperate. You think that I wanted to drive a bargain from you against your will."

I glance over, but not up toward his hooded face. For some reason, I'm too nervous for that. I keep my eyes instead on his hands.

"I know that you guess at my power, Psyche. Well, it is considerable." He turns further toward me. "Please understand, if I had wanted to take you away by force, I could have done so at any time. I did not need your predicament to achieve it."

Now I do look straight up at him, and my face is flushed for other reasons.

"Am I to congratulate you?" I say sharply. "On your restraint?"

He stiffens.

"I only meant…"

"That it is normal to abuse one's power?" Of course that's how his world works, and mine too. Whoever has power wields it over those with less. Men over women, women over slaves. And gods over all of us.

"What I am trying to say"—his voice is cooler now—"is that I helped you because I did not want to watch you suffer." Under the cloak, he shrugs. "I had hoped that once you were here…that you would come to feel…"

A wave of heat ripples through me. He shakes his head.

"No matter. You need rest. I have distracted you for too long."

Wait, I want to say, as he moves toward the door. Wait, and finish. *Feel what?*

But he's already gone.

He does not come back that evening, nor does Aletheia. I watch the flowers at the window until the sun drops down behind them, and then I watch the stars. Sleep does not come. I toss and turn; my bones seem to itch under my skin. Is this what healing feels like?

But my thoughts itch too, restless and insistent.

It seems there may be cruelty in a god, and kindness in a demon. What has he shown me these last days, only kindness? I think of the riddle he teased me with in the weaving-room that day. *Gods and demons are in the eye of the beholder,* he said. Now I let the words dance in my mind for a moment, I let myself fancy them as true. But it can only be a fancy, and only for a little while.

And yet the thought comes to me, strange and uncomfortable: I do not want to leave him.

Foolish thought. Of course I want to leave here. And I *will* leave here, as soon as I can. He will have to lock me up if he wants to keep me from escaping again. But something in his voice and manner, something heavy and sad, tells me he won't do that.

I think if I could see his face, this strange spell would fade. If I could see whatever cursed, monstrous thing he is, whatever truth he is adamant that I should not witness. This whisper of insanity in my brain would be silenced, then.

I tell myself to rest. To close my eyes and banish these senseless thoughts. But there is no denying it—just as there is no admitting it. When I'm falling asleep it's his voice I hear, a voice like wind in the cedar trees. And it's his scent, like the drift of incense through slow night air, that I find myself straining to catch, hunting it on my hair, my skin.

It's night when I wake again. I'm disoriented, and at first I think it's the pain of my healing limbs that has woken me. But it's not that. I hear the sound of the bedroom door closing.

"Who's there?" I say sharply in the dark.

There is quiet, and then in the darkness the quick sizzle of fire, and a candle bursts into flame.

Twenty-two

The flame seems suspended in the blackness, its small light floating on a dark sea.

His black cloak makes a deeper darkness than the night, and I see his golden hands wrapped around the taper, and the faintest outline of his jaw, uplit from the candlelight. It's the closest I've ever come to a glimpse of his face, and the sight of it teases strangely at me. There is nothing hideous about the flicker of it that I see. And then I remember to be afraid. What is he doing here, in my bedroom, in the middle of the night? Why does he come here in darkness, when I should be sleeping?

"Psyche. You are awake?"

For a moment I think of feigning sleep. But surely he can see the whites of my staring eyes—and besides, he is not easy to lie to.

"I am awake."

The silence is thick as he gathers words. I realize he has come here to tell me something, and my first thought is for my family. His voice is heavy; my heart clenches. If he has news of them, it cannot be good.

"You are determined to leave," he says at last. "I know that the escape you attempted, you will attempt again. And again." The candle lowers; he sits down on the corner of the bed, opposite me.

"A woman of good sense, I think, would stay. But you will not. Am I correct?"

I stare into the darkness.

Will not. Cannot. It's all the same. There's nothing I can do about Sikyon's destruction now. But I can't hide in here while things get worse.

"I must face my fate," I say finally. "Whatever it is."

His head turns away from me. I can read him so well by now, but in the darkness I still struggle. Is he disappointed? Angry?

"It is foolish of you. But, if you must go…" He breaks off for a moment. "If you *must* go, if you *will* go...there is something I can give you."

He reaches, then, inside his cloak, and pulls out what looks to be some kind of necklace: a leather string with a white stone medallion. The medallion has an eye carved into it.

"This," he says quietly, "is a Shroud. There are only a few of them in the world."

I gaze at it. I have never heard of such a thing.

"What's it for?"

And why is he giving it to me?

"Wear it and you will be hidden from the eyes of the gods, when they search for you."

I feel his gaze—but what he's saying makes no sense.

"Hidden?"

"I cannot offer you complete invisibility," he says. "No charm can grant that—but it will help. You must understand, Psyche: Aphrodite can track you as a hound tracks a rabbit. She could spot you a thousand leagues farther than the sharpest-sighted eagle. That is why mortals cannot flee the gods. That is to say, *unshrouded* mortals cannot flee the gods."

He drops the medallion in my palm.

"But while you wear this, she cannot catch the scent, and her sight is dull." I hear the frown in his voice. "Even so, try not to draw attention to yourself. Keep among crowds."

I stare at the talisman in my palm. Can this be real? Is it some kind of hoax? Does the demon speak from some delusion? It is hard to believe I am holding an object of the kind of power he claims.

I turn my face up toward him.

"But…why are you doing this? Why are you giving this to me?"

He's silent.

"You are a fool to leave," he says then. "But if you insist on leaving…I made a promise to save you. You need not boast that I lied to you." He watches me. "Put it around your neck."

I reach, but a twinge of pain in my arm stops me. In this moment, my injuries were the last thing on my mind.

"Forgive me, I had forgotten. Here: I will do it."

He takes the amulet and leans forward. He moves the hair away from the nape of my neck, his hands gliding over the skin there. I shiver, and he notices. His thumb hesitates, then grazes the skin once more, as if to test its power. This time, I swallow down the shiver, and he hesitates only a moment longer before pulling back.

"Wear it under your clothing," he says. "Some may know its significance, and those that do will seek to take it from you."

I run my hand over the stone. It is polished and cool. I'm sure kings have cleared out their coffers for objects of lesser power.

"You're not angry with me?" I say slowly.

"I *am* angry," he says, and from his voice I would almost believe he hated me, were it not for the gift I'm wearing at my neck. "I'm angry that you're such a little fool. And I'm angry that I..." He stops.

"No matter."

I don't know what to say.

I have called him my captor these past days and weeks, in my head and even aloud. But that is no longer the right word. If I am honest, I don't think it ever was. He has been haughty, he has been high-handed with his manners, but I think he did try to save me the only way he knew how.

And he's saving me again.

When I go, none of this will seem real. I will wonder if I dreamed it up: the honey-wood scent of him; the roughness of his voice and the softness of his hands. The air about him like the air before a storm, crackling and smoky and sweet. The song that my skin makes when it touches his. The wind-rush in my blood when he speaks my name.

I cannot explain these things, or justify them, but there they are.

"Aletheia can pack you some supplies," he says. "You will leave tomorrow, if you are well enough."

Suddenly, it's as though he wants me gone. It's goodbye.

Just as you wanted.

Except not quite what I wanted.

I touch the cool edge of the medallion. How strange that it should have worked out like this.

"So I must bid you farewell now," I say.

He inclines his head, but does not speak.

"When I was a child," I say abruptly, "I played with a little girl who was blind. When we met, she put her hands to my face. To feel it; to see it with her hands."

"Indeed." His voice is detached and withdrawn.

"Might I do that now?" I say into the silence. The fabric of the cloak ripples as he turns.

"Why?"

I touch the medallion again.

"I owe you a great debt now. I know I cannot thank you face to face, nor bid you goodbye that way. But this would be a little like that."

I can feel his stare on me.

"You wish to do this?"

"I...I would wish to remember something of you." I hesitate. "I will wear the blindfold, if you wish."

He is very still, and when he speaks, it's halting.

"Very well," he says.

I nod, my throat dry.

The blindfold lies on a small table near my bed. I gather it in my fingers, feeling his stare on me as I do so. I take a breath, and tie it on. Strangely, it feels like home: now that it is no longer my enemy, it has become like a friend. I know its dark and silken world.

"Why are you smiling?" he says, and immediately my smile disappears. My hands are hot; my skin tingles.

"I see nothing now. Will you take my hands?"

There is a hesitation, and the soft movement of fabric. I picture him lifting back his hood. I can hear him breathing.

"Very well," he says again.

And then his hands fold over mine, and a surge rushes through me. I'm embarrassed by how hot my hands are, but I stop thinking about that as he leads them through the air and—gently, but to me it's sudden as an explosion—places my palms against cool skin.

It's like all my senses are fighting each other at once. Or like a brand-new sense, suddenly coming alive. The tips of my fingers are electric, a thousand points of sensation. It's like lights going off behind my eyes. His hands guide mine over his face. His forehead, the downy hair of his eyebrows. The tender skin, impossibly tender, that marks the sockets of his eyes. I feel the sweep of his lashes as he blinks, and he moves my fingers down over his closed lids.

Am I breathing? I'm not sure.

I hadn't expected him to trust me like this. My fingertips graze over his eyelids, feeling the tremor beneath, the slight flutter as though it's an effort for him to keep them shut. My fingers brush the lashes again and travel down the slope of his nose, and across to his cheekbones.

He is beautiful, the thought comes to me, as sure as the sky.

The thought is strange, yet not strange at all.

His hands tighten on mine, his fingers around my wrists, his thumbs in the center of my palms. I can hear his breath, and no doubt he hears mine.

My fingers inch down toward his mouth. I try not to let the least sound escape me. I feel the bow of his upper lip, that little pucker at the center, yielding beneath my finger. One finger traces to the corner of his mouth—am I imagining that it quivers?—and then back over the bottom lip, smooth and full. I feel his breath now, the movement of air against my exploring fingers.

And I don't move, can't move. I just breathe.

I should take my hands away, but I don't.

And then *his* hand is there, warm against the nape of my neck. Cradling the back of my head. Drawing me closer, inch by inch.

Until finally, his lips touch mine.

*

A shock runs the length of my body, rattling me like a bead. And yet inside the shock I am calm, weightless. I am the eye of the storm. My body is a raging wind, but in the center…in the center, there is a holy kind of emptiness. I feel a thread of heat rush from my throat and through each vein. The tips of my fingers pulse. The pit of my stomach contracts. Time warps, suspended. Nothing is real but this.

"Psyche," he murmurs into my mouth, but my name is a word that lost all meaning a heartbeat ago.

His voice is a caress. A plea. A demand. I feel the shape of his jaw against mine as he draws back for a moment, taking air. My lips are cold and empty without his.

It doesn't matter that I cannot see him, I feel where he is the way I'd know a fire in the room. I reach out my hand and it finds the back of his head, the nape of his neck, the tendons there pressing strong against my hot palm.

I have hated him, I have *wanted* to hate him. But I cannot find these thoughts now, the things I thought he was. Whatever he is, it is not evil. I feel it in his breath, in how he touches me: with such desire, and yet with humility.

With such care.

His cheek grazes mine; one hand rests against the brooch that pins my *chiton*, and I feel him toying with the clasp, his teasing touch waiting for permission.

"Yes," I whisper, and the loosened silk slides free. I feel his hungry smile against my skin.

His hands lever me back against the bed. Silk rustles beneath us. Darkness like water. His hands at my throat, my shoulders, my collarbone, his fingertips grazing the length of my arm.

I want everything from him.

And he wants all of me.

Before, in my life in Sikyon, with Yiannis, I thought perhaps I knew desire…but I knew nothing at all. I thought desire a pleasant thing. Like the smell of fresh flowers, or sunlight on skin. Now I know better. Desire is not comfort. Desire is not peace. The only peace in desire is in knowing it will be gratified, and the hunger sated.

I give myself over to sensation. The caress of his hands, the crisp whisper of the sheets. I'm in a daze, my words gone, reduced to mere sounds. There is only pleasure and then more pleasure, and just when I think no more could be possible, I am proven wrong.

The darkness wraps around me. The world trembles.

Until finally, we see stars.

*

I wake from a dreamless sleep, deeper than I've ever known. It seems as though I have traveled a very great distance over many aeons, only to find myself conscious once more, waking into this mortal shell we call the body. I breathe softly, touch the fabric that still wraps my eyes. And I shiver, remembering the hours that passed before I slept. It seems like a dream, and yet I know it was no dream: my body still bears witness.

My mind is groggy as I tweak the corner of the blindfold. The windows seem blacker than before, and the candle long is extinguished. It's ocean-dark in this room.

But he's here.

I remember falling asleep with his arms encircling me, but even now, he has not retired to his own chamber, as I assumed he would. His body isn't touching mine, but I can feel the warmth of him, the spell of him. I roll onto my side and take a breath. Through the thinnest of light, the barest shades of grey, I can make out the back of his head.

I see the curls, thick, lush, silky: even in this blackness I can see the sheen of them, and I have to force myself not to reach out and bury my hand in them.

And his back…I inch closer, peering in the darkness, to make out every curve of it. The broad shoulders, like a diver's. The gleam of his skin. The sharp line of his spine, the firm shape of muscle.

I feel the heat rush back into my body at the sight of him. To see him, to see just this much of him! A warm joy spreads through me, deep and heady. I drink him in, all that I can see. My eyes seem to hurt with it; I have never looked this fiercely before.

The urge to reach out and touch him is almost overpowering, but I don't dare. It might wake him.

Instead, slowly, I slide myself up onto one elbow. I can see more of him now: his ear, a perfect whorl, the darkness at the center of it strangely bewitching; the curve of his strong neck. The side of his jaw; the very edge of his cheekbone. Those glorious curls, the way they spring from the soft skin beneath his temple, thickening over the broad dome of his head. I open my mouth, as if I could drink in the smoky scent of him and hold it in my throat.

Dare I?

My heart thunders. I should not. I know I should not.

But it's dark. It's not even really looking.

The voices in my head argue, but the argument is only for show. The part of me that sits below the mind, the darker place where instinct rules, has already made the decision. I sit up, all the way up now, and hold my breath. On hands and knees I lever myself forwards, careful not to brush his sleeping form with my hair.

And I see him, at last.

For a moment, it feels like blindness. I don't know how else to explain it.

He's the most beautiful creature I've ever seen—his lips, his face, the broad, soft brow relaxed in sleep—and every artist who's ever tried to capture beauty has failed, failed miserably, because nothing I've ever seen, nothing I've dreamed of, comes close to this. But it's more than beauty—much more than that. I don't know how to describe it, except to say that it's holy.

It's like looking at the first and last sunset.

It's like seeing the world be born.

Not a demon, my mind whispers.

Not a demon.

A god.

And then, he opens his eyes.

Twenty-three

They are golden, like the sun. And for the briefest of moments, before he has time to focus, I see him without him seeing me. And it seems to me then I'm looking not at his eyes, but through them. For just an instant, I leave time and space behind.

I see everything there is in the world: the long grasses in the fields, stirred by the wind's breath, and the beetle swaying at the grass's tip. I see the living and the dead, and every star in the sky. I see the beating heart at the center of the earth.

I see futures, so many of them, all the futures that could be. I see him, and myself by his side. I see war, and blood, and love, and rebirth.

And then it's over. The visions leave my head like a fog clearing and I'm looking at his golden eyes again—which are focused on me now, and full of horror. His arm darts in front of his face, as though to shield me from some hideous thing.

"What are you doing; what have you done? Look *away*," he growls. "Little fool, look away!"

But I don't.

"I warned you, Psyche! You swore it."

"I know who you are," I say. Because I do. I knew it the moment I saw his face—or if not then, the moment he opened his eyes. I know his name like I know my own.

"Why did you hide yourself from me? All this time…You had me believe you were a monster."

"I am one, to mortals!" His voice is full of fury. "Now you will suffer, and I will lose you!"

"I don't understand…"

"The sight of my face…" His words tip between anger and dread. "It brings madness upon them."

Madness? I don't know whether to shudder or laugh. One could call what I've been feeling "madness," I suppose, but it is the sweetest madness I have known.

"But look, I am not mad. Whatever curse you think you've brought on me, you are wrong."

He is silent for a moment.

"Perhaps…perhaps if it was dark enough…perhaps it spared you…"

"There is nothing wrong." I don't care what he says; even his fear doesn't make me fearful. Not when I know joy like this. I nudge his hand, trying to uncover his face.

"I am fine. Everything is fine. See?"

But he's shaking his head.

"You made a vow. It cannot be unsaid."

"Then I will make a new vow," I say. "A better one."

Because I know who it is that lies before me now. It is the god of love himself, and his name bubbles up in me: a well of joy, begging to be spoken.

"Eros," I murmur.

*

Even though I whisper it, it's like the world stops. The walls seem to shake with it. I feel the echo, shuddering through the room and reverberating up to the heavens.

Eros.

Eros.

Eros!

His hand is over my mouth now, but it's too late. I don't know what's happening, but I can tell it won't be stopped. I can't find my voice, to ask questions or even to cry out.

Around us, the walls continue to tremble. The floor shakes harder. My hair swings against my shoulders; the bed seems rattled by an invisible hand.

"What's happening?"

He knows: I can see in his face that he knows. He throws my discarded *chiton* at me.

"You must leave here. Now."

Leave?

"Can't you forgive me for this one thing? It was an impossible promise! I had to see. I had to know."

"I know," he says. "And now we both must pay the price." His voice is sharp, but his face is full of a terrible sadness, which is worse. "I do not ask you to leave as punishment, Psyche. Soon this place will fall. And you must not be here when it does."

I stare at the walls, the cracks like webs, growing furiously in all directions. The grinding sound of stone on stone. On the ceiling, cracks are spreading like tree-roots. Whatever's happening is outside his control, and that frightens me: he is a god.

"Can't you stop it?"

"Psyche, *go!* For once in your life, you must trust me!"

I stare at him, his radiance, his furious eyes. The shuddering is everywhere now. I don't dare look up at the ceiling to see the cracks.

"What about you?" The way everything's shaking, I have to talk between rattling teeth.

He makes an impatient noise.

"I am a god. Stone will not crush me."

Then why are you so afraid? I want to ask. Because he is: I can see it in his eyes, in everything he tries to hide.

"You wished to run from here, so run." His voice is harsh, the cold voice I used to hear and hate. I stare at him, and the pain wells up in my chest. This doesn't make sense. It isn't fair.

"You won't come with me. Why won't you come with me?"

His gaze shifts as if to find mine, but he stops himself in time. He refuses to look at me, no matter how much I want him to.

"You will not see me again, Psyche. Forget what you can."

Forget?

Forget?

And then I feel a terrible shaking, a shuddering. It's as though the very bones of the earth are creaking, as though some great edifice is about to give way. I become conscious of something else in the shadows. There, by the bed: the shadows are building something. A form. Almost human.

"What is it?" I whisper, the dread multiplying.

"It's broken, Psyche. Run, before you are ruined." His voice sounds distant, far away. "I can't come with you, don't you understand? You must run. Run, before she gets here."

"Before who gets here?" I shout, frantic now. But I already know.

I had forgotten, for a moment, whose son he is.

He does not look at me—does not, or cannot. Either way, his face is stone.

And with one last sob I tear myself from the bed and hurl myself toward the doors.

*

The earth seems to heave beneath me as I run along the corridor; the torches rattle in their sconces and the flames flicker madly. It's only when I reach the courtyard that I think of Aletheia—did I leave her inside the palace walls to die? And once I think of her, I think of the gate. She has the key, and it is locked. I will perish in here after all.

But when I throw open the door to the stable-yard, the huge gate stands open. Aletheia must have already fled.

A clamor from the stables stops me from racing out into the darkness. Whinnying, stamping; desperate noises. The horses are still tied up in their stalls. A chunk of plaster smashes to the ground beside me, and I race across the yard and into the stable. I start with the farthest stall first, scrambling to loosen the ties on the chestnut mare as her eyes roll wild with frenzy. No sooner have I finished than she bolts away into the night. I set the next two free, then steady my breath as I enter the final stall. The black stallion watches me with big dark eyes. I try not to feel the fear, but my body remembers all too well. If he attacks me now, no one will come to rescue me. These walls will fall on me in the darkness.

"Will you trust me?" I say aloud. "I'm here to get you out."

The stallion snickers softly, his breath a warm cloud.

There's no more time to waste.

The knots are tighter, or else my fingers are shaking harder: I can't seem to loosen them. I let out a howl of frustration. The dust kicks up from the ground, getting in my eyes. I tear at the knots, seeing images of the abandoned palace whose rooms seemed to be crumbling even as I ran through them; and the Hearthstone in the great-room, its black surface sheared in two as though some great axe had severed it.

All the things I saw as I ran away, and left him behind.

What have I done? He said none of this could kill him. And yet he seemed weakened. Faded. Trapped.

I shake my head: a mortal cannot kill a god. But this place will kill me fast, if I don't run.

The knots give way, and finally the stallion's free. But instead of running like the others, he doesn't move.

"*Go,*" I shout. Tears of frustration well in my eyes. "Run, you stupid creature!" I shout. "I can't save you if you won't save yourself!"

But he's not running. He's…

Waiting.

For me? His eyes are on mine, wide and black and urgent. And I can read exactly what he's thinking.

Stupid creature. I can't save you if you won't save yourself.

I take a breath, grab a hold of his mane, and hoist myself up. And this time, he lets me.

He takes off, faster than I knew a horse could run. My

stomach roils, my hands break out in sweat. I try to bury myself deeper in his mane, grip harder. I'm no great horsewoman, and I've never ridden a beast like this one. We burst through the open gate and into a dark, mountainous place. Are we in the mortal realm? I want to look, and yet I am afraid to. But dawn is coming in: I see its rays in the distance. We're on a sloping hillside, the silhouette of vines and olive trees against a purple sky. The shapes are dark, yet...not unfamiliar. I suppose we could be anywhere, and yet it feels like a place I know. The horse pounds forward over earth and stone.

I don't know how to begin to think about what has happened.

Eros.

Aphrodite.

I touch the medallion around my neck. I don't understand what just happened, but I fear something in me will break if I let myself think about it. Right now, I must do as the horse is doing: one foot in front of the other, onward.

But I can't help it. I have to look back.

I turn precariously in my seat—and suddenly I understand. I know where I am. I know what I'm looking at. The vines and olive trees, the sloping hillside. I know exactly why it all feels so familiar. I remember what he told me, my first night:

The mortal realm overlaps this one, like footprints in the sand.

As the stallion tears down a chalk-white road in the hillside, I stare back at Sikyon's temple. The Temple of Eros. All along, I was this close—and yet, a world away.

A realm away.

How the magic works, I cannot say. Sikyon's temple was built with simple stone, by mortal hands, and yet the place I have just come from was no mortal place. The temple, I suppose, is a threshold of sorts.

Was a threshold of sorts.

The path jolts beneath us, stony and uneven. But though my hands are balled in the horse's mane to keep me upright, I barely feel it. I can't take my eyes from the crumbling temple behind us. Soon it will be in ruins.

I watch another row of marble pillars splinter like bones, and a whole section of the roof collapse. I squeeze my eyes closed against it all: the dust and grit, the fear and confusion.

What has happened to him?

And what will happen to me?

The horse's frenzied pace has finally begun to slow. I secure my hands tighter in his mane, and remind myself to breathe. Right now, there is only one thing I know.

Where I'm going next.

Twenty-four

In the grey pre-dawn light the ruins rise up like broken teeth. Instead of wide streets and noble, elegant buildings, the ground is strewn with rubble in every direction, and mounds of stone.

Oh, Sikyon. What have they done to you?

Razed, as though the fist of a god rammed right down upon it from the sky.

I breathe unsteadily.

And this, too, is to be my fault? The feeling is unbearable.

I don't want to ride on, but I must. It cannot all be destroyed. But even the horse seems to falter at the sight of so much devastation. His large back sways as we turn down what was once the main street. Now it is nothing more than a series of ruins. Great chunks of rock stand in the ground, trails of dust marking their fall from the mountain above. To my right, down the mountainside, I can see the paths some of the falling boulders took, wide enough to push a cart through. Even the buildings that are still standing look precarious and unsafe. Through windows and gaping holes, I see the signs of abandoned life: kitchens with their pots and braziers shattered; cups and bowls and children's toys jumbled on the earthen floor. Thin, mewling cats roam in and out of the abandoned homes. Everything smells of dust and desolation.

My home.

A home that betrayed me.

And yet still, it was my home.

By the scale of this ruin, there must be many dead, and yet there are no bodies here, or none that I can see. It makes me think this place was not abandoned straightaway. Some panicked and fled immediately, I suppose. Others waited, tended to the dead and dying, took the time to pack up their homes, and loot the abandoned ones.

I walk from house to house, looking to see what has been left behind. In some places, a little; in others, a lot. How many of my townspeople escaped? Hundreds? Thousands? Just a few?

I urge the black stallion through the streets, but it seems to me he already knows where I want to go. Maybe he's drawn, just as I am, to the whisper of disaster. At the next crossroads I study the churned-up mud: many feet—horses and humans—have passed through here, moving every possible way. The survivors did not leave as a convoy, then, but fled piecemeal, in families and groups.

Past the agora, the ruin is not so absolute. Here, too, the cats roam freely as if they, now, are the true owners of Sikyon. But here and there I see shadows move behind windows; shutters twitching as I pass. It has not been entirely abandoned, then.

I see a flicker of movement to my left: a child, picking their way nimbly from the rubble at the back of a house, tripping as they run off, their arms full. Carrying some looted bounty, I suppose. They're glancing back at me as they run. I must be what scared them off.

"Hey!" I call. "Come back! I won't hurt you. I just…"

But they've already gone.

I lead the horse down the dirt roads to the outskirts of town. When we reach the streets around my old home I slow his pace, the beat of his hooves like a tremor in my spine.

The door of our house hangs wide open, and I dismount with a fast-beating heart.

I loop the horse's reins over a door post and step inside.

"Dimitra?" I call. "Father?"

My voice ricochets back to me. Of course I did not expect them to answer; of course they are not here. And yet, for a moment, I imagined…

I walk through the rooms and find them emptied out. Anything of value that can be carried is gone. Taken by my family as they rode to safety? Or by the looters who came after?

I have heard what it is like in times of war or disaster: the belongings of the dead are shown little respect. Their homes are overrun, their heirlooms melted down. The very rings are pulled from their fingers.

I just never thought I would witness such a thing in my lifetime.

I thought we lived in a protected place. In a protected time.

Our town is one favored by the gods—that was what our king used to say.

I walk through the rooms, which feel cold and no longer mine. It's not just the emptiness, not just the fine layer of settled dust. Before, the rooms would seem to turn their faces toward me when I entered. Now, they look blindly past me. They don't know I'm here, or if they know, they no longer care.

This was the place I longed for when I thought myself a prisoner in a demon's palace. The only home I knew. The place of all my memories.

I trail a hand along the wall, and make my way from my old room to Dimitra's, and then to Father's—it used to smell of him, but now it only smells of dust and stone. I open the great wood chest where he kept his clothes. Most of them look to be still here. If he packed some for a journey, they were very few. I run my hands over an old, grey cloak at the bottom of the chest, and pull it out.

I rub the light wool cloak between my thumb and forefinger. My head throbs. I dare not close my eyes, I dare not stop moving. Because if I pause for an instant I will think of him, and the enormity of it all will paralyze me. My cloaked stranger, my demon husband: the one who told me to forget him.

I know what happens to mortals who fall for gods. It never ends well.

And he is Aphrodite's own son! No wonder he feared her wrath. No wonder he knew she'd hunt me forever: I'm the reason her own son went against her.

And what will she do, now that she knows what he has done? How he cheated and defied his own mother, to save me? I finger the medallion at my neck. I can't un-see that look in his eyes, the pain of betrayal, the awful resignation.

Enough. I must push these thoughts from my mind.

My father's room is not so empty as downstairs. The looters did not bother with much here, I suppose—

These things are valuable only to a loved one. The tray where he keeps his brush and soap and scent; his liniments, and the picks he uses for his teeth. And there at the back, a wooden box I know well.

Too sharp for little fingers.

The small, jeweled knife my mother brought with her from Atlantis. The only thing of value she owned. The sheath is old and slightly rusted when I lift it from the box. I slide the knife out to examine the blade.

Still sharp.

I don't know how my mother came to possess such an object. I asked my father once and I think he was uncomfortable; it seemed to me that he believed my mother might have stolen it. She had lived a hard life, he said, before she came to Sikyon. But for a weapon it was a pretty thing, he admitted. Why should she not treasure it the way other wives might treasure a rich bracelet or a diadem made of gold?

The opals in the hilt catch the light, flaring like tiny flames. I don my father's cloak, and slip the dagger in one of its deep pockets. It can be dangerous, for a woman traveling alone.

I start, then, at a noise from downstairs. Just the horse, growing restless outside? Or a stray animal perhaps, overturning something in the kitchen. *Or something else altogether.* I move quietly to the head of the stairs.

If someone is here to loot, they can have what they like. Most things of value are gone, and what is left I don't care for. But I'm remembering the shadows in the windows that moved as I rode by. Watching me. In a pillaged town, looters may come for more than jewels…

My hand closes around the knife in my pocket. I take a few silent steps down the stairs.

"Lydia?" I stop short.

It's no marauder—just our old neighbor, Lydia, who taught me to weave when I was only waist-high.

"I—I thought you were an intruder. Here for looting." My breath catches in a foolish half-laugh. Her milky eyes look me over.

"Psyche." Her voice is solemn and unsurprised. "So you are not dead after all."

"I am not." Though I almost feel it, today. Walking through the devastation of Sikyon, a part of me seems to have died with it.

Lydia's gaze is steady. I notice that, though she looks much the same as before, her clothes are covered with a layer of dirt, and there is a small gash at her left temple that is still in the way of healing.

"Your sister said she saw the monster that came for you. That he was the size of a tall man, but all shadow. And that later he sprouted terrible wings, and carried you away."

"It is so."

"But he did not kill you."

"The opposite," I say, and my throat constricts.

Despite her milky gaze, her stare seems to pierce me. She taps her cane and steps closer. Her face is puckered and wary.

"But you are changed," she remarks. "You fly too close to the sun, girl. I see it in your face. Already you have been singed."

A question burns in me, but part of me dares not ask. If I don't ask, I can never hear the worst. But I force myself to speak.

"Can you tell me what became of my family? My father, my sister. Are they alive?"

"They were when they left here," she says. "What they are now, I know not."

My heart quickens.

"So they survived..." I gesture. "All this?"

"They were gone before it happened—the king expelled them, not so many days after his men brought you to the rock. They were allowed to bring what their wagon could carry, and the rest was forfeit." She looks at me. "A few days later, we suffered this collapse. Some said the gods were angry at the king's harshness: that we had been wrong to expel your family, and to sacrifice you." She sighs, adjusting her weight, leaning harder on her stick.

"Others blamed you." She pauses. "But you did as you were bound. If the goddess was thwarted it was not your doing."

My stomach sinks, hearing her account of it.

"Do you know what direction my family took?" I say. "Where they may have been headed?"

She shakes her head.

"If they knew it, they did not speak of it to me." Her pale eyes rove slowly, taking in the empty rooms.

"Were you here?" I say haltingly. "When it happened?"

She nods.

"It began in the middle of the day. When the sun was high. It came out of nowhere. Creaking and rumbling, and then a great thundering. Slowly at first, and then fast." Her fingers tap out a quiet, aimless pattern on the handle of her cane. "For some, there was time to flee. For others, none. The poor took most of the damage. The wealthier end of the town was mostly spared. Such injustice...but it is ever thus."

It's hard to look at Lydia's face.

"Some of us wanted to stay and rebuild, but we did not find much support; too many were afraid. They said that it would be tempting fate to stay. I never saw carts packed so high—gold, jewels, food and wine." She shrugs her bony shoulders. "I told them they were wasting their time. Places aren't cursed: people are. Any if a person is cursed, they're cursed wherever they may go."

I feel the air sharp in my throat. "You believe that?"

"I do."

Her pale gaze travels over me.

"I must go looking for them," I say aloud. "For my family. But I don't know where to begin."

She shakes her head.

"I have no answers for you, child. I am no oracle."

Her thumb rubs the polished wood at the top of her cane. I stare at her.

No oracle.

They're idle words, and yet they spark a thought in me, a thought that shivers through me. There *is* a place that I can go for answers, but it is an uncertain road, to be sure. I look out the doorway of the house that was once my home.

An uncertain road, but it's all there is left.

Twenty-five

The path to Delphi starts high in the mountains. It's colder than I expected for late summer, and I keep the hood of my cloak pulled close around me.

In the horse's saddlebags I have the few valuables I found that had not been taken. A handful of coins; a gold signet ring of my father's. There was no food left in the house, but the garden had not yet been fully dug up, so I was able to forage a little there, and put the grains and vegetables I gathered in a sack to take with us, along with a full waterskin. Along with the coins, I'm hoping that will last long enough to get us to Delphi. After that, I'll have to figure something else out.

I noticed something else, when I was fastening on my bag of meager provisions: a quiver of arrows, hooked to the horse's saddle. I would have noticed them earlier, I suppose, if I hadn't been so distracted. Out in the barn I found an old bow, and now I ride with the quiver of arrows slung across my back.

Poison arrows. I wonder what he carried them for. And then I think of the things he said to me; the lessons, as I see it now, that he was trying to teach me.

What is a god but a demon by another name?

Just because he is the god of love, does not mean he isn't dangerous. All gods are dangerous. I should know that by now.

Either way, I'm glad of the extra defense. When Father taught us combat, Dimitra was always better with the sword or javelin, but I could shoot an arrow straighter than she ever could, so these won't go amiss.

I adjust the quiver on my back, and look out over the mountain road, the azure sea in the distance. Soon it's nearing sunset; the sky is clear except for a patch of thick clouds blowing in from the west. A flock of birds flies overhead—they circle once, split apart, then knit back together. Although I ride alone, with not another soul in sight, I wonder how many traveled along this mountain pass a short while ago, in the exodus Lydia described. As for us, our road will go west from here, before taking us down through the mountain passes to the coast, and then we'll follow the bay around toward the crossing at Patras. Then we'll go east again, skirting Nafpaktos and Galaxidi, until we finally reach Delphi.

The stallion snorts and shakes his mane; I almost think he welcomes the journey. That makes one of us.

I reach a hand forward and stroke the side of his great muzzle.

Ajax, I remember. That is this noble creature's name.

"You have done me a great service," I say to him. "I hope you will not regret it."

I had half-expected him to turn against me, the further I led him from the temple. I thought perhaps he would pull away, seeking to return to his master, but he rides as easily with me as if we were old friends. Even so, I have the sense that all of it is on his terms: I have not forgotten the way it went before, when I tried to ride him out of there against his will.

As stubborn as his master, I think, but it only brings a tightness to my chest.

You will not see me again, he said.

Forget what you can.

The words echo through me. Did he mean it? After all that happened between us? Perhaps he hates me now. I betrayed him, after all. I broke a vow, somehow I brought his temple to the ground. He warned me—it was the one thing he made me promise.

If only he had told me the truth, I think, but I know well enough why he didn't. Better to let me believe he was monstrous, if it kept me from the temptation of looking. If it kept me from a curse of madness.

So am I mad? Perhaps. If love is madness, if desire is

madness.

It sounds wrong—it sounds stupid and dangerous—to use words like that. Words like *love*. But what else am I to call this? First I hated him. Then I desired him. Then I began to love him. All against my wishes, against my better judgment.

And I cannot forget that feeling, when he first opened his eyes. It felt like falling through time, as if the future and the past had compressed into one. And the most strange and wondrous part of all: in each instant, *he* was there. As though the memories of the future were already made, as though the whole of our lives had already been intertwined. Whatever part of our mortal selves is deathless, I *felt* that part of me sing out. How can I describe it, except that I felt certain our fates were bound?

But that cannot be.

It must not be. It is impossible, and worse than impossible, it's dangerous.

He will return to the Pantheon, and forget me. What was it he said, before? *Your lifetime, your father's and your father's father's, are nothing to a god.* He may not forget me overnight, but what does time matter to him?

I lower my head, and turn into the wind. We ride through the night. I'm tired, but not tired enough to sleep—and besides, I feel safer up here, on Ajax's broad back. There are few places to seek shelter on these open roads, and no telling who or what might come across me as I slept.

I bring my fingers to the Shroud that hangs around my neck. I suppose it must be working: the earth has not opened up to swallow me yet, nor has some dreaded creature emerged from these mountain passes.

Did he really think he could rescue me from the cliffs that day, and keep the secret from her? Did he really believe she would not find us out?

Gods can be fools, I suppose, as much as mortals can. But he was right about one thing: the wrath she has for me will only be redoubled now.

I think of all the little things he told me, the oblique comments that meant nothing at the time. The family he spoke of, the two brothers he'd been parted from in childhood. I know who they are: Aphrodite may be married to Hephaestus, but none of her children come from his seed—she is the goddess of love, but not loyalty, and her three sons are all born of the war-god, Ares. And of these, Eros is known to be her favorite. The youngest; the one she raised to be like her, a love-god, while Ares raised the other two in his own image.

A dangerous family, to be sure.

Still, whatever offense Eros has caused to his family, I suppose it is nothing to mine. I finger the knot in the medallion's leather string again. I had better ensure it does not loosen. The moonlight picks out the path ahead, but my eye can only follow some small distance before it blends back into brush. It would be easy, I think, to get lost up here. I am tired, but I keep my eyes open, and the threat of sliding off of Ajax's broad back is incentive enough.

Morning comes, slow and red. I reach a village, and then another one after that. The path becomes a road, and after a while I see others on it—here and there another horse-rider, here and there a person on foot. I keep the hood of my cloak up, and my eyes on the path. I don't want their attention. I don't want them to ask where I'm from or why I'm traveling this way. I don't want them to notice that I'm a woman, and young.

When dusk starts to fall for the second night, I think about stopping. I'm exhausted. How long is it since I slept?

I ask around to find a room before the darkness thickens. The *xenodochoi,* the villagers who offer up their rooms for travelers, do so as a holy act—but they are more eager to host some guests than others, that much is easy to see. The first door is opened by a woman, who narrows her eyes at me and tells me their house is full. The next door is opened by a man, and although he says there is room for me, I do not like how he says it. I dismount to ask some children playing in a small square. They eye me curiously; one of them has dark eyes that remind me of young Hector Georgiou.

"Try the house with the red door, after the shrine," the boy says. "Kirios Hieronymus is good to wayfarers."

Sure enough, when I knock the door opens quickly, and a stocky man with deep brown hair ushers me in. There's a free room, he says, and a table with bread and wine for me if I wish it.

"Will you have this for it?" I take my father's ring from the bag and show it to him.

He looks at it, looks back at me, then shakes his head.

"Keep it, girl," he says gruffly. "You may eat as a guest tonight."

I take my bread and wine in the one large room where other travelers are dining. I seat myself in a dark corner; they barely notice me come in, so deep are they in conversation.

"You've felt the storms, have you not?" one of them is saying. "If you knew how to cast for omens, brother, you would know it. Something is amiss with the gods."

"Something is always amiss with the gods," another says, waving his companion's words away with a mouthful of wine. "They fight more than we do down here."

"Be that as it may," a third one says, "whatever her priestesses decree, we'd be fools not to follow."

"Whose priestesses?" I say at last, and the men go silent, turning my way. They stare, but I don't lower my hood.

"Why, Aphrodite," the first of them, a tall, whiskered fellow, says. The others are tight-lipped, seeming unsure whether they ought to share such speculations with a woman.

"Her priests have issued a decree," the whiskered man continues. "Those seeking her blessing are no longer to worship her son, the god Eros."

The piece of bread falls from my hand. What can this mean? As the whiskered man's companion said, we are used to the gods and their fighting—but this seems different.

"Rumor has it the temples of Eros have been falling. We are not to rebuild them, the priests say. Even his shrines are not to be used. Likenesses and statues are to be covered or put away."

I swallow, feeling a chill go down my spine.

"But surely such a thing will not happen. He is one of our gods. We can't just…*stop*."

The men look at each other.

"There are many gods we have stopped worshiping over the years," one says finally. "Our ancestors worshiped the Titans."

True enough. The Titans were an ancient race, and I suppose no one has worshiped them in these lands since Zeus brought his clan to Mount Olympus—but that was many years ago.

The man shrugs. "No doubt with every generation, some are lost."

I say nothing. It is too hard to fathom. Gods cannot be killed, and yet…what he is describing sounds almost like a death.

"Well," one of the other men says, "I reckon it's time we turn in." He eyes me as he says it, and there's a hesitant rumble of agreement. Left alone in the room, I finish my bread and wine slowly, then climb to my room and lock the door. I push the weight of the bed against the door, and through the night I lie with my mother's knife beside the pillow.

At first light I slip out to the stables, untie Ajax, and pull my aching limbs up over his back. Ajax, I think, suffers none of my exhaustion. Even on these dusty paths, his black coat looks sleek and unsullied, his mane as lush as ever, and the walking does not appear to tire him. Nor does he show any reluctance, any instinct to pull against me or run off. And I know that is not because he is tame—he is a wild creature, much wilder than I. I can only judge that he is here by choice; that he remains here, with me, by choice. I whisper to him as we walk on.

"I have heard strange things of your master last night, Ajax. I do not know what to make of them."

The roads are empty enough, and if anyone thinks me a madwoman for conversing with her horse, they keep it to themselves.

By the time the sun is halfway through its ascent, I have my first glance of the sea, and something about the sight brings tears to my eyes. By noon, we are riding by the coast. It is bracing, euphoric even. I feel something stirring as I watch the waves glinting under the sun, the blue ripples laced with gold. From the high vantage point of Sikyon, though the sea was within sight, it felt remote. Not so now as we ride through these flat lands, along this endless briny expanse—dancing, ever-shifting. My mother was an island girl, the child of fisher-people. Perhaps that's why my blood seems to rejoice at the sight of all this.

We have to wait a while for a ferryman at Patras, but the crossing itself takes no more than half an hour, with the currents in our favor. I give him an extra coin because I can tell he's not pleased about Ajax; it's a large enough ferry, and not unusual for a rider to cross with their horse, but the great stallion looks bigger on the boat than he did on land.

I avoid the center of Patras town, heading east with the bay as soon as we land. Soon its outskirts give way to villages, poorer ones than those I passed through yesterday: these are squat mud-and-clay houses, with small rough statuettes outside the doors for protection. I see that the villagers here pray to Hestia and Hecate for the most part. Hestia, to keep their fires burning and their homes tended. As for Hecate, the goddess of darkness, I cannot say; perhaps fearful things happen here in the night. Open fires have been lit here and there along the road, and flies congregate in pockets above what smells like goat meat. Children play on the dirt path, and their parents call at them to stay clear as I ride by. I ride through the night again, and on the third day, I begin to spot other travelers headed to Delphi.

They stand out—they're pilgrims, like me. There is a hum of anxiety about them; in some cases, desperation. Some are sick, or carry sick children with them. The sight pulls at me. It is not hard to imagine what questions they bring for the oracle.

But it is not only the poor who go this way. I see rich men, too, borne along in fine carriages with many servants. Rich and poor, young and old: I spot more and more of them, and by the fourth day, there are a flood of us. Military men and others who look like farmers; women from all walks of life, accompanied by their husbands or servants, and two who ride with no male companion at all—I see their curious glances find me, perhaps wondering the same of me as I am wondering of them. A man and a young boy; a group of soldiers on horseback; a man in shackles, shorn: I guess at all the questions these many people carry with them for the oracle. Some questions will be life-changing, some seemingly small. Some querents come to be relieved of their fears, others to confirm them. Some will beg for miracles they do not really want.

Perhaps, like me, they seek and fear the truth in the same degree.

*

The town of Delphi is small, a cluster of innkeepers and merchants selling trinkets to the pilgrims. But the crowds! I had expected some, but not this! It is busier than I had ever imagined. The temple is above the town, high on a mountainside, and from down here, milling with the crowds, I can only see flashes of color amid the foliage. A winding path leads uphill, a series of switchbacks toward the shrine at the very top where the oracle sits. The *Pythia*, they call her. They say she can answer any question you ask, but that does not mean she *will*.

There are priests and priestesses in red robes, trying to impose some order on the crowds swarming around the foot of the hill. *Zealots,* a man next to me mutters under his breath. I understand what he means. Now and again we had passersby come to visit our temple in Sikyon, but they were nothing like this. Here, the crowd is full of intensity, the air practically hums with it. I, too, am unnerved by those who make too much of religion; the kind who become glassy-eyed, like sleepwalkers, when they talk about their god. I think there will be many such here.

"An orderly line, please," someone is calling, and two priests walk firmly down the path, maneuvering stragglers, forcing us into some semblance of a line.

I've had to pay a man at an inn to keep Ajax under his watch; everyone must climb to the oracle's shrine on foot, there is no other way. Paupers and princes, all must go the same path.

"Look here!" A wealthy-looking man with a gold coronet and a retinue of military men catches one of the priests by the edge of his robe. "We have gold, and plenty of it. I come on an errand of the king of Thebes. Can't you show us to a place further up this line?"

The priest looks at him.

"We have many errands here, from many kings. And what good is your coin to us? Here we live on the mercy of the gods."

The man falls back in line with a snort of disgust, and soon he's bargaining with those lined up ahead of him, exchanging coins to move a place or two along.

We wait, and the hours pass; the sun moves through the sky. Finally I am near the top of the line—surely it cannot be long until I am brought forward—and now that I'm so close, half of me has the urge to disappear. Not everyone believes in the oracle's proclamations, and perhaps I will not believe her myself, once I know what she has to say. But I'm very much afraid that I *will* believe her…and that I may not like what I hear. Like everyone else, it seems I am afraid to know the truth, when it comes down to it.

A priestess with a coil of braids crowning her head comes down the line. "The oracle cannot see everyone, you are too many today. Some of you will have to come back tomorrow."

I don't know whether it's disappointment or relief that makes my heart clench, but the rest of the crowd seems to feel no such indecision. They are angry: there is murmuring, then arguing, then shoving. When I feel a hand on my shoulder, I am sure someone is about to throw me to the ground. They want my place in the line, and don't care how they get it. But then I realize the hand is a woman's, and a voice, low and soft, is saying my name.

Twenty-six

I whirl around. She's familiar, but for a moment not familiar enough at first for me to place.

"Melite," she says, seeing the uncertainty in my eyes. "Melite Georgiou."

Georgiou. Of course. She's little Hector's mother. Memories flash through my mind, sudden as a knife. Yiannis helping me into the chariot, Father hoisting Melite's son up to stand beside me in our chariot. Everyone smiling, proud in the sunshine.

Another lifetime. Another world. I swallow down the memory.

Melite looks older than she did before. She is perhaps only ten years my senior, but the blue shadows around her eyes have the look of someone with years more than that.

"Your cloak hides you well," she says. "I was not sure…I thought my eyes must be playing tricks on me. They play many tricks, these days."

"You thought me dead."

"I heard differing accounts," she admits. "Some said you had been carried off by a demon. Some said by a god. Some said you were swallowed whole by a serpent." She looks at me. "Either way, I did not expect to see you again."

"Nor I you," I say honestly, but if she asks for the truth of what happened to me, I must lie.

"I doubted whether I would ever see anyone from Sikyon again."

Her large brown eyes look at me with such a heaviness, it's hard to meet her gaze.

"You know what happened to us, then?"

I nod. Does she blame me for it? Does it anger her, to find me well and unharmed?

"We lost him." She speaks quietly. "Hector. We lost him in the rubble." She swallows. "My daughter survived. So did my husband and I. But Hector…we lost him."

The pain curls in my throat. *Hector*. I think of the crown of flowers on his head; his boyish, sweaty palms. The faint fuzz on his upper lip. Just a child.

Gone.

I raise my head and force myself to look at her.

"Tis lypes mou," I manage, but my voice is shaking. Is this really all I have to offer her—my sorrows? She will never see her only son again.

She stares back at me, and in her gaze I see Hector: all that he would have been, all that he will now never be. I understand what she meant, when she said her eyes play tricks on her now. She sees him still. She will always see him, perhaps.

"I don't blame you, Psycheandra," she says at last. "I don't know why those boulders fell, or what it is that stirs the finger of the Fates. The tempers of the gods are beyond my ken. But you went to the cliff to save Sikyon; you deserve no blame for what came next."

I wish that felt as true in my heart as it sounds on her lips. I cannot help but think now, what if Eros had never intervened? Hector would not be dead then.

But I remember what Eros said when I voiced that thought before. *A life is not a coin that can be traded for another.* For better or worse, no such bargain exists. I was saved, and now I have my life and must use it. My grief won't bring back Hector, nor will guilt or regret. Instead I vow to one day do something great in his name.

"We will keep the memory of him burning," I say quietly.

"Tha thymithoúme," she responds. *We will remember*.

We look at each other in silence for a while, and then she gestures, indicating over my shoulder.

"They are moving," she says. "You are being summoned."

*

She sits on a three-legged stool, before a deep opening in the rock. Across the divide there is a small bench, where petitioners are to sit, I suppose. When I see her round, young face, I can't help blinking in surprise. I had expected an old woman—wizened, ancient, a crone. The Pythia has served at Delphi for hundreds of years, after all, not that anyone truly believes it's been the same person all that time. Despite the girl's young face, her lush, thickly braided hair is bone-white. She regards me with large, pale eyes.

"Sit, daughter of Sikyon," she gestures.

I take my seat. *Daughter of Sikyon*. Is it her gift that speaks, or was I asked for that information earlier? I can't remember.

"What do you wish to know?" she says. Her voice is light, like a child's. Somehow, after these days of riding, and these many hours of waiting, I'm tongue-tied. I have questions buried inside me that I haven't yet figured out how to ask. But there is one above all that drove me here.

"My father, my sister. I was told they escaped the devastation of Sikyon. Is it true?"

"It is true," she says. A lump forms in my throat when she speaks the words and I cannot look at her. The relief, the gratitude, is too overwhelming. *I did not hope in vain.*

"Then I must find them," I say. "Where are they?"

She does not speak for a while, and I grow restless. Has she not heard me? Does she refuse my second question?

"Nowhere, yet," she says at last.

Her words do not make sense—they must be *somewhere*—but she speaks them so definitively.

"You will not find them if you search now," she carries on. "It is not your path."

I stare.

"My *path*?"

"Your path is through the gods, daughter of Sikyon." She

keeps her cool eyes on me. "The god who is your husband. Aid him, and he will aid you."

A cold, prickling feeling spreads over my skin. *Husband.* She knows everything about me already. And she speaks as if this god and I were still bound together; as if those reckless promises still endure. But he told me to run. To forget.

"*Aid* him?" I repeat. She must see how absurd the notion is. "What need has a god for mortal aid!"

She gives me a serious look.

"Your god is…much diminished. A god's temple is his place of strength. A container for his energy, his power. Eros's temple is broken, and that has weakened him."

I swallow.

"His temple at Sikyon, you mean? Did I make that happen?" But I am sure I already know the answer.

Her unblinking eyes are fixed on me, making the hairs on my neck stand up.

"To break a god's vow, in the god's own temple…it creates a deep rupture in the fabric of things. An unraveling. It is like a tremor in the earth—one that the gods may sense."

"So it *is* my fault."

"Blame is irrelevant," she says. "What was fated came to pass."

Fate. That slippery word that I am coming to hate.

"The rupture you spoke of," I swallow. "Was that what brought the goddess to him?"

I remember that shadowy form taking shape in the corner of the room. Eros's doomed expression. He knew she was coming; that something had alerted her.

The oracle nods.

"Aphrodite's third son is her great pride. The one made in her image: a god of love, whose beauty can transfix the eye. Since his boyhood she has made a companion of him, and bound him to her with oaths of loyalty. She is a doting and jealous mother. Eros thought to defy her wishes and keep his defiance a secret, but he was found out. To the goddess, his actions were a betrayal of the worst order."

My stomach turns over. It's nothing I didn't already know, but hearing her speak it aloud fills me with dread.

The oracle shoots me a curious look.

"Her pride in him was so great that when he was still a boy, the goddess boasted that no human could look upon him without being driven mad by his beauty. Whether she meant it as a prophecy I do not know, but a prophecy it became. The boy could not roam freely like the other gods—not without causing pain and destruction. When he left Olympus, he learned to cloak his face."

She adjusts her seat, leans closer.

"And yet you do not seem mad," she says.

My heart flutters.

"I do not feel it. Perhaps—perhaps the madness is just a legend," I say.

The oracle merely raises her eyebrows.

"Perhaps."

Her gaze comes to rest then on something over my shoulder.

"You are armed, I see." She reaches out a hand. "May I?"

I hesitate, then realize what she's talking about, and pass her the quiver of arrows. She slides one out and examines it. The arrows are of two different colors, I notice for the first time. Half are made with a dark wood, cedarwood perhaps; the other half are almost white, like birch.

"Love and death," the oracle nods. "You must be careful which you choose."

"I—I'm not sure I understand," I stammer.

She gives me a patient look, as though she knows that deep down, I *do* know.

"This one," she points to the birch wood, "has the effect of a love spell—an infatuation, if you like. The other, instant death. To mortal creatures, that is." She fingers one of the cedarwood arrows, then drops it back into the quiver. "Eros may be a love-god, but he is the son of Ares, too. Be careful. They need only pierce the skin to take effect."

She hands the quiver back to me. I hesitate.

"You said Eros was weakened," I say finally. "After the temple. What do you mean?"

The oracle looks at me like she's been waiting for me to ask, and my stomach sinks again. There's something she's preparing me for, something she wants me to do.

"His powers are much diminished, and in his weakened state, Aphrodite has imprisoned him. She has hidden him from the eyes of the other gods, and conscripted her other sons to guard him."

I listen, my heart quickening.

"To what end? When will she release him?"

The Pythia shakes her head.

"When she has bent him to her will. When he is broken."

Broken. I stare out over the mountains of Delphi, the dust-brown earth and the scrub of green; the blue of distant hills. Aphrodite and her two other sons, three against one. What does it mean, to break a god's will? I run my finger over one of the cedarwood arrows, its smooth feather-tail.

"But what can *I* do? I am a mortal. He is a god."

"And so you think yourself powerless?"

"Gods have all the power that matters." I am impatient now. "All they leave us with are prayers."

She cocks her head to the side at that, as though considering my words.

"Nevertheless," she says finally, "you must decide."

I stare at her placid, quiet face. I open my mouth, then close it again. This is madness.

"What are you asking of me? What aid would you have me offer?"

The Pythia nods.

"You must go to Mount Olympus. You must ascend its

slopes."

Olympus! Mortals don't go to that place. It simply doesn't happen.

"It will be difficult. Do not stray from the path. Do not become distracted. You must listen carefully to your instincts. There is a great river that divides its peak. You will find him on the other side."

"But…you said he has been hidden there. How am I to find him?"

She nods.

"Do not let your eyes grow dazzled. You must seek out the darkness, daughter of Sikyon. You will not find him in the light."

A knot grows in my stomach.

"What darkness?"

But her lips only tighten.

"You will know it when you see it," is all she says. "If you are watching."

I swallow hard. Maybe Herakles, or Theseus, or some other god-child could make it up to the top of Mount Olympus, but I have heard things about the mortals who dare to seek the gods' own realm, the ones brave or foolish enough to climb the slopes that were made to keep us out. There are stories of monsters, of spells darker than in any tales of the Great Poets. It is arrogance to think that we can journey at will through lands we were never fated to walk. And yet apparently I am to attempt it.

"And will he be returned to me?" I say. "If I do this? If I go?"

She blinks slowly.

"You have a chance."

"A chance," I repeat. "A good chance?"

Her gaze moves away: she does not like my demand for guarantees. She gives a tiny shrug.

"A chance," she says.

A chance.

My heart's beating fast. The quiver of arrows is still in my hand. I replace it, very gingerly, against my back. *Mortals don't play with the gods*, a voice inside reminds me.

Or if they do, they lose.

There is silence then, as if she believes we have reached the end of our time. And indeed, I see that two guards are walking this way, ready to escort me out. No one is allowed too much of the oracle's time. But I can't make myself rise. My legs won't do it.

"You said my path was with Eros," I say quickly. "That he would aid me, if I aided him. You mean that…that if I succeed in this, he will help me find my family?" My chest tightens. "I *will* see them again?"

She inclines her head. It seems a long time before she speaks.

"They are alive. But according to my sight, you will not see them again as a mortal."

Her voice is soft with understanding, and my throat swells. A grief I can't swallow. The blue hills blur. Her words are lodged in my chest.

I am not to see them again in this life.

I must wait out its end, when we are reunited in Hades' realm. I feel weightless, strangely numb.

I have always known that I must wait until the hereafter to meet my mother. But I had not thought to wait until then to see the rest of my family, too. I had thought to have their companionship through much more of this life.

I bow my head. The tears do not come. I feel them inside me, but they do not come.

"I will grieve them," I say quietly, and the oracle nods.

"Such are our lives, daughter of Sikyon."

I stand up, stumbling, as the guards draw in. Before they reach us, she glances my way again.

"You said now that mortals have only prayer, and no power." Her eyes find mine. "I counsel you to remember, prayer may be power too."

Her words tumble around me as the guard's hand closes around my arm.

Twenty-seven

My head is pounding so hard, I don't know how I make it back down the hill. A priest is there to guide me, but nothing is more than a blur.

Mount Olympus.

I am no hero. No god-child or great warrior. Herakles might very well ascend to the home of the gods, but me? I have no strength or skill to best whatever lies in those hills—whatever guardians have been placed there for the very purpose of keeping mortals like me out.

Fate, the oracle said. But what is it, in the end? Perhaps it means only the path I choose; perhaps the path I choose *becomes* my fate. Is that what Eros meant, before?

"Psyche…"

A soft voice pulls me away from the pounding thoughts inside my head. I blink, and see that Melite Georgiou is nearby. We are in a small, sandy enclave at the back of Delphi's hill, a sort of antechamber, it seems, for the pilgrims who have heard their answers. We are allowed to wait here, I suppose, before venturing back out into the clamor. I look around at the other faces, the expressions of those recovering from what they have learned. Some look merely dazed, one or two are grieving. But Melite's face looks peaceful, at least.

"She tells me Hector does well in Hades' realm." Her voice is low with emotion. "She says he made the journey with great courage for one so young, and that he was well received there. She says his uncle has claimed care of him in the Underworld." She takes a deep, unsteady breath. "I asked if he was sad there, if he missed me. She said that it's different, there. That there is no sadness, the way we know it here." Her eyes find mine. "I suppose that means he doesn't miss me. I suppose…I suppose I am glad of that."

I don't know what to say. I take her hand, briefly.

"And you?" she says.

I look toward the path out of here. Beyond is the milling crowd, and beyond them, the road. Beyond that, the mountains.

"I am to go to Mount Olympus," I say.

Her eyes widen.

"To Olympus? But…not to *climb* it?"

She might as well say it: it's a fool's errand, and likely as not you will die there.

Well, and if I *should* die there? I think of Hector, and the legions of our kind who have already left the mortal world behind. Hades' realm awaits us all eventually. It is only a matter of years.

"Mortals do not travel past the foothills," she says gently.

"Nevertheless," I say, "I must reach it." I don't explain to her that I go on this fool's errand because of a reckless wedding vow, or because I looked into a god's eyes and saw all my forevers there.

Or because the gods are mad.

Or because I carry love and death in a quiver on my back.

Melite studies me a moment more.

"In that case you may journey with us, if you choose. As far as the foothills, at least."

"Are you sure?" I say. I am not sure what the rest of her party will make of me.

She shrugs. "We travel to Thessaly, you are on the way. The roads north of here are more dangerous than those to the south."

Melite's offer is a good one and I would be foolish to turn it down. And yet I am not sure that she likes me very much, or desires more of my company on her journey. What can I be for her except a bad reminder?

"Why are you helping me?" I ask, and her eyes travel over me.

"Hector," she says at last. I understand all that she means by it.

Because Hector would have wanted it. Because Hector liked me. Tears seal my throat as I think of her son, her child. Truly, the gods can have no sense of what it is to be mortal, of the grief we endure. If they knew, they surely would spare us it.

"Thank you," I say, and bow my head low.

*

The sky is purple, the road ahead long and winding. Olive trees make black shapes against the sky. There are six of us in the party: me, Hector's parents, his sister Kypris—a girl of perhaps fifteen—and another couple, Melite's brother- and sister-in-law. They are from Sikyon too. They didn't know me at first, not with the cloak covering my hair and half of my face, but then Melite said my name and their eyes widened in unison. Still, they did not protest when she proposed my joining their group. It's lucky for me that they seem to be of the same view as Melite: that I am a victim of the king's, and that it was the king's conduct that brought about the downfall of our town. I feel treacherous, a snake in their midst. Their home—our home—is in ruins because Eros rescued me against the goddess's decree. They have paid the price I did not.

The daughter, though—Kypris—I see her face as we ride along, the way it twitches when her glance comes to rest on me. It's not hard to see that she hates me. Unlike the others, she doesn't believe I'm so innocent.

The Georgious have two wagons, one for Melite, her husband, and Kypris, and the other for the brother- and sister-in law. The men drive the wagons, and I trot alongside with Ajax. Melite addresses me from time to time as we ride, quiet comments about the state of the road or, as day turns to evening, the dying light and changing views. But mostly, we ride in silence, and I think that's for the best. She is thinking of what she has lost, perhaps, and so am I. Perhaps I should be thinking about what lies ahead of me, but instead, it's grief that's making itself known.

But according to the oracle, I won't see them this side of Hades' kingdom. At least there's a chance, I say to myself. The oracle was certain about some things, yet about this, she was not quite so certain.

I look sideways at Melite's face. For her there is no chance of seeing Hector in this life again.

As the sun starts to dwindle, the mountains come into sight, distant but clear. There is Olympus, the tallest in that great range, rising against her sisters like a god herself, her flat peak lost in the clouds. I never really thought I would see Olympus—let alone seek to climb it. This mountain is the stuff of legend, the stuff of dreams and nightmares.

We tie up the horses and stop to make camp for the night. Melite and I prepare the food. Hector's sister pushes by me to gather kindling.

"Careful, Kypris," Melite says, but the girl doesn't look back. I have no doubt that she knocked into me on purpose, nor do I blame her. I look off into the woods, and wonder if there are bandits or bears out there. I wonder what would be greeting me on these roads if I were here alone.

Or what will greet me on the mountain that awaits.

It strikes me that I could simply turn back—I could turn back right now if I wanted. But I know that I won't. I can't, while I remember that night; while I remember what I felt looking into his eyes. If Fate is anything, surely it is that: the strange thing that happened in my soul, subtle as the whisper of feathers. It was a *knowing*. That is all I can say.

"Dinner," Melite announces, and we gather in the firelight. The night is calm, the fire is warm, but we are a somber gathering.

Melite puts a bowl of stewed mutton in my lap, but across the fire I catch Kypris's eyes, and suddenly my appetite is gone.

I leave the stew at my feet until it turns cold.

"Time to turn in," Hector's father says, when the rest have had their fill. He glances up to the dark sky and bright moon, and I think of Artemis and her chariot, riding through the sky: goddess of night-time and of the hunt.

Which of the gods are loyal to Aphrodite, and which have their allegiance elsewhere? I pull the hood of my cloak a little tighter, and feel the cool stone of the medallion against my throat.

Soon pallets are rolled out in the wagons. There are none extra for me, so I bundle some spare fabric on the floor and make a pillow of my arms. I stare out at the stars and think that I will never sleep—except it seems I do, because suddenly I start awake in the darkness, with a stranger's hand over my mouth.

Twenty-eight

My brain kicks, my thoughts still foggy but full of terror.

Bandits, I think at first, but it is no bandit. It's Kypris, with a kitchen knife in her hand. Her eyes flash at me. I cannot say what she sees in mine, but it's not fear. I am not afraid of her. I am not even angry at her.

"I know who you are," she hisses. "You don't fool me. You are the reason my brother's dead."

Her teeth are sharp pearls in the moonlight. The knife trembles in her hand.

"You bewitched all the boys in Sikyon. First you bewitched them, and then you let them die. The goddess sent us a punishment meant for you. *You* were supposed to die, not us. Not Hector."

I feel a wave of sorrow inside me. Her fight is not with me. It's not I who am her enemy. It's the gods who wrong us all, but she is too young to see it.

Then again, maybe she will never see it. Maybe she will become a woman, and then an old woman, and live all her days in anger.

Her furious eyes are too focused on my face; she doesn't see my arm in the darkness, circling around to grip hers. When I clamp her around her skinny forearm, she lets out a small, muted cry of rage. She doesn't drop the knife. I don't need her to.

"I'm going now," I say. "You will never see me again." I keep a hand on her arm as I move toward the side of the wagon, bringing her with me; Ajax is tied up right nearby.

"I am armed, with a sharper knife than yours in my pocket. The quiver of arrows on my back belongs to a god. Don't seek to fight me, Kypris. Think me a killer if you wish, but you are not one."

Keep your innocence while you can, girl.

She stares at me, her breath shuddering, her knife-arm frozen. A paralysis of hate and doubt.

I walk away and don't look back. I untie Ajax, throw myself onto his back, and ride into the night.

*

Now that I am alone, the roads seem darker. The world is silent, just the slow clop of Ajax's hooves stepping rhythmically against the dirt, and the sound of small creatures rustling in the shrub. At least, I hope they're small. Under the moonlight, I can almost imagine we are ghosts, the two of us: the ghost horse and his ghost rider. I am still adjusting to my seat and my legs ache, my skin sore and chafed around my thighs. I ride with my cape pulled fast across my head, and our two forms throw long shadows over the road when the moon moves from behind a cloud. There are no other riders: night-time is not for journeying but for making camp and resting. I, however, will not stop till dawn. For one thing, Kypris may rouse her family and tell them what happened—or tell them a version of the truth that turns them against me. I think it's best I don't see the Georgious' wagon again. Besides that, I am a woman alone. I am safer on Ajax's back than asleep by the roadside. But as we walk on through the night, the road starts to blur before me, the moonlight pulsing strangely, like a throbbing in my mind. When my legs scream with pain and I'm too tired to stay upright any longer, I give in and edge Ajax off the path. I can tell by the faint streaks in the east, it's only an hour or so till dawn. I'll feel better when it's light.

"Only a few more hours ahead of us now," I tell Ajax softly. Hearing my own words aloud I feel a shiver down my spine. I don't know whether it's excitement or dread.

In the rough growth to the right of the path there are brambles, but Ajax makes his way carefully around them. We go about twenty paces from the road before I ease him to a stop and dismount. I tie him to a tree there, although it feels almost an insult to do so. But he lets me, and doesn't complain. I look into his eyes, put a hand against his nose. His honey-colored eyes gaze back at me. Steady, somber.

"Thank you, Ajax."

I pile some leaves under me, dismiss the pain screaming in my muscles, and wait for sleep.

*

There's a chuckle, and a crack of breaking twigs.

"Nice full saddlebags," a voice says. "Some coin in there, I shouldn't wonder."

"And the girl," says another voice. "Tasty enough, isn't she?"

The first voice is disinterested.

"Have her if you like, but let's get the rest first."

Dawn is breaking across the sky. My heart pounds in my chest. I feel for the dagger but it's not here; I must have left it in the saddlebag. My arrows, though, are with me, under my cloak, and my bow is on the ground. I reach for them quickly and jump to my feet.

"Don't touch me. And don't touch my horse. I'm armed, and more dangerous than you think."

The two men are to my left, just a few paces away, one with his hand on Ajax's bridle. There's a pause, and the thickset one chuckles.

"She's feisty, your girl."

"I'm warning you," I say, and notch an arrow from the quiver. Gods help me, I'll use it if I must. I've never taken a life before, but I suppose now I'll see if the oracle's words were true. I can't let them take the saddlebags. They carry all of value that

I have, including my mother's knife, and the little food I have to last me on this journey.

"These are cursed arrows," I say. "They will find their mark, and they will kill you. They are poisoned at the tip."

"Now, now, my lady." The scrawny one laughs, but nervously. "No need to get so excited."

But with a quick dart, his companion reaches for the bags strapped to Ajax's side. He means to use Ajax like a shield between us. But his reach was too sudden and violent, and Ajax is rearing up, whinnying ferociously, his front hooves kicking the air. As he brings them down, he sends the big man flying to the ground. I wheel and point my arrow toward the scrawny one.

"Go now! Run, and take your companion with you, or it will be the worse for you."

His eyes are wide. He nods wordlessly as his mouth opens and closes.

"Get up," he kicks the other one. "Get up and let's be gone!"

They scramble toward the road and I watch them go.

Ajax paws the earth, then with a great tug, tears his rope right off the tree: the branch breaks clean away and whips to the floor, dragging a pile of twigs with it as he moves toward me. I was right, then: he could have freed himself with one sharp tug whenever he liked. But now he nudges his great head down toward my shoulder.

"Thank you, Ajax," I whisper.

As we canter down the road, Delphi at our back, I stroke his mane.

"I have never been very good at making friends, Ajax. But I think perhaps I have found one in you."

Twenty-nine

Olympus.

From a distance, its summit sheathed in the clouds, this great mountain looked like another world. But now that we are drawing close and are almost at its base, the height of it seems more incalculable, more impossible, than ever.

I wonder, not for the first time, if I am perhaps too suggestible. The oracle told me this was my path, so I took it. And yet there is nothing stopping me from riding on, past this place—all the way to Thessaloniki or further, across the great wide curve of the Aegean, like the outcast I am.

That is a lie. There is something stopping me, and I know exactly what it is.

Perhaps Eros told me the truth, when he said gods were only demons by another name. Love is surely a curse, desire a peril. Because what pulls me toward Eros now, pulls me toward the place that any sensible mortal should avoid.

I draw Ajax to a slow halt, and we stand at the bottom of the mountain, looking up. It's a considerable ride from the nearest village, which is unsurprising. Mortals fear this mountain; no one will build their homes near the base of it. The gods' temperaments are volatile, and if they should descend from their home angry, you don't want to be the first village they meet. I wonder how long it will take me to reach its summit, *if* I reach its summit. I have few provisions with me, just a loaf of bread in my saddlebag taken from the inn.

I stare up at the thin dirt path that leads up from the base of the mountain. It is so unassuming, I almost wonder if I have got the directions wrong. But no: I'm sure this is the place.

I check the saddlebags once more, and the knife I now

wear strapped to my waist. Finally I check the quiver of arrows, making sure they're secure against my back.

Love and death.

A perfect pair.

Ajax's breath comes softly, its warmth stirring the air. Summer is toward its end, now, but it seems hotter than ever, as though it has found a new strength in its death-throes. Dawn has come and gone and it's mid-morning now, the air ripe with heady scents. A bee buzzes nearby.

Come on, Psyche.

I always wanted to prove the value of a mortal life, didn't I? Perhaps this is my chance. I glance up again at the narrow path, and the green slopes that tower like a wall before me.

Is it madness, to attempt what I'm about to do?

Certainly it is. But perhaps I am getting used to madness by now.

"Come on, Ajax," I say, but the horse's ear merely twitches.

"Come on," I say again, nudging with my heel, and this time he moves. I cannot say I blame him for his reluctance. I pull my cloak tighter around me despite the summer warmth, and I wonder in passing if Eros ever got used to this—to always being cloaked out in the world, always hiding himself from prying eyes.

The path is even steeper than it looked from below. My legs clench hard around the horse's broad back, and I hear Ajax's damp snorts of effort as he climbs the rough track. Tree roots snake in front of us, thick as my arm. There is a wet, heavy scent to the air—perfumed, almost. As we climb, the heat seems only to cling more thickly, as though the season itself grows more intense. Soon the last beads of dew on the grass are all gone, though it is hours still till noon. The animals are hiding from the heat, perhaps—aside from the intermittent buzz of a bee, there's hardly any sign of life, only the long grasses and the many wildflowers, and overhead, now and again, the glimpse of a soaring eagle. We make our way through the exposed sun. Though I see trees uphill, there are none along this portion of the path.

At the next pass I pull Ajax in and turn us around to see the view. It's already astonishing—cascading hills around us, and ahead the mist of faraway blue that I know is the Aegean sea. But I have only to look over my shoulder to see all of Mount Olympus that still towers before us.

"How long do you think until we can see to the summit, Ajax?" I murmur, because the trunk of the mountain is still cloaked in fog, and it's impossible to estimate how much road remains ahead. I wonder how many mortals have passed this way before me.

It is said that great heroes of legend were invited to the gods' acropolis at the top of Olympus. In the early days of man, it is said that our kings went there regularly. But later the invitations became fewer, and the mortals who journeyed there did so against the gods' will, and by strength and cunning instead: Ixion and Bellerophon, and the famed Herakles. Heroes and god-children, not regular folk.

Certainly no women.

I set my jaw, and turn Ajax back toward the uphill path.

Those are only the tales men tell, and men's tales are never the full truth of the world. Besides, I have the oracle's words to sustain me, and I carry a god's own arrows.

We climb on, and the sweat beading at my hairline breaks free now, rolling down my temples and the back of my neck; the sun beats down against my shoulders. Ajax, I know well, is no ordinary horse, and yet it is the first time I have heard his breath sound strained, or felt shivers travel the ropy muscles of his back. When we round a bend and find ourselves suddenly on a great plateau, I feel my body sag in relief. We have been on the ascent for hours now, five or six or more, perhaps, judging by the sun's position.

A meadow opens up before us, wildflowers in bright clumps dotted everywhere. I know some now by name, after my education with Aletheia in Eros's gardens. Celandine and yarrow, harebell and flowering sage. There are trees dotted around the plateau too, tall ones with many bare branches and piles of leaves beneath, as though the world up here is turning to autumn quicker than down below, in the valley. And as I watch, I spot movement in one of the trees. I hold my breath as I study the dark mass clustered there, moving slightly. Crows? Then a shape breaks loose from the cluster, black against the blue sky.

Vultures, I decide. It has the shape of a vulture, I think, and it circles and swoops as vultures do: some dead or near-dead creature in the grass must have caught its eye. But it is odd, to see a group huddled together in a tree like that. Vultures do not hunt in packs.

No matter. These are vultures of Olympus; the rules of the world I know no longer apply.

"Forward, Ajax. They will be no threat to us, and besides, they are far enough from our path. We will move quietly; they are occupied with their prey."

I nudge him, and reluctantly, he complies.

But as we ride through the meadow, another black shadow breaks free from the treetops, and then another. I pull my hood back, the better to search the sky. At first their circling seems lazy, speculative. But I cannot help but feel, then, that their circles are drawing closer. They fly higher, now, too high for me to see more than a blur, but they are almost directly overhead.

And then one of them drops, and banks, and drops again. There is an uncanny zeal in it, and I lean in to Ajax, urging him to go faster. I can't shake the feeling that the creature is carving a path directly for us, unnatural as that seems. But a few paces later Ajax shies and kicks, and I feel, more than hear, the clamor of wings above me.

Unwillingly, I look up. A great, grey wingspan stretches over us, wider than the greatest eagle, and a foul smell drifts in the air—the smell of carrion, of death. But the worst of all is that above the grey, withered-looking wings, there's a face that looks almost human.

Nausea roils my stomach. These are no birds.

These are harpies.

*

"Traveler!"

The stench of death drifts toward me again, roiling the fear in my belly. "You seek to pass this way?" Her voice is womanly, not the squawking or rasping I expected. I hesitate.

"I seek to continue my ascent."

"Then you must pay a toll," she says, and I hear the glee in her voice. Harpies are known for their greed, they are thieves at heart. And yet all the stories I've heard about them have done little to prepare me for the horror of being face to face with one, for how my mind stutters and my hands tremble. But her demand can be met, at least. I open one saddlebag, feeling around for some trinket that will please her. A silver cup I took from the table at home—less valuable than the ring, but shiny.

"I have little to offer," I say. "But take this."

I hold it above my head, and the harpy's eyes turn this way and that, like a bird's, inspecting.

"No!" Her voice is unpleasantly merry, as if from a secret joke. "*That* will not do."

Ajax whinnies and stamps, wanting to be gone; I feel the same.

I lick my dry lips and put the cup away. I do not wish to part with my father's ring to this fetid creature, but I will if I must.

"This, then." I hold it up. "It is gold. A family heirloom."

"You wish to trade in petty baubles?" She laughs, and now I hear the dry, scratching cackle. Her head turns upward toward the skies.

"Sisters! Come! We must collect."

The two other distant shapes begin to wheel and drop.

"I have offered you what I have!" I shout, but my voice is lost under the flurry and flapping of wings. "Take what I have or let me pass, there is nothing else I can give you!"

I cover my head with my arms as her companions descend, falling like stones from a great height. A shrieking laugh pierces the air, and one of them calls out behind me.

"Give us what you wear around your neck," she cackles. "*That*, mortal, is the treasure we seek."

Thirty

There's a rush of wings, a sudden blindness all around me. A foul, thick sound, chafing and rustling, like rats scurrying in the dark. I can't breathe.

I duck as low in the saddle as I can, and slide an arrow from the quiver—one of the cedar-woods. I struggle to notch it while their wings flap around me and my heart beats wildly. I feel a talon at my neck, scrabbling. The harpy will gladly hurt me, but that isn't her first goal: what she wants is the Shroud, to lift it from my neck and carry it off.

Does she know what it is? Can she tell?

"Move, Ajax," I whisper.

He pushes through the circle of beating wings and the harpies rise a few feet, cackling, then easily regroup. They have the advantage and they know it.

"Faster," I whisper to the horse, securing my arrow, steadying my grip. It will be better if I am a moving target: they will not trap us quite so easily, then. But shooting from a galloping horse will not enhance my aim.

"You think you can run from us?" One of them swoops down, and I feel the scrape of her talon against my skin, and feathers, oily and rough. Without looking, I know she's drawn blood—but she doesn't have the Shroud. The leather string stays fast around my neck. The harpy's claws are fierce, but made for tearing apart prey, not for delicate tasks like this.

Which is little comfort, I realize: she can always tear me apart first, then take the charm after.

Another of them makes ready to swoop, but before she does I show her the bow I'm pointing toward her.

"I carry the arrows of a god," I shout. "Do not test me!"

They only laugh. Two of them wheel and plunge toward

us.

I let the arrow fly.

It misses, and more cackling breaks out. Sweat runs down my back, and I feel the sting on my neck where the harpy's talon cut me. I pant, and with shaking hands manage to notch another arrow.

The harpies wheel, taunting me. I aim, but they are five times faster than me—I no sooner lock one in my sights than it's swerved away. I will just have to aim in their direction and hope for the best.

I release the second arrow, and watch as it arcs wide into the sky, landing harmlessly in the meadow. Sweat stings my eyes; my breathing is labored. I have few arrows, and I cannot afford to waste them. But it looks like I mightn't even get the chance to notch another.

"Take it, sister. Take the charm!" one of them coaxes, and the great grey wings cut through the air toward me, blocking out the light. I think fast.

I clasp the Shroud against my neck with my left hand, and with my right I whip another arrow from the quiver and grip it like a knife.

I feel her drop toward me—a gust of cold, foul air—and this time her talons close fast over the leather string. But I pull down with all my weight to stop her from flying off with it; her strength lifts me half-out of the saddle. Then I turn and plunge the arrow deep into the dark, oily feathers.

She shrieks, dropping me in an instant. I watch her retreat to a tree branch, huddling in on herself, hissing like a cat.

"There are more of those," I shout, "for the next one who comes for me."

I look down at my arm, where a trail of her blood is dotted. If she dies, will her companions retreat? Or will they come after me in vengeance?

The one who seems to be the leader wheels, circling until she is in front of us once more. Her wings open wide as she glides down to my level.

"Very well," she hisses. "Keep your charm, for now." Her wings beat once, hard, and she hovers above me.

"We shall take it later. We shall lift it from your corpse instead." She drops toward me once more. I have another arrow ready, clutched in my fist, but she doesn't come for the Shroud, nor within reach of my hand. At first I don't understand what's happening—all I hear is a ripping, tearing sound but the pain does not come. Then I realize: it's the cloak she's ripping from my back, shearing it as easily as if it were paper. And then I lurch as I feel wings by my leg, and realize she's snatched one of the saddlebags, too. But not the one with the gold, not the one I offered her before.

She's taken the one with the food.

In the grass lie the torn remains of my father's cape, shredded like some helpless creature. I feel naked without it. My *chiton* is light cotton, damp with sweat.

"Keep climbing, girl," she squawks flapping back toward the tree. "Keep climbing, and we will come for you tomorrow, when your body lies cold on the ground!"

Her words make me shiver, but I will not wait to hear more. If they come for me tomorrow, it's still better than today. I snap the reins hard, refusing to look at the tatters of my father's cloak again.

"Go, Ajax, as fast as you can," I breathe into his ear.

*

I'm shivering.

I'm trying not to fear the unknown, but it's hard not to wonder what else waits for me on these slopes. It's a thin line, is it not, between courage and foolhardiness?

And now my bread is gone, along with my waterskin. I will have to find food and water on the mountain, if I am to survive this place, and there is none of either on this stretch.

There are woods ahead though; maybe there will be a stream there, and some berries I can forage. I kick myself for keeping the bread in my saddle-bags; for not allowing myself even a crumb since starting out today. I should have eaten the damned stuff when I had the chance. *This is what comes of self-denial,* I think with gritted teeth. I was always taught that self-denial was among the greatest of virtues. Now I think it's just something people with more power made up, to keep people like me from complaining.

We're entering a forest, and I shiver again.

It seems to me the air has grown colder. I inhale it, smelling its crispness, dry and bright where only hours ago it was thick and humid. And the landscape around us is changing, too. The lush grass grows browner and the trees sparser, their canopies less dense. Leaves begin to litter the ground, first singly, and then in small, wind-tossed piles of yellow and orange.

It is not my imagination, then. On this accursed mountain, the seasons cycle through at some unnatural pace. And it starts to make sense, what the harpy said to me. In the height of summer, I could travel comfortably without any cloak. But I wonder how long I will last out here, as I ride higher into the mountains. The harpies' plan begins to sound quite efficient now. Easier not to kill me, and let this monstrous mountain do the work for them, leeching my life from me slowly.

I look upwards, to where the great body of the mountain still soars higher, its peak buried still in the fog. I cannot tell how much farther there is to go.

Well, I suppose there is only one answer.

I must go faster.

I must scale these cursed slopes before they have the time to kill me.

*

It's dark in the forest, all its foliage cloaked in colors of the waning year: rust and crimson red, browns and dying yellows. I try to ignore the hunger in my belly. When we round a bend and hear the babbling of a stream, I pull Ajax to a halt.

Lack of water is more dangerous than lack of food, and in the high summer heat, we have lost much.

The stream isn't hard to locate—we almost stumble across it at the next bend. I will have to drink my fill here, without a waterskin to refill. I stroke the horse's warm, shivering hide and nudge him toward the stream so he can drink first.

But Ajax doesn't seem interested.

"What's got into you?" I nudge him again with my foot, but he turns his great head away. I slide from his back—the ground is wet here, squelching beneath my sandals, and the mere sound of the stream makes my mouth water. I take Ajax by the bridle and give it a tug.

"Don't you understand? It may be days before we come to running water again."

I try to reason with him, but he tugs his great head back away from me. I sigh—I have no solution for this strange display of contrariness. Hopefully, there'll be more streams uphill, and a horse can go longer without water than I can.

I crouch down, trying to find a dry-ish part of the bank to bend and drink. But Ajax stamps his foot and whinnies loudly, making me turn.

"What has gotten into you?"

A thought comes to me, cold and sharp, as his golden eyes meet mine: *I should be listening better*. I turn back and stare down at the crystalline, flowing stream. There should be grass, shouldn't there, on the bank? The earth here is wet and mulchy, but nothing grows on it. I step a few feet away, and rip up some tiny yellow flowers and a handful of grass. Then I go back to the bank, and scatter them into the stream.

The water's fast, and carries them swiftly around the bend.

But not so fast that I can't see them curl up like a dead

thing, and shrivel to black.

*

I scramble back, my heart thumping. Ajax whinnies softly, treads the ground where he stands.

"Thank you, Ajax."

He snorts, and moves his face briefly against my palm. I look into his gold-colored eyes. I'm embarrassed to have doubted his instincts, which clearly are better than mine. My heart stays in my throat until the sound of the stream disappears behind us, and even then, the forest makes my skin crawl. I'm glad when we're free of it, back on another broad and sloping plain.

The world is brown and withered now. The rich reds and russets are gone, giving way to brown and grey. The sky is heavier than it ought to be at this hour, and I wonder if it will rain. I drop the reins for a while to rub some warmth back into my limbs, and wonder how much worse all this will get. I touch the Shroud around my neck once more: I find it hard to believe that it's working, when I've never felt so hunted in my life. Only belatedly did I think how I ought to have waited until the harpies had moved along to other victims; then I could have gone back and collected the two lost arrows from the wild grass where they fell.

I suppose the gods will hear word of me soon. The creatures of this place must whisper it, whenever they see a mortal on these slopes.

It begins to rain at last.

At first it is just a drizzle, then a steady patter, and soon a driving, pelting wall. I pull the hanks of wet hair from my face, barely seeing Ajax's mane before me, barely hearing the slush of his hooves through mud. I can't see far in front of us, and at this rate I'm afraid of losing our path. I push a rake of rainwater from my *chiton*, and move the reins to my left hand.

"Ajax, what do you see, boy? Any trees nearby?"

We're already soaked, but surely there's somewhere around here we can take shelter.

Then in a brief gap in the rain, as if through a grey window, I glimpse a copse of dark green trees. Despite the wintry season, their foliage is still thick and lush, a dense canopy of evergreen. .

"That will do!" I exult, and bury my hands in Ajax's mane, steering him off the path. It's not far—we'll be able to find our way back again as soon as the rain stops.

When we pull up under the trees, it's like stepping through a doorway into some protected place. Instantly the hammering of rain fades to a soft splashing outside its circle. The sheltering trees are tall, and their canopy so dense that barely a stray drop makes it down to us. I dismount, wipe my face, and coil my hair tight to wring out a gush of rainwater.

"Greetings, lady," a strange voice says.

Thirty-one

I whip around.

Greetings, the voice seems to echo, redoubling on itself. *Greetings, lady.* But there's no one here. I move slowly, keeping my back against Ajax's warm flank. The circle is empty. There's not a soul to be seen.

"Are you a wraith?" I say. "Show yourself!"

There is silence and then a beat before the whispers begin again.

She hears us.

Hears us.

"Lady, we mean no harm."

The voice is light, almost childlike.

No harm; no harm, the echoes come.

"Then why can I not see you?"

We, the voice said. Not *I.* There are many of them, then—whatever "they" are.

"You do see us," the voice protests. "We are here. Around you. Above you."

I stare. There's nothing here but this great ring of spruce trees. As I look at them more closely now, I see there is something different about them. Despite the wind and rain, their boughs do not sway and saw, and their leaves appear to be dry. Each trunk is lithe and long, unusually perfect. I thought when I entered that this circle seemed a protected place. But perhaps I did not understand the nature of that protection.

I clear my throat, my fist tight on Ajax's bridle. "Are you dryads?" I demand.

There's a faint hiss, almost like a sigh, that seems to drift from many places at once.

"We *were* dryads, lady," the voice comes. "Hunting

companions to the goddess Artemis. She had many, but we were her favorites. We were the nimblest, the fastest, and…" The voice becomes coy, then: "deemed by all, the prettiest."

A stray raindrop trickles from my scalp and down my forehead, blurring my vision. Dryads are much like nymphs, I tell myself. And certainly, the nymphs in Eros's gardens meant no harm. The childlike voice goes on:

"When a mortal poet stumbled across our party, he wrote great ballads in our honor. The goddess—*you* know of whom we speak, lady—became jealous. All because the mortal poet praised us so lavishly. All because he called some simple tree-nymphs the finest of goddesses."

The finest, the other voices chime, like whispers.

"And so she cursed us," the voice resumes, tinged with longing. "While other dryads may roam among their forests and transform at will, *we,* lady, know no freedom now. These trees are our cages. We must stay here forever."

Forever, the echoes ebb and flow. *Without end.*

I swallow, the hairs on my neck prickling, and not just from the damp and cold. These plaintive voices are so melancholy and strange—beautiful, in fact. But there is something cloying about them too, something that seems to fill the air too thickly, making my thoughts move slower than before.

"I am very sorry," I say. Indeed, it is a painful story.

"Yes, we have suffered at the hands of the goddess too, you see." The voice pauses, and I hear a note of excitement now, a shiver that seems to ride the gusts of wind from outside. "But now we can help each other, lady. We will help you, and you will help us."

I stick close to Ajax; his warmth soothes me. I feel his breaths through his flank.

"I have little to offer," I say. "I am just a mortal. I came here for a moment's shelter. All I want is to wait out the storm and continue on my path."

"But we will show you a quicker path," the voice says. "We can tell you how to reach the summit before nightfall."

Before nightfall. I shiver. I still see no end to this mountain. How many more hours, how many nights, must Ajax and I ride?

"You do not want to be here at nightfall," the voice says, as though it knows something I don't.

There's a quivering and fluttering around me. The trees are restless and unquiet now, almost nervous.

Nightfall! the eager echoes come. I hesitate.

"We were supposed to stay on the path. The oracle told me."

"It is a safe path, a protected one," the voice persists. "Known to the dryads but not to mortals. It will be our gift to you."

I stroke Ajax's mane. His head butts against me, soft and restless. He is not comfortable among these voices, this strange glade. I cannot blame him. And yet what they're offering…

"And what is it," I say, "that you seek in return?"

"Petition for us," the voice says. She pauses. "We know whom you seek, lady. We know the one you journey to reclaim."

The son, the son. The voices stir with excitement. *The goddess's son!*

"State our case to him," the leader says. "Ask for his help."

I look away, out past the safety of the leaves. Water cascades down the canopy outside. So it is not really my help they seek, but his. I am only to be a messenger.

"And what if he cannot help you?" I say. "Or will not?"

She pauses.

"Our bargain is for the attempt, lady. We ask only that you carry the message." There is something urgent about her voice, I think. She is trying to please me. I wonder why she should try so hard, when the bargain sounds like it's more to my advantage than the dryads'.

I rub Ajax's mane as he snorts and stamps. The sooner we move on from here, the better. The dryads are making him so agitated, I'm half-afraid he'll bolt without me. But I must consider the offer I've been made. It is a good one, after all, since the trust is all on their side. For all they know, I won't honor my bargain and Eros will never hear of their petition. But I would never cheat them like that.

I had always thought of immortality as an extraordinary gift, but only now does it strike me what a risk it can be, too—a curse is a curse forever, a miserable situation preserved for eternity.

"I thank you for your offer," I say at last. "If I manage to rejoin Aphrodite's son, I will offer your petition in good faith."

She accepts! faint voices chatter.

A rain droplet falls from my wet hair onto my neck, and trickles slowly down my spine. I push down the queasy feeling in my stomach.

"Then come into the heart of the glade," the voice says. "We will show you with our branches; we will point your way."

I tug on Ajax's reins and lead him, reluctant, to the circle's heart, where the biggest tree stands. This one, then, must be the leader, the mother tree.

"A few paces more, lady," it says.

I don't know what it is, but something about the voice…there is a sweetness there, something artificial, that disquiets me. I *want* to secure the bargain, but the hairs are standing up on my neck, my breathing has quickened. I don't move forward. A few paces in front of me is the trunk of the great mother-tree, its bark thickly ridged, with a great whorl that makes me think of a tremendous cyclops-eye.

I stand my ground, and open my mouth to say something—what, I don't know.

But then Ajax tosses his neck, gives a last whinny, and bolts—with my arm still caught in the reins. I stumble forward, crying out as my shoulder jolts with pain. In the second it takes to loose myself from the tangle of reins I topple to the ground, my shoulder protesting, my lungs heaving. The reins whip through the grass in Ajax's wake as he hurtles out of view, and my eyes prick with furious tears.

No food or water. No cloak. And now no horse.

How long will this cursed journey take on foot? How am I to survive it?

Then I feel a cool, rough grip across my legs. It tightens, and there's a rustling sound; another rough touch snakes across my back, drawing me in, binding me tighter. I gasp through the tangle of my disheveled hair.

The mother-tree, the leader of the dryads: she has roped me in against her trunk, bound me tight with her great tree-limbs. One heavy branch imprisons my shoulders, another my waist. Smaller ones shackle my ankles.

Ours now, the voices say. *She is ours.*

Thirty-two

I can't move. I'm immobilized, arms at my sides, feet locked.

"Why do you do this?" I force my heart to beat steadily, and my voice to stay calm. "I undertook to do you a favor, a fair exchange. Who will plead your case if you do not let me go?"

"You are more useful to us like this," the voice answers. Her tone has changed. It is not so plaintive or so cloying now.

"You are the one Aphrodite seeks. The troublemaker. If we are the ones to catch you, she will thank us."

Thank us! Free us!

My heart thunders in my chest.

"So I am to be your bounty?"

"You are to be our tribute," the voice answers.

My throat is dry; my mind races. There is one thing, only one, I can think of. My quiver of arrows is pinned against my back, and the great branch holding my shoulders keeps me from raising my arm. But my mother's knife is still strapped to my waist, and I think I have just enough movement to reach it.

Perhaps it's just fancy to think that a knife will do any harm to a dryad, but it's all I have. Even a small wound may cause a shock, enough to loosen her grip for just an instant, and an instant will be enough.

I don't have time to doubt myself.

"Do not kill me." I play for time. "You will arouse the wrath of my husband. You would not wish to be cursed by the gods a second time?"

But as I speak I use my one free arm to burrow down my side, snaking toward the sheath belted at my waist. I feel the hard, jeweled hilt under my palm. The branches tighten—do they feel my movement? Do they suspect?—and I think my arm will be locked, after all, at my side, and that I will die like this, like a fly in a web. But the thought makes me wrench harder. My shoulder cries out again in agony, but the knife is in my hand now. Without a second thought I raise it and bring it down hard, hoping to cause just a split-second of pain, enough for a moment's disruption.

But instead there is a terrible, unearthly shrieking. My blood runs cold, and I feel myself falling, suddenly untethered. I'm on the ground: the great tree has released its grip, its branches flinching from me as if scalded. The branch that pinned my shoulders lies severed on the ground. The tree's agonized call reverberates inside my head. The knife…it did this. It traveled through wood as if it were butter, as though it were nothing at all.

The voices echo and flurry, calls of horror, so frenzied I can hardly make them out. But there is one word I hear.

Adamantine!

I know what adamantine is, but it makes no sense. This little blade in my hand cannot be that.

But the dryads are in chaos, and the mother-tree still cringes from me, so I don't stop to think, I don't stop to wonder. I jam the blade back in its sheath, then dash as fast as I can through the circle of trees, back out into the rain, as far beyond the dryads' reach as I can get. I race in the direction Ajax went, and I run until my lungs sting before I remember that I must not travel through the open fields; that the path is the safest route, if not the shortest.

What was I thinking, to leave it at all? The oracle warned me not to stray from it. What need had I to avoid some mere rain? And then to trust the dryads' promises! Betrayal is second nature to the gods—and those I just encountered were barely even gods anymore. They were what a god may become, if it is locked up and starved of all that is natural to it.

The path is muddy and waterlogged when I get back to it,

but I tramp along it nonetheless, letting the wet dirt suck at my sandals. My shoulder throbs faintly; my hair smacks against my shoulders in wet hanks. After being astride a horse for so many days, walking feels like an unnatural motion, newly painful. But none of that is what I think about.

Adamantine.

I think back to the stories told at my father's knee: adamantine, the only substance that can sunder a god. But it cannot be. Surely the dryads were mistaken. What happened was simply the work of a very sharp blade—even a dryad's tree is only made of wood.

And yet the feel of it…it makes me shiver even now to remember it. It moved through wood as no blade should, as no blade *can*. It was easier than parting water.

I take the knife from its sheath again and stare at it. There is some wet smear on the blade—tree sap, I suppose, only this is sap from a dryad's tree. I turn the blade side to side, and it seems to me the sap has a purplish glow. *Ichor*. There is a touch of that in all immortal blood, according to the stories.

I bend and clean the knife against the wet grass, then return it to its sheath.

Adamantine.

If the dryads were right, then how came my mother by such a thing? How came a fisherman's daughter to possess such a dangerous treasure? By theft? As a gift?

I am told that Atlantis is an unusual place. It is an island more beautiful than most, more perfect and more lush—which is why they say it belonged to the gods once, before they tired of it and ceded it to mortal kings. It is rich with resources, gold and silver and precious gems, richer than other parts of the Hellenic lands, and so the mortal kings fight over it even today. Many strange things have washed ashore on its beaches, and gods roam there still, upon occasion.

I shake my head. Still nothing explains *this*.

My mother must have known the blade was special, I

decide. But perhaps she didn't know quite *how* special.

If only I could ask her.

But I know this much: if the knife is truly of adamantine, then it is the rarest, most dangerous kind of object there is.

My stomach turns at the thought. I do not feel powerful carrying such a thing. Perhaps I should, but instead it feels as though I have placed a target on my back. If word gets out, which it will, then surely I will become the greatest enemy, not just of Aphrodite, but of all the gods—for the thing I carry can do what not even a god can do to another god.

It can end immortal life.

I swallow the cold feeling in my throat. Part of me would like to get rid of the blade, but that would be foolish now. It will not stem the dryads' rumors, and it is the best defense I have. Perhaps I will have the chance to make a trade with it. I can buy our freedom, perhaps—mine, and Eros's.

A small voice laughs within me. *You are a dreamer, Psyche,* it says.

I wipe the rain from my face—it is lessening now, but the air grows colder. The mud path gives way to stones and crags, and here and there the rocks are sharp enough that they threaten to poke right through my leather soles. My thighs feel weak, the muscles strained with overuse, and the impact of each step seems to judder through my bones. The air is frigid now, the coldest I have known. When I exhale I can see my breath before me. I pull the *chiton* tighter around myself and remember the harpies' threat, to come for me when my body lay cold on the ground.

I lean into the uphill path.

I miss Ajax. Not just the speed with which I traveled on his back and his steady footing. I miss his presence. I didn't listen. I chose wrongly. And now he is gone.

The sound comes distantly on the wind: a chorus I remember from Sikyon, one that would make the farmers look nervously at each other, and ensure all the hen houses were secure.

Wolves.

I cannot tell how far away they are, but they are ahead of me at least. The wind is in my favor, carrying their howls back to me, instead of my scent toward them.

The rain starts to fall again, but strangely. It's softer, colder, feathery. I put a hand out, watching it land against my skin, slow and milky. I have heard of this. Father said that in the northern lands it happens sometimes. The water in the sky is so cold it changes shape and texture, forming this odd, feathery rain they call snow. I push on as it grows thicker, muting the world around me.

Then I round the next bend, and let out a gasp. This white rain, this snow, has coated everything. It lies thick on the ground and edges every tree-branch with white. The sky is white, the earth is white. How is anything supposed to survive in such a place? How am *I* supposed to survive?

My wet clothes are beginning to freeze, and the chill is making me shake enough that the quiver of arrows strapped to my back rattles. Only three of the cedarwoods are left now. If only I had been able to collect those left behind in the harpies' field.

I walk on, the wind at my back, the world like crystal. There is fog, now, as well as the snow. I seem to trudge through it for a very long time. And then I stop, hearing a noise at my back. It's almost muffled by this snow-covered world—but not quite.

I turn, and see him. A young wolf, perhaps born just this year. But large enough already to kill me, quick enough to corner me with one spring. He bares his teeth at me, his hackles all risen. A deep growl curls from the back of his throat.

Danger. The word comes into my head as if someone else has placed it there: as though it's not my thought, but the wolf's. And though it's surely just a fancy, it makes me remember something useful. He may be just as scared as I am, and may attack, not for food, but because he sees me as a threat.

I drop my eyes a little, bending my body lower so as not to look like I'm challenging him.

Pass, I think, and step away from the path. I push the word at him, an invitation, not a command, pushing it toward the place the word *danger* seemed to spring from. Maybe if I think it hard enough, my whole body will show it; somehow I will make the creature understand.

And perhaps somehow he does, or perhaps it is the fact that another great chorus of howls drifts now from some distant place. The young wolf snaps his gaze to the hills beyond me. He darts one last, brief look my way before darting forward and disappearing into the shadows and the thick snow. Only then does it strike me that I could have used the knife. I could have thrown it as he ran, and had a pelt tonight, to keep me from freezing.

But it's too late now, and besides...the wolf may not have heard the promise I made him in my head, but to me it was a contract. *I will not hurt you if you will not hurt me.*

If only I could make such a contract with the winter air. My breath's coming fast, and each intake chills my throat, a cold burst that flares in my lungs. The light is not yet gone, but the sun is below the horizon, and the moon is out. I wonder if I will survive the night out here.

Is it better to keep walking, or try to find a place to bed down? But if I bend down in the snow, it is surely a guarantee of never waking. And every step is a step closer to my goal.

To reaching him.

Will he be glad to see me? Will he berate me for how I left him, for the fall of his temple? Memories flash through my mind of my first days in his palace. His haughtiness, his amusement. As though because I was mortal, and a woman, my emotions must be flimsy things. At least, that is how it seemed to me then. But there were assumptions I made, too, about his intentions and his character. I did not understand how much he had risked, all to offer me the one contract that would stand between me and death.

And what now? Even if I reach him; even if I free him? Eros belongs in the Olympian halls, where I could never be welcome.

I shake my head. *One foot in front of the other.*

The snowy landscape grows bluer, the fog thickens. The sound of my feet on the icy ground is like crystals breaking. Ahead I can see where the path narrows and dips into the earth, a gully of sorts, though any water that once flowed at its base is dry now. Rocky walls rise up on either side, banks of sheer stone with trees at the top.

I cannot see how far it goes on like this, before the path returns aboveground. I will be sheltered from the wind, which is an advantage, but I don't like the idea of being down there for very long, unable to run except along a straight line, and exposed to anything that might be prowling above.

I walk on, and hear my footsteps grow louder as the walls of the gully rise on either side of me. The snow on the bottom muffles my step a little, but not fully. It's a fraction warmer down here at least. Above me, the trees climb higher, almost meeting in the middle over the ravine, black shapes against the foggy sky. It will get dark much sooner down here, I realize. Perhaps if I don't see light after this next bend I should turn back.

I put my hand to the steep wall, feeling my way. The stone is cold and hard. That's what's making me shiver, I suppose, and causing this sudden prickling feeling.

When I round the bend, instead of more light, there's less. The world is almost black. But there, in the darkness—I stop in my tracks. Pinpricks of light, forty or fifty of them, hovering there like tiny, greenish stars.

Until a pair of them blinks.

Thirty-three

A howl rises out of the ravine. Shadows, black shapes charging through this dim underworld, all in my direction. It's not like with the young wolf: I know exactly what these wolves see in me, what they smell on me.

Prey.

I turn and run, but I know each step is only closing the gap between us. One step of mine is five of theirs. I have moments, only a matter of moments, and I can't escape them like this. I need to get out of here—up these walls, and over the top. But the walls are sheer, hard stone. Nothing to give me purchase…

Then a wild idea crosses my mind. Will it work? It's all I've got.

I pull my mother's knife from its sheath, and then, panting, I ram it into the stone wall, knee-height. It buries itself deep in the ice and rock, right up to the hilt. Despite myself I shiver at the feeling. Stone might as well be soft flesh to this blade.

Another howl. They're closing in. I can smell them now, the wolf-pack. My balance will have to be perfect for this. I take a few steps back, then run toward the knife, and leap—and as I hoped it would, my foot lands on the hilt like a step in mid-air. No ordinary knife would take my weight like this, but this is no ordinary knife. And with this foothold, I can reach the extra height I need—up to the gulley's rim. I grab on with both hands before I can tip over from my teetering position on the blade's flat edge. My hands bury themselves in the loamy earth at the top of the gulley walls. There are thick roots tangled in the earth, giving me something to grip onto.

The eager howls close in on me as I claw one hand further up over the edge, then haul one leg up. I just manage to clear it over the gulley wall: I'm hanging half-in, half-out, as the wolves' jaws snap below me and their eyes flash in the moonlight. I can smell the blood-and-iron tang of their hunger, and it seems to me I can *feel* them, the bristle of their fur, their biting anger at finding me just out of reach. One springs at me, then another, missing me by a few hands-worth. I pull harder, scrabbling in the tangle of rope-like roots, pulling myself bit by bit toward the cold, biting air that says freedom. And at last I roll over the top of the gully, my breath heaving. A baying howl comes from below me.

*

I don't wait any longer than it takes for me to get my breath back. The wolves are clever enough to trail me to the beginning of the gulley and around the top if they want to. So once I can manage the shaking enough to make use of my arms, I pull myself up into the branches of one of the tall trees lining the gulley's edge, and start to climb. I climb higher and higher, until at last I come to rest in a broad fork, high above the ground. I snap off the smaller twigs, gathering what vegetation I can to pack in around me. It's a sort of nest, I suppose—a prickly, unpleasant one, but it may help trap a little warmth. If it is enough to keep me from freezing in the night, I shall be grateful.

Once I have unraveled some of my *chiton* and knotted it around the branch to keep myself from falling out of it in my sleep, I stare up at the moon for a long time. I think of Eros, and the certainty that has driven me this far, a certainty that sometimes feels like the madness he said would befall me. Where did it come from, this conviction in my blood, this feeling that my fate would be twined with his for the rest of my days? From one look into his eyes? From some words an oracle said? How can such a thing be real—or trustworthy?

If I succeed, if I free him, I will have atoned for what I broke when I broke my vow. But more than that, neither he nor

I can hope for. No union between a mortal and a god may last—they serve only as cautionary tales for other mortals through the ages. And yet…there is some conviction that comes, not from the mind, nor from the eyes or hands or any other sense, but from somewhere deep in the bones.

I will find you, I think. I will find you, because I must.

I will continue our story.

And then I suppose I must fall asleep, because I am trapped in my strange eyrie no longer: instead, I am back in Eros's palace, in the weaving-room, and I am not alone. Three women stand at the loom before me, and they turn to me, surprised, as though I have interrupted them in the middle of their work. I know from the moment I see them that they are gods. It is like when I looked on Eros's face, except the only feeling that surges in me now is awe, an instinct to drop to one knee and bend my head low. But I resist the urge, and stand my ground.

"Greetings, Moiraie," I say. "I know who you are."

For I recognized the Fates at once. One is a maiden, younger than me. One is an old woman, grey-haired and stooped. One is middle-aged. The youngest holds a ball of woven silk, and the old woman...I see the glint of silver shears, held lightly in one hand.

"And we know you, Psycheandra." The middle one speaks. Her voice is neither warm nor cool, neither kind nor unkind. "We have met before."

Met before? I do not know how to contradict a goddess.

"On the day you were born," she adds. "You would not remember."

A chill goes through me. What is she saying? What can such a thing mean?

"It is true then. I am cursed."

Her eyes travel over me.

"Perhaps, perhaps not," she says. "You don't understand the Fates, mortal. Our loom is not like yours. Yours only goes one way, where our fabric is woven in many directions at once: backwards, and forwards. Warp and weft go hand in hand. Nothing is finished until it's finished."

"And how will this story finish?" I say. I had thought this was a dream; I do not think it now.

None of them speak, but the eldest one, the one with the shears, turns toward me then. Her eyes are more ancient than the earth. She raises her hand with the shears in them, and I realize that she means to throw them.

Time slows down as the blades flash, the shears turning over and over in the air, sweeping in a great arc toward me. Does she mean for me to catch them? Or does she mean for them to cut me open? But the image dissolves, swirling like a vision in choppy water. And then I open my eyes, and a gasp of cold air fills my throat.

It's morning.

And I am still alive.

*

Once I am sure that the wolves are nowhere in sight, the first thing I do is return to the gully to collect my knife. I clean it and sheathe it again at my waist. The morning air smells like ice, and the cold covers me like a second skin—and yet, its chill does not seem to hurt as badly as before. My strange night's sleep seems to have healed me a little. Even my shoulder, wrenched so badly when Ajax ran away, seems to have regained full movement.

The gulley isn't so threatening now, in the morning light. Sunlight filters down through the trees, less dazzling than up above where it bounces off the snow and blinds the eyes. Still, I am glad when I can see its end, the glimpse of sunlight ahead. The path starts to slope uphill to high ground again. I hear something—a river?

But once I step out of the gulley, I have to grasp at a tree for support. The fog is all gone now, and I can see what's ahead of me. A river indeed, and beyond that, on the other side…

Blazing marble; spires taller than my eye can register. It's like looking at infinity, too dazzling to contemplate. Pillars of crystal catch the light, splintering it into prisms everywhere.

The city of the gods.

I close my eyes, then try again to take it in. Great staircases that wind and weave, seeming to float impossibly in the air. A great dome at the heart of it, and twelve great spires that seem to pierce the sky, the clouds clustering around them. Staircases that link the spires like a coronet among the clouds. And the whole thing drenched in light, as if in this place the sun shines from every corner of the sky at once.

I blink again, and realize something else. There, across the river, it is spring. The banks are thick with hyacinths and violets; trees creep into blossom with pink-and-white blushes; anemones sprout at their feet. I can almost see the warmth in the air, the pale golden glow of it.

A great river divides its peak, the oracle said. *You will find him on the other side.*

Am I supposed to make my way through this great acropolis of the gods? They will hardly welcome me there, and a tremendous glass wall flanks the base of it.

I remind myself to think one step at a time. I have made it this far—the fog I have been traveling through was surely the fog I saw before at the mountain's peak. Ajax must be a magical creature indeed, if we were able to scale so far in such a time. I imagine the horse beside me still, huffing gently and stamping the ground. I suppose he knows this place. Perhaps Eros has taken him here many times.

I look back at the dark river, where on this side the snow is still banked high, right up to the water's edge, and the river itself is a corridor of broken ice, huge tables of it bobbing on the black, frigid depths. The bridge looks to be of a scanty sort, just rope and planks, swaying slightly in the breeze. I must hope that the ropes are tight and not too threadbare, and that the whole construction is enough to hold me.

I step up to the river's edge and look down. Where it's not covered by great sheets of drifting ice, the water is black. No sign of life—no waterfowl, no fish, not even moss. I suppose it's too cold for anything to live in it. In the gaps between the ice, the surface is as steady and calm as a black mirror.

An ice-wind blows off the river and another shiver wracks me, but I take a couple of long breaths, forcing my limbs to be steady. I imagine the feeling of heat; of a strong fire crackling in the hearth of my father's house, and turn again to the bridge. The river's not so very wide, really. The bridge is perhaps thirty paces, maybe less.

I take another step and set one foot on the bridge. The movement sets the rope swaying. I'll need to keep both hands tight on the ropes if I'm not to fall into these icy waters. I take a deep breath, and then step on with my other foot. The bridge sways gently, almost rhythmically, and I take another step, and then another. It feels stable enough after all, moving predictably with each small shift of weight. Soon I'm five paces in, and then eight, and then twelve. A harsh, icy wind blows my hair into my eyes and I blink, shaking it free. No matter: I'm halfway to the other side.

And then I take another step, and the water explodes around me.

Thirty-four

It happens so fast, all I understand at first is the roar of breaking ice and thrashing water. And the shadow—the great shadow that suddenly towers over me. Something has reared up out of the water, weaving side to side, scaled and silver, and I'm trapped as the water sluices wildly over the bridge. While the bridge rocks like this I can't run, only clutch fast to the ropes while my heart explodes in my chest.

A great water-serpent, white-bellied, silver-scaled, towers over me, its three heads weaving together in a horrible, mesmeric dance. What a fool I was, to think I was about to reach my journey's end! To think that the banks of anemones and sunshine were actually within reach!

The beast's scaly lengths twist and turn like some monstrous vine. Its three heads are searching as it weaves about—searching for me, I know, and yet not seeing me. And I think I know why. There is something blind in the way these heads move. Although there is one great eye in each grotesque head, they are large and pale and empty. This creature is used to the murky depths, I conjecture: not the bright daylight where sun bounces off dazzling snow. No doubt its vision at night or even at dusk would far exceed mine, and I'd be ripped to shreds already. But here, at high noon, I have at least this one advantage. I keep my body down, ducked close to the slats of the bridge as it sways beneath me.

My body is weak. I have not eaten, nor hardly slept; my arrows are all but gone. As for my dagger, its blade is only the size of my hand: even if I were to somehow sink it into the hide of this creature, the beast is enormous. Adamantine or no, the dagger would barely dig into the outer layer of blubber.

I force myself to think clearly. I watch the monster's blind, weaving dance as it hunts. If it doesn't rely on sight, then it must rely on smell or sound, or both. Right now in the frigid air, with the wind died down, I doubt it can find me by smell.

Which means it will seek me out through sound. One more footstep, and it will know where I am.

I cannot risk a mad dash across the rest of the bridge. The rope swings too wide for me to move fast enough, especially here at the center, where its arc is widest.

I'll have to slow it down before I can make my escape.

I feel in the quiver for the poisoned arrows. There are three left. Hopefully it is enough. Will they kill the beast, or merely injure it? Is a monster like this even mortal? But the poison stopped the harpies, I reason: even if it could not kill them, it must be powerful enough to have a strong effect.

First things first. I slip my right foot out of its sandal, as carefully as I can so as not to lose purchase against the bridge's wet planks. Then I lunge, and fling the sandal over the side of the bridge. It hits the water with a smash and the creature rears, listening intently. *I was right.* Faster than I knew such a gigantic beast could move, it dives.

But it must know it has been tricked. The three heads search underwater only a few moments before they resurface, searching, sniffing. And now my arrow is notched and ready.

Wait for the moment. I think of my father, standing beside me in the woods as he trained Dimitra and me. I always released too early, he said.

Wait for the moment.

Each eye is large and clouded, almost white. In that moment of stillness, I release the bowstring, and the arrow flies true, landing straight into the eye of the creature's third head.

It lets out a howl of pain, and thrashes as though it can shake the arrow free. Within moments, it seems, the head hangs limp. But the other two heads hiss and rage, still: if anything, they hiss and rage worse than before. I had hoped one arrow would be enough for the beast, but now I see its three heads must live three separate lives. If I am to take out all of them, it must be one by one. Two more arrows, two more heads: I cannot afford to miss.

One head rears and then another. I glimpse a forked tongue, fangs. The fear inside me is so bright it doesn't feel like fear, but courage.

I notch another arrow, breathe deeply once more.

Now, Psyche.

I let fly, this time toward the left head. I can feel the arrow's trajectory even as it spins through the air, and the monster howls in rage as the arrow lands, exactly where I wanted it to. It lets out an unearthly wail, and my blood chills. I suppose this creature is only as violent as the gods that created it—does it deserve this fate? Perhaps not, but there is nothing to be done. I must cross this bridge, I *will* cross this bridge. And for that, it seems, the serpent must die.

It's bent over the water now, as though trying to find its own reflection in the black depths, seeking to understand what has happened to it. I notch the last arrow to the bow and breathe deep. From the recesses of memory, my father's voice comes to me:

Steady does it. That's right.

And then Dimitra's voice:

Don't be a sissy. Just take the shot.

I focus. I breathe. I will the arrow beneath my fingers to fly true. I release.

And the arrow just grazes the side of the beast's head.

Cold shock runs through my body. *It can't be.* My first two shots were perfect. How could this have happened? My last arrow…

I fumble in the quiver, hoping I've miscounted. *One more arrow, let there be one more.* But the only arrows that remain are the birchwood ones, the love arrows, useless as dust.

Unless…

I freeze, as the thought takes shape in my head. The idea is outrageous. Dreadful. Yet perhaps it can work.

But even as I quietly slide one of the arrows out of the quiver, the beast has reared its head again. Its rage seems redoubled, its one remaining head slashing madly through the air. My plan cannot work like this. I must direct its gaze back toward the water, toward its own reflection.

I loose the slipper from my other foot: I'm barefoot on the wet bridge now, and the sodden planks slide too easily underneath me. But I grip the rope, and hurl the slipper wide.

As it hits the river's surface, the creature cocks its remaining head, shifting it slowly in the direction of the sound. I see its single eye searching, its hesitation.

Look, I urge it in my mind. *Look down.*

And it does. I let the arrow fly—and this time, it flies true, burying itself easily in the flesh above the creature's one remaining eye. The monster starts, jolts, but does not look up. Its gaze stays locked on the water's surface exactly where it was before. The great eye stares back at itself, unblinking.

Mesmerized.

I wait, barely daring to breathe. A moment passes, then another. I shiver on the bridge. A wind sweeps through and the bridge rocks again, but though the slight creak of it makes me wince, the monster doesn't so much as glance my way. As I watch, it bends even further over the water, as though to study itself more fully; it turns its head one way and then another. And then it lets out a call that makes me shudder from head to toe. I have heard its cries of hunger and rage, and even pain. This was none of those: it was some kind of mating call. I swallow down the bile in my throat.

I could hurl a rock into the river, I suspect, and it would not turn my way. It strikes me that after all, perhaps the poisoned arrows are the less evil of the two. Love—at least, this kind of love; this mad, senseless infatuation—might be the greater curse.

I turn, gripping the rope, to look toward the far shore. A mere fifteen paces away. The icy air flays my back, my *chiton* frozen solid in parts. And yet so close in front of me is this vision of spring, bright and green and strewn with flowers. I have to close my eyes for a moment to gather myself. I tell myself not to look back—the doomed beast, the frozen river, the desolate lands behind me, I must will them from my mind now. I must move forward.

Breathe, Psyche.

I take a step, and then another. And then two more. Soon I am ten paces from the far bank. Then five. Then only one step remains.

The grassy verge is hyacinth-strewn and perfumed. Just one step more will do it. And yet my feet freeze where they are. I don't know if I could bear it, if it should all turn out to be a mirage—and why shouldn't it be one? Since I began this journey, betrayal has never been more than a breath away. Why should this moment be different? Perhaps the moment my foot touches the ground, the hyacinths will shrivel to ash, the ground will turn barren and hopeless. And I don't know if I could survive that.

But I've come this far. I breathe in, breathe out. I open my eyes.

And my foot touches the ground.

Thirty-five

Sunlight washes over me.

The hyacinths move softly in the breeze, and a great warmth goes over and through me, like fingers through my hair. I fall to the ground, and the ghost of what seems a hundred winters leaves my body. I allow myself one glance behind me, but when I do, it's like looking through a window to another world. The black and grey shapes of the river, the bridge, the monster—all of it seems fuzzy and unclear. I wrap my hands around the Shroud and for the first time since I began this journey, I really believe I may reach its end. Around me the air is scented, rich as wine. I lie collapsed on the grass, feeling the breath warm my lungs, listening to the cottony sound of petals moving together in the warm breeze. When I feel able to move again, I grab onto a handful of the long grass and pull myself to my feet.

Above me is the great citadel, the realm of the gods. I suppose I should be afraid, but the city itself is like a spell, too dazzling in its beauty to look away. I'm ready to start walking again—and then a cold breeze stops me. The air here is so mild that the chill seems out of place, like it belongs across the river, on the winter side. But the wind isn't coming from the river. It's coming from a dark, round opening under the hill. An opening just high enough for a person to pass through.

A cave.

The gaping black mouth looks wrong against the bright greenery and riot of blossoms, a void where life should be.

But then I remember something.

Do not let your eyes grow dazzled.

The Pythia's words come back to me, ringing like a warning in my ears.

You must seek out the darkness, daughter of Sikyon. You will not find him in the light.

Could this be what she meant?

I take a deep breath, and draw closer to the mouth of the cave. Cold air rushes toward me as though seeking me out. But there is no sign of life at all, only the small damp rivulets that coat the walls, slick with moss and dark-rooted plants. Beyond the first few paces, the cave grows dark.

I don't much like the look of it, and yet instinct nudges at me. What if this *is* what the Pythia meant? The city above is as dazzling as a lure, drawing the eyes and the mind like moths to a flame. But I was told I would not find him in the light.

I feel for the dagger at my waist. I may be all out of poisoned arrows, but at least I am armed. Once I'm holding it in my hand I notice it seems to be emitting a faint glow. I step closer to the mouth of the cave, into the deeper dim. Sure enough, the blade glows brighter. There are some minerals, I have heard, that glow in the darkness. Is that all this is? Or is it the sign of some other, unnatural thing?

I shiver, and look down. And there, drifting in a puddle of water at the base of the tunnel, I see it: a black feather, brilliant as a raven's, large as a crane's.

And I know whose feather it is.

I take a breath, and step deeper into the tunnel.

*

I walk for what seems a long time. Every time I turn and look behind me, the mouth of the cave is still visible, close enough that it seems I could return to it in only a few paces. But I know I have been walking for much longer than that. And the further I go, the more my other senses, too, feel distorted. The blue-white light glows around me, creating shadows and phantom shapes that make me jump and gasp, yet turn out to be nothing. This endless dark does strange things to my mind.

Memories surface, recent ones and old. I see scenes from my childhood again. I walk through the rooms of our old home as if in a dream. And then other things come to me, the horrors of the last days. I see Hector's sister Kypris, her teeth bared, a knife glinting in her hand. I see the ruined streets of Sikyon. I see the eyes of a hundred wolves.

And then I take a step, and feel my balance give as my foot finds only empty air. I cry out as I tumble through the darkness…then land with a damp thud onto a watery, unpleasant cushion. It's moss, and at least it broke my fall. I blink a few times, feeling the pain flow through my body—that was no little distance I fell. Then I sit up to find myself in a tremendous cavern.

It's dimly lit by a faint reddish glow, and the great walls of rock are three times the height of a man. The cavern itself must stretch a great distance, for I cannot see its end. But not fifty paces from me sits a great stone chair, with a figure in it.

Eros.

It must be. Breathless, I sheathe my dagger, and drag myself from the moss.

"Brother?"

My breath hitches in my throat at the sound of his voice. It's him. It's really him, at last. But he can't see me—they have blindfolded him, and bound him to the stone chair with shackles of some dark metal. It is those shackles that give off this dull red glow that lights the cave.

I step closer. Simply to see him is a shock all over again. The face that has swum up in visions as I slept; that I have seen only once before, but which has burned in my mind since. Here is that face again, and it is a thousand times brighter, a thousand times more beautiful, than any picture I can carry inside my head. The hair that curls like polished wood, his golden skin; the flush in his cheeks and the hollows beneath that sharpen them. He is carved more finely than the finest statue, but there is a warmth that breathes in every inch of him that no statue could ever achieve. To see him defies everything I think I know of beauty.

I take another step closer.

"Speak! Who are you?"

My heart thunders. I swallow hard, and reach out a hand. When I touch his arm a shiver tears through me, hot and bright. He starts, yet still I cannot bring myself to say his name: I did so once before, and when the word passed my lips, the sky fell.

"It is Psyche," I say. "I am here. I have come for you."

Thirty-six

"Psyche?" His voice dies in his throat.

Gently I reach for the blindfold and pull it free. His eyes blink open, and every thought disappears from my mind. I have experienced it before, and still I was not prepared for it: this vertigo, this feeling of plummeting through time itself. I'm at the center of all things: the past and the future and all the paths between them open to me like a flower. Light runs in my veins.

"Psyche," he says.

My name has never sounded so beautiful.

For a moment we stare at each other.

"You are well. You are safe. But..." His voice is full of wonder. "How is it that you look upon me, and are not mad?"

A question I, too, have asked.

"Perhaps your face is not the curse you think it is—perhaps it never was." It seems like something Aphrodite would lie about: a jealous mother trying to keep her son close, preventing him from consorting with the mortal world.

He shakes his head.

"But...but how came you to be here? You could not possibly—"

He sits up straighter.

"Unless you are not Psyche all, and just some trickery of my brother's."

"But—of course I am Psyche." He thinks I'm an illusion of some kind; a trick? I think fast, and pull the Shroud from beneath my robe. "You alone know I wear this. If I were just an illusion crafted to deceive you, whoever crafted it could not have known of this."

He breathes more easily, but as he stares at me the wonder

in his eyes only grows.

"But…how came you to be here? I know this mountain, and it is not hospitable to humans."

His understatement almost makes me laugh.

"I went to Delphi," I say. "The oracle told me what had befallen you, and I came to find you—though I admit, I came close to not succeeding."

His eyes—those glorious eyes—continue to study me. And then the look on his face gives way to pain.

"She should never have advised you to come here. You have done more than I dreamed a mortal could do. And yet…you cannot free me from here, Psyche. You must leave now, while you still can."

"*Leave* here? After all this?" To turn around and go back, now! Surely *he* is the one who is mad.

He just shakes his head.

"I cannot get you out of this place. But there must be some exit you can take, and you must seek it, quickly, before…"

"I'm not leaving without you!"

He bangs his fists on the stone chair; the chains rattle.

"Psyche, do you see these shackles? Who do you think made them?" He glares. "Hephaestus is blacksmith of the gods, Psyche! No one can free me from them, still less a mortal! And one or other of my brothers will be coming soon, to check on me: I cannot risk them finding you here."

I kneel before his chair, and draw the dagger from its sheath. Perhaps there *is* such a thing as Fate. For how else would such a knife lie at my belt?

"There is something in my possession," I say, "which may cut even the steel of Hephaestus."

Eros just stares at me. His face twists when he looks at the dagger, as though the sight of it causes him some pain.

"It is cursed—my ears ring with the sound of it."

I hear nothing, but he winces as though some high whine has pierced the air.

"I will be sure," I say, "not to let it harm you."

But he simply stares.

"Psyche, what *is* it?"

"If it is what I think it is…" I force myself to meet his eyes. "Then, adamantine."

His lips draw back, his face turns pale. For a moment he is silent.

"*Adamantine*?" He shakes his head. "*You* possess a blade of adamantine? It cannot be. No more than three such are known to exist—and *you* have one?"

"I think so."

His beautiful face clouds over.

"You tell me you have scaled Olympus, as no mortal has in centuries, and you look on my face without harm; now you say you carry a weapon that can kill a god? What is it you are keeping from me, Psyche?"

My throat tightens.

"Nothing! What do you accuse me of? I have done all this for *you*!"

Fire dances in his eyes. "What do I accuse you of? I say that you have lied to me."

I throw down the blade and stare at him.

"I *have not lied.* I do not know why I can look upon your face without paying the price, and as for this knife, it was my mother's—how she came by it, I know not. As to how I made it through this cursed place, perhaps some god or other chose to aid me. Or perhaps," I glare at him, "just *perhaps,* I am braver and stronger and have more fortitude than you are ready to admit!"

His eyes lock on mine, neither of us willing to look away. And then his face softens, and he shakes his head.

"You are right, Psyche. Forgive me."

I close my eyes, savoring the sound of his voice. When I open my eyes, he's looking at me. I take up the knife again.

"I won't bring the blade any closer unless you trust me to,"

I say.

"I trust you," he says, his eyes still on mine.

I go to examine the shackles, but when I try to grip it I cry out in shock. The steel burns like fire.

"I cannot hold it," I say, ignoring the pain in my hand. If I cannot hold the shackle steady as I cut, how am I to slice through it safely?

"Try and slide the knife inside the shackle," he says. "Then pull outwards."

It's a good thought, but when I turn the dagger on its flat side and ease it underneath the shackle, against his skin, I hear him swallow a gasp. The very touch of the ore must cause him pain.

I get a hold, then pull the knife back toward me—but it cuts faster, slicker, than I expected, and I yelp as the blade swings back too sharply in my direction. I steady my arm just in time.

"Psyche…" Eros says, but he doesn't need to say *be careful*. I'm trembling now.

"I saw it cut through stone." My voice shakes. "And through wood as though it were butter. And yet I did not expect…" I don't know what to say. The more I see of it, the easier it is for me to believe a blade like this can kill a god. And the harder it is for me to believe that my mother came by it innocently. I think Eros was right to be suspicious, though not of me: there is more here, there must be, than meets the eye.

Eros stares at the blade in my hand.

"I have only heard of adamantine, never seen it," he says quietly. "Zeus forged the blade when he killed the god Kronos, and a second when we went to war against the Titans. There was tale of a third blade, but if it existed, its whereabouts was unknown." He looks down at the one in my hand, wondering.

"Zeus never spoke of where he got the ore; he refused to. The two blades we know of are under lock and key in the inner sanctum of the gods. The vault cannot be opened unless all twelve Olympians unite to do it. That is how dangerous this is."

I look up at him, then away.

"Is it true that it can kill a god?" My mouth feels dry as I ask the question. "I cut a dryad's branch with it, but the dryad did not die."

Eros shakes his head.

"A tree will not die unless it is felled or its roots destroyed. But if you sever the limb with adamantine, it will never grow back—that is the difference between adamantine and any other blade." He looks at me. "You have heard of Prometheus and his punishment?"

I know the story: every day an eagle plucked out his heart, and every day the heart grew back.

"Immortals regenerate, Psyche. They may be injured, they may suffer pain, but the wound will always heal. Except," he says, "a wound inflicted by adamantine ore."

I turn the knife over in my hands, trying to absorb all that I'm hearing.

I move down to the shackle on his leg, and though even the merest touch against his skin seems to scald him, he is careful not to flinch. I cut through this one just as easily as the first, and more smoothly now. We both watch the metal fall away.

"It is incredible." He pauses. "And yet, not the most incredible thing to have happened to me today." His voice carries the meaning of his words, and I know his eyes are on my face. I don't look up. I can't. When we are free, I tell myself, and gone from here: *then* I will gaze and gaze upon him. But it is so hard not to look at him. And the scent of him! I had forgotten. Instead of a dank cave, we seem to linger in a forest, where the wind carries the rich scent of cypress and cedar, of sandalwood and myrrh.

I'm leaning in to start on his leg-shackles when I freeze.

"What was that?" I whisper.

But one look at his face tells me all I need to know.

Someone is coming.

Thirty-seven

"Hide yourself." He looks at me. "*Now.* And no matter what, do not come out—no matter what you hear. My brother must not know you are here." He's pulling at the chains, moving them back into place.

"No!" I say. "We have time, if I hurry. I'll cut the other ones. Then you'll be free. You can fight him."

He winces, and his eyes meet mine.

"I am not the god I was, Psyche. Before, I could have matched either of my brothers in a duel, but now…" I hear the pain in his voice, the pain of acknowledging weakness.

"But your brothers do not have this," I say, holding up the dagger.

If I thought I had seen Eros angry before now, I was mistaken. Now I see what anger really looks like on him.

"You want me to arm myself with adamantine? I will not end immortal life, Psyche—less still, my own brother's!" He swallows, mastering himself again. "We must wait till he has gone. If you arrange the shackles as before, he will not notice they are broken. And then you must hide, and fast."

"But…"

"There is no other way!"

I want to argue, but instead I push the shackles back around his ankles, quickly arranging them as they were. In the dark, unless you were looking closely, you would never know. And then, even though turning away from him feels like a lead weight in my chest, I move quickly to a nearby boulder that's high enough and wide enough to shield me. I run toward it and huddle behind it, sheathing the dagger to hide its light.

What did he mean, that I must stay hidden *no matter what I hear*?

A chill of foreboding goes through me.

I know a little of his brothers. Deimos and Phobos: the twins. My countrymen paint their faces on our shields when we go to war, to horrify the enemy. These are gods who turn brave men into cowering children—at least, that is what is said. They, too, are the sons of Aphrodite and Ares, but the twins were raised by their father only. There is no love in them at all, only battle and terror.

Footsteps echo in the tunnel above us, very close now. And then I hear the sweep of wings, and I peer around the boulder to see a figure descending smoothly from the drop I fell down earlier. This other gods is tall like Eros, and golden-skinned as well; he shimmers, too, with the aura of a god. But instead of Eros's black wings, this one's are white as a dove's. He moves swiftly through the room, and alights before Eros's chair. His immense wings fold in and my heart hammers in my chest. I hope he cannot hear my quick breath. I have not seen his face; perhaps I do not wish to.

"You have done something, Eros." The sound of his voice is like the clashing of knives. "The river runs with the *ketos*'s blood."

A *ketos*—so that's what the creature was. I should have known my presence on this mountain could not be hidden long—not when I have left such a trail of destruction. But Eros seems surprised. After all, he knows nothing of how I got here; of what I had to do. Though perhaps now he's starting to guess.

"I have done nothing to your creature." His voice is steady. "How could I have? I am in chains, brother, as you well see."

"And yet you are troublesome still," the other god sneers. "Have you no sense at all in that pretty head of yours?" He reaches out a hand as though to caress his brother's curls, but instead gives a sharp push, so that Eros's head snaps back on his neck. I set my jaw; I must not make a sound.

"I already know you do not. Betraying our mother over some little mortal girl!" His white wings stir, like a dog bristling with anger. "But I do not think it was an accident that the beast had arrows of *your* making buried in it. Who have you commandeered to help you? Some other fool god? Some mortal idiot who believes he is heir to Herakles? Whoever it is, the Olympians will punish them when they find them. We do not like the guardian of our river to be treated so."

"That's as may be." Eros's voice betrays no emotion. It's the voice I remember from before: the voice that tells me he's steeled himself to keep every feeling at bay. But I know him well enough now to detect the anger he's trying to hide.

"Think what you wish, but I know nothing of the monster's fate." He looks up at his brother. "Why so suspicious, Deimos?"

Deimos. So that is the brother who stands before him.

"You know nothing of it, you say? We shall see."

He flicks a hand toward Eros. I see nothing, no disturbance in the air, but whatever power flows from this white-winged god is instant: Eros's breathing becomes labored, his eyes screw shut, his whole body stiffens. And after a moment he begins to shrink back in his seat as though suffering from some great pain.

"Tell me the truth," Deimos says. "Tell me the truth and I'll stop."

Eros's head shakes side to side. My heart constricts; it's too painful to witness. A god, reduced to this! And yet, if he did not have such mastery of himself, I can see he would be writhing in pain.

Whatever torture this is, it continues. Eros answers none of Deimos's questions or taunts, but when a soft moan escapes him, Deimos pounces again.

"Something you'd like to tell me?"

Eros shakes his head.

"Have it your way, then."

Whatever pain he's inflicting must be redoubled: Eros is crouched down in his seat now, cringing, his breath coming in hard, fast pants. I want to scream, I want to hurl myself on this monster called a god—this creature who takes pleasure in his brother's suffering. But Eros told me to stay hidden, no matter what I heard. I tell myself I must stay where I am.

Then Eros's eyes flash open. He knows where I am; his gaze meets mine. And in his eyes I see a pain more dreadful than anything I've ever imagined. A pain that no one, god or mortal, should ever be expected to bear. And I can't stay hidden any longer, I can't.

I get to my feet, the dagger in my hand.

"Please stop."

The god Deimos whirls around. His face is a cruel distortion of his brother's. He has the radiance of a god, but here it inspires dread, not exultation. This is the face the word *god-fearing* was meant for.

"*This*, brother? Your little mortal plaything?"

His deep voice is filled with disgust. Eros looks at me, his eyes bright with pain. Yet again I have flouted his orders.

But this time I had no choice.

"Great god, I petition you. Please: he is your brother. Relent from this." I get on my knees. My heart batters; I cannot think that he will listen, but the oracle said prayer was power, and I will try.

Deimos only sneers at me, with that face so like Eros's.

"Stupid creature. Didn't anyone ever teach you to respect your gods?"

It grows so fast, the darkness. I'm in a mist, a fog—but is the fog in my mind or in the air around me? Are my eyes closed? I can't tell.

I try to take a step forward, but my body will not move. And then another feeling grows, starting in my feet. It seems to come from the earth up, like ice grips a plant from the roots and spreads upward.

The voices...is it the madness the oracle spoke of after all; has it finally come to claim me? They seem to speak to me from the very walls. They get clearer, and soon I understand they're speaking to me.

Look what you did to us, they say. *Look what you've done.*

I hear little Hector's voice, and his mother's; I hear Dimitra, and my father, and all the voices of Sikyon. I hear voices of strangers, of those not yet born. And all of them despise me. I wish I could block my ears to them, but there is no end to it, this chorus of malice—their voices shake with it. It seems as though I am back out in the Olympian winter, but now it is the winter of my mind. Everything is cold.

Endless.

Hopeless.

There will never be light again.

I see things I have long refused to imagine. Now they flock to me. My mother lies dead in a white room, the blood of my birth pooling around her. I see Dimitra, a small child, whimpering in the doorway, the blood reflected in her eyes.

I see other things, too, horrors that have not come to pass, but seem invented to torment me. Eros standing over me with a wolf's smile, his teeth bared, sharp…teeth digging into my chest, ripping my heart from inside my ribcage. My sister, with the face of a Gorgon. My father weeping on a battlefield, ringed by a circle of men who taunt him with their knives.

They're not real, I try and tell myself. *They're creations, evil fantasies.* But my voice has no conviction in it. And I'm so cold. So very, very cold. I can't think, can't cling to anything except this feeling: the dread in my stomach, and the ice in my veins. I'm dying, I realize. This must be what it feels like to die.

Please, I try to say, but nothing comes.

The world is pain, a voice says. *Pain and fury. Nothing but this.*

And I feel in my bones that it is true. There is nothing else but this aching dread, this horror. Nothing but disease and war and death and hopelessness…

The horror sticks to me like a thousand webs. I can't find

my way out. Am I breathing still; am I dead? Somewhere out of dim memory I remember Eros's voice, commanding me to breathe.

Breathe, Psyche. Breathe.

It's not real.

It's. Not. Real.

I force my eyes open.

"Psyche!" Eros calls.

But his brother is in the air above me, his pale wings beating. *Deimos.*

His face sings with malice. He's not tired, I can tell from his eyes—we haven't even got started. This is just to whet my appetite. I can feel what's waiting for me, the horror of it, and I know, I know without a shadow of a doubt, that it will kill me.

That he *wants* to kill me.

And I did not come all the way here to let him.

I force myself to move. Just unclenching the fingers of my right hand is like pushing a boulder uphill. It takes everything I have. But with that small movement comes a flood of warmth, as though the ice has started to melt. I fumble for what's strapped to my waistband, and my fingers close around it, smooth and cold.

I must move quickly. I imagine myself back in our old house, parrying with Dimitra with our wooden swords. Dimitra's aim was always better, but I practiced harder.

I whip the blade from its sheath, draw back, and fling it, all in one smooth motion. I hear the sweet keen note it makes as it cuts through the air and I know I've never thrown a blade so fast, nor so true. It's almost as though it knows where I want it to go.

I *feel* the cut it makes as though it were my own flesh. And I hear it, the slicing-through of feather and tissue. A scream to split the sky.

And a god falls from the air.

Thirty-eight

Cold rushes through my body—no longer frozen but a wave, a torrent, moving from the ground up through my body like fetid river water. I choke, spewing it out at my feet. And for a moment my mind sings with emptiness, as though I have just rid myself of the deepest poison.

The god Deimos is sprawled on his knees, one of his white wings lying severed at his feet. His back is bloody, one wing still intact, the other just a stump, a mound of raw flesh. He screams again, staring at the sight before him. He's scrabbling to pull himself forward through the scattered feathers, and the blood.

"What have you done! Brother!" He turns, howling, to Eros's chair. "She has brought adamantine here! She has brought death upon us!"

The look in Eros's eyes is like a knife through my heart. He did not think I was capable of such a thing. Even though his brother is a monster, he was still his brother—and a god. Now he crawls, with a wound of pink raw flesh below his shoulder blade.

"I am ruined," Deimos cries, in a voice that begins as a snarl and ends as a sob.

My stomach swirls with more bile. I needed to survive. I aimed for the wing only, not the heart or face or hand. But looking at the young god now, his blood mixing with the earth…

"Brother!" Deimos calls again, and I see the pain in Eros's face.

"No mortal may do this and live!" Deimos's hand is bloody; he keeps feeling for the wound at his back, trying to touch it. "You will avenge your family. She will die at your hands for what she has done!"

Eros stares at me, then at Deimos. I can't read what he's thinking. For once, his emotions are totally opaque to me.

"She will not be killed." His voice is steady, resonating through the cave. "Not by my hand, nor by yours, nor anyone's. I am her husband, and sworn to protect her."

Deimos stares at him, livid.

"Swear to avenge me and kill the girl, or you will die!"

"You have heard me, Deimos," Eros answers, and now I hear the tremor in his voice—whether from sorrow or from anger, I can't tell.

"Do not insult me by asking again."

Deimos's words shake too—with disbelief and hatred.

"You choose *her* over me? This murderous, foul thing? She will kill you in your sleep!"

The words sicken me. I would never hurt Eros, never…and yet this pool of blood on the floor, this maimed creature crawling on the earth: I did that.

"I do not choose her *over you*." Eros's voice rises, though he is still imprisoned in his chair. He looks at me now.

"I choose her, I will always choose her"—his gaze turns back to his brother—"but I do not choose her *over you*. That was your choice, not mine. Remember that she has but one life, Deimos, and you would happily have stolen it from her." His voice thickens. "She spared you, Deimos. Her aim is true. If she had wanted that knife through your heart she could have done it. She did not."

Deimos howls again and arches his back.

"You are a fool, brother. You have always been a fool!" he shouts. "You are bewitched, a traitor in thrall to a mortal whore!"

"Watch your tongue," Eros spits. "Call me what you will, but you'll insult my wife no further."

Deimos calls out from the ground.

"Or what? You will kill me, too? I suppose she's promised

you a share of that adamantine! You're plotting against us now."

"Don't be a fool," Eros scoffs.

"Me? *Me*, the fool?"

Deimos lunges, and snatches something from the ground: the knife. As he holds it aloft, it still drips with blood. I cry out as he swivels around, bracing himself to drive it into Eros's leg. But Eros sees it too; he levers back his leg and kicks, landing a foot against his brother's jaw. I see Deimos's head snap back as the knife skitters across the floor to land at the foot of Eros's chair. Eros picks it up and I feel Deimos's fear—but all he does is cut the two remaining shackles. He stands, and Deimos stares; the stump on his back quivers.

"You *dare*."

Eros walks slowly across the room to where I'm standing.

"Psyche."

I find it hard to look at him. But the touch of his hand—*that*, I feel. I feel it like a promise, like the first green shoots of life.

"Psyche. Take my hand. We must go. Now."

I want to move, and yet the command seems not to make it to my feet. I take a step forward, but my whole body shakes. And then I feel him taking me in his arms—just as he did that first night. Only I can feel now how weakened he is, how changed. *I did that.* I caused this change in him. This weakness.

He lifts me; my neck rests against his shoulder. His great wings unfold.

I glance back, although I know I should not. The blood on the ground is almost black now, mixed with mud, but white feathers mark the darkness. Deimos hisses at the sight of me.

"Run while you can, worm." His eyes burn with a fire I know will haunt my dreams.

*

Once clear of the cavern, Eros draws in his wings and lowers us to the floor of the tunnel.

"I cannot fly far," he admits.

"I can walk," I say, but he does not put me down. He walks on with me cradled against him. I struggle with the words I want to say.

"I'm sorry. I did not wish to hurt him." There's silence for a moment.

"If you had not stopped him, he would have killed you. And then I would have killed him."

His face is dark, and so are the words: they should not warm me, I think, and yet they do. When I look at his face it's as though my lungs have been tied shut, and I have to force myself to inhale. I can see he's deliberately avoiding my glance, his eyes on the tunnel mouth ahead, the circle of sunlight. Why won't he look at me?

"What your brother said, before…" I hesitate. "You believe me, about the dagger? You know I would never mean you harm?"

"I believe you."

My head swims; letting my eyes close, I lean back into him. The smell of the woods at night. Of incense swinging in the temple.

What will happen to us? I want to ask, but I don't know if I want to hear the answer.

At the entrance to the tunnel he puts me down—and there, like a vision against the sky, is a black stallion. As though he had been waiting here for a thousand years and could wait a thousand more. At the sound of his master's feet, he whinnies.

"Ajax," I murmur, and his tail swishes, ever so gently. He waits quietly until we reach his side, then kneels—kneels! I have never seen such a proud creature do such a thing—to let us mount. Eros sits me onto the broad back first. Then I feel his warm weight behind me and he gathers the reins. Ajax rises, and without Eros seeming to command him, breaks into a gallop. As he hurtles down the mountain it seems to me we move faster—much faster—than before. There is magic in his stride now. I suppose it is because he rides with a god on his back.

The mountain, too, is changed. It feels silent, watchful—as though its creatures have retreated to eye us from their lairs.

"News will travel fast," Eros murmurs in my ear, one warm arm around me, clasping the reins. The small of my back presses against his chest. "We must put as much distance between ourselves and the mountain as we can by nightfall."

I look at the silent wilderness around us. The enormity of what has happened is starting to sink in. I know—I have always known—what happens to mortals who get involved with the gods.

"They will kill us," I say quietly. "They will find us, and they will kill us."

"They will not harm you, Psyche." His warm voice buzzes at my ear, his chest against my back. "I will not let it happen."

"And who will protect you?" I whisper. "Your powers are weakened. If they come after us…"

"They will not find us," he says, and there is a finality in his voice.

We hurtle out of the winter storms, past the falling snow, past the ice and white-coated forests.

"We will make for the crossroads of Elassona," Eros says. I know the name of Elassona. It is a great meeting-place: the roads there go in all directions, bringing travelers north to Illyria and Macedonia, south to Corinth and Sparta, and even across the seas to east and west, as far as Persia or Italos.

"And from there," he says, "we will travel south: to the Gulf of Patras, where the crossing is shortest; then from Achaea to Elis, and find passage west, to the isle of Atlantis."

Atlantis?

"Why Atlantis?" I say; my head is spinning again.

"It is where my father fights."

Ares. The god of war.

The war at Atlantis has been on and off for many years—its resources are too plentiful for mankind to leave it alone. But recently, I hear the battles have renewed with new fury.

Of course the god of war camps there.

Atlantis.

My mother's home.

We hurtle through the dank autumn leaves, the brown mulch, and then the amber, still-crisp ones.

"You think your father will help us?" I say, and when he doesn't answer, I wonder if my question got lost in the wind. I'm about to repeat it when he speaks.

"I cannot say." His voice is flat. If he feels hope, he refuses to let it show. "But he is fearless as to the opinions of his fellow gods. He may side with us for principle, or if not that, for sport."

I think of the oracle's words to me: *a chance,* she said. And now I think *a chance* may be enough.

Eros tells me of his brothers, how, once Aphrodite declared that Eros had betrayed her, the twins were quick to seek their mother's favor. How they would do anything she asked of them.

"She has stolen them from my father's side. I think he will not be pleased with that, either."

I shiver. It is not much to depend on—the whims of angry gods.

"I did not kill the *ketos,*" I blurt out. "Not quite." And I tell him about the last arrow. I need to tell him the story. I don't know why, until I stop speaking and find I'm shaking again, and then I realize: I want him to comfort me somehow. To tell me that the power in those arrows wasn't as evil as it seemed. It seems to me that it *must* be an evil power—to make a creature fall in love against its inclination, against nature, against all reason; even to its own destruction. The power to manipulate and control, distort and exploit.

But if he knows I'm looking for comfort, he won't give it.

"I cannot change my powers, Psyche. They are the ones I was born with. I told you, didn't I? One man's god may be another's demon. I am what I am."

"But you're no demon," I say, though I think I hear a note of pleading in my voice. Because I want it to be true. I want him to be capable of only good things. But deep down, don't I know better?

He doesn't say anything to that, maybe because of what happens next—a sight so arresting, so beautiful, I catch his arm. Is it an omen? A white doe stands on the path before us, watching us, motionless, unafraid. And then she turns and bounds into the forest, back uphill.

"Beautiful," I breathe. Something in the sight was so mesmerizing, so perfectly bewitching.

But behind me, Eros is breathing faster.

"Forward, Ajax!" he says in a low, hard voice. "As fast as you can."

Ajax flicks his dark mane, the touch of it like silk against my forearms. Now we're going so fast, the world is a blur.

"What is it?" I say, my voice barely audible now over the sound of hooves. My teeth meet with a jolt at every pace.

"That was no ordinary deer," Eros says, and I hear his jaw shut, too.

"That, Psyche, was my mother."

Thirty-nine

Aphrodite.

"Are you sure?" I say, despite myself.

He makes an impatient sound.

"She does not follow us," he says. "Perhaps because she does not have Ajax's speed in that form." He takes a breath. "She goes back to Olympus, I suppose, to gather allies. But she does not know where we are going. We must keep her from guessing where we are bound."

I shudder. Deimos may not fly again, but that need not stop him from chasing after us to the ends of the earth. Nor will it stop his twin brother, I am sure.

"What about the other gods?" I say. "Will none of them defend you? Can they condone what she did to you; how she took you and kept you prisoner?"

"Perhaps not condone," he says. "But whether they will condemn her is another matter. Hephaestus for one will take her part, and Zeus listens to Hephaestus more than he listens to any of the others."

Because Hephaestus's weapons are what keep Zeus strong. I understand what he's telling me: right and wrong will take second place to brokered loyalties. The gods watch for their own interests, just like mortals do. And if Zeus takes Aphrodite's part, we have little hope with the other gods. Surely none of them would risk defying Zeus.

"Adamantine, Psyche…" he goes on. "It is the thing the gods fear most. To bring it to Mount Olympus—to bring it to their home—I fear they will view it as the greatest of treacheries."

"But *you* didn't do it," I say. "I did. And I didn't know..."

But I would still have brought it. Even if I'd known what it was.

"It doesn't matter." Behind me, his voice is low and contained, the way it is when he's trying not to feel.

"I'm sorry," I say. Could all of this have been averted, if I'd stayed my hand a little longer? If I'd let Deimos continue a few moments more?

Eros pulls me closer against him and I feel his warmth in my body, even while the chill still covers my heart.

"Do not be sorry," he says quietly. "You saved me from great pain." He hesitates.

"My mother brought me to that place to punish me, yes—but also to re-make me. To re-make my mind, my loyalty. To make me forget you, and my own self."

I close my eyes against the wind, the hurtling road.

"Even a god's mind cannot hold out forever. I don't know how long it would have taken her to break me, to take my mind apart and mold it back to how it once was—compliant, obedient, her devoted son." His voice is sharp. "But… you came for me."

It occurs to me that he is an outcast, an *ostrakon* now, too: such things exist even among the gods, I suppose. But despite the chilling things he speaks of, all I feel is his warmth behind me and his voice in my ear. We're clear of the mountain now, flying along the open road to Elassona. The sun behind the trees looks watery and strained and a bluish cast is in the air; there is no warmth in this evening at all. But something warm and bright blooms in my soul.

*

It is evening by the time we reach Elassona. We have avoided any villages or encampments till now, taking back roads only, but Eros insists I eat tonight. Since he has no cloak and cannot accompany me, I ride Ajax into the marketplace alone. Quickly I barter for some bread and cheese, then on impulse stop at another stall selling hides and wool, thinking they may have a cloak to sell me.

"For a tall man," I say, "and with a deep hood, enough to cover his whole face."

He looks at me strangely, but finds something that will do the job. He stares at Ajax the whole time, and when I try to pay, nothing will please him except to try and buy my horse from me. I tell him that I cannot sell, that the horse is my husband's, but he only looks at me more narrowly. It is a relief to be back on Ajax, riding toward the forest again. Ajax knows the way.

Eros is waiting for us in a small grove, ringed around with laurel trees. The sky is turning golden now, and in its light Eros glows, the most beautiful sight I have ever known. A confusion of awe and desire goes through me. *Can this really be?* I feel shy: it was easier when he sat behind me and I did not look upon his face. Did all that happened between us before truly happen? Did I once share my bed with a god? The memory assails me, like something I dreamed once, and heat flushes through me.

He reaches for me, to lift me down from Ajax's saddle. Our eyes meet and I see his soften. But he says nothing, just places me gently on the ground.

All it takes is a wave of his hand, and laurel trees twist and grow, their branches sliding and interlocking with a sigh and a shudder. They twist into a canopy: a living treehouse more delicate than what any sculptor could craft.

"You are tired," Eros says, his voice veering toward abruptness again. "We will sleep here for the night."

I look sideways at him.

"You haven't changed much," I say. "Still making decisions for me."

He turns sharply, then sees the look on my face and understands that I am teasing him. His eyes glint.

"*You* haven't changed much. Still lacking in gratitude and manners."

"Manners!" I say. "I'll teach you manners!"

"Not if I teach you first," he says, and hoists me into his

arms, lifting me over the threshold of our tree-home for the night. Its branches slide across the gap after we enter, sealing behind us, but an enchanted glow lights the space inside and turns everything a dim gold.

He sighs my name, and I bury my face in his neck and listen to his heart beat.

"Does a god's heart always beat so fast?" I murmur.

He brushes the hair back from my face and looks down at me.

"Yours beats much faster," he says. "Yours is thundering. You must want me very badly."

I see the gleam in his golden eyes. He's teasing me right back.

"Are you going to continue to torment me like this?" I say.

"Always," he says, staring at me.

And just as I think he's going to stare at me forever, he finally lowers his mouth to mine.

They say when you die your life flashes before your eyes. I must die a little, because every moment I've ever lived seems to flutter through my mind in an instant—and then after that, a blissful emptiness. I am an empty husk, nothing in me but warmth and want.

This is what mortals pray to Eros for, isn't it? To feel this.

I draw him toward me, but he stills my hand with his. Then with the other hand he pulls the brooch from my *chiton*, and pushes the fabric slowly back from my shoulder. He bares my skin inch by inch, his eyes never leaving mine, unwrapping me slowly, like a gift. I can tell by the pulse in his throat he'd like to go faster, but he's showing off his self-control to me, his capacity for discipline.

I have no use for discipline now, and as soon as I can wriggle free, I show him that.

And it's a long time before we come up for air.

*

Afterwards, we lie panting, his bronze flesh next to mine. He runs a finger over my bare skin. I am beaded with sweat, my hair tousled. And despite having spent until there was nothing left to give, I feel desire awakening in me once more.

I will never have enough of him, I think. Never.

And that thought, if I truly let myself think it, brings me pain.

"What is it like to be immortal?" I turn to him. "How does it feel?"

I watch his finger trace patterns on my skin.

"I do not know how it is to be any other way." He pauses. "I do not envy you mortals. You have so little time. And yet…you find purpose, much quicker than we do. Quicker, and perhaps deeper."

I swallow. His words remind me of other things, and as I stare at the ceiling I tell him what the oracle said about my family.

"I am grieved to hear it," he says.

I gaze up at the ceiling's interweaving tapestry of vines and leaves. It occurs to me that the oracle's words were both blessing and curse, all interwoven like the vines. The blessing is in knowing my family are alive. And yet, not to see them again in this life…

Perhaps the oracle is wrong, I think. But oracles are never wrong.

"You are courageous," Eros says at last. "All you mortals. We are not tested as you are."

"I did not think you admired mortals much," I say. I can't help remembering the disdainful way he spoke of mortals when I first knew him, in his palace. As though we were some lesser form of life.

He frowns.

"For a long time I knew no better. I was not raised to honor mortals." He looks at me. "But then, you too made free to tell me how much you hated my kind, did you not?"

I thought you were something else, I want to say, then stop, remembering his words about demons and gods and the eye of the beholder. Maybe I *do* hate his kind. Or maybe I just hate how much power they have.

"I thought you had cheated me," I remind him. "I do not like to have my choices made for me. Nor to feel tricked."

He looks at me for a while, his eyes wandering around my face. One hand reaches out and plays with a strand of my hair.

"I tried to persuade her, you know, once I knew my mother's plans for you. I tried to change her mind. Despite how I wanted you, interfering in your life was not my first resort." He shrugs. "But I admit, I was not used to having to explain myself to mortals, nor consulting their opinions. The gods would say that mortals rarely know what is best for them."

The words sting, but I let them settle. They are arrogant words, but not without truth.

"I suppose it is true, we rarely know what is best for us. And yet everyone bears their own mistakes better, I think, than any choices forced upon us." I look at him. "Could you not just have told me from the start? Could you not have let me know who you were?"

He runs the side of his thumb along my face.

"And would you have believed me? I think you would have been ever more suspicious, then. You would have thought me the worst of demons then, trying to deceive you." He looks at me. "Besides, I have a god's pride, Psyche. It was taught to me from a young age. I thought that with time, your feelings would change."

I frown at him.

"Without ever seeing your face?"

And yet, he was not wrong. I can't deny it. My feelings *did* change.

"I did not believe it would be possible for you to ever see my face. And if you had known the truth of who I was…I did not want your awe, Psyche. I did not want your worship. I wanted your desire."

I turn to see his face better in the dim glow.

"You had it," I say. "You have it." I hesitate. A question pulls at me.

"I know your powers have grown diminished, since the temple at Sikyon fell." I look at him. "I suppose it is all my fault. Is there anything I can do, to help you regain them?"

A shadow passes over his face. He doesn't answer for a moment.

"Sikyon was one of my chief temples: its collapse left me vulnerable, but only for a short time. That alone would not have left me as I am now. Do not blame yourself. It is what my mother has done. She has made the people take her side over mine, forbidding them to worship me."

I recall the conversation I overheard at the inn outside of Delphi.

"But...does that really matter? Whether people worship you or not?"

He looks at me.

"More than you can imagine." He sighs. "Mortals always think our powers come from some magic source: nectar or ambrosia, or something in our blood. Perhaps it's to our advantage that mortals believe such things. But that's not where true divine power comes from, Psyche. That comes from one source only: worship."

I stare at him. What he's saying makes no sense.

"But then...anyone could become an immortal," I protest.

He gives me an impatient look.

"Immortality is not the same as power, Psyche. A nymph or a dryad, for example—they are immortal. They are born that way. It's their *ischys,* their life force. It's different from a mortal's. But, while the nymph or dryad may have a little power of their own, it will only ever be a little. They cannot turn a battalion of men into a flock of pigs; they cannot bring down mountains with a wave of their hand; they cannot set whole plains alight or cause a storm that splits the sky. *That* is great power, and that comes from worship alone."

I frown, trying to absorb what he's telling me. It's not what I was taught as a child. It's certainly not the message the priests give out.

"You mean, even Zeus..."

"Zeus is the most powerful of all the gods, but not because he was born that way." Eros looks gravely at me. "It is because he captured the favor of the people for his deeds, and they prayed to him in droves." He shrugs. "His brother Poseidon thinks *he* should rule the Pantheon, but he will always be second in command so long as the mortals worship Zeus in greater numbers."

Thoughts tumble through my mind. It is all so different to what I thought I knew. The gods depend on *us*—what a new and foreign thought. I think about the great heroes of legend, god-children like Herakles, or Theseus, or Perseus. They were worshiped, too, in their time. Is it from this that their powers grew?

"So, as my followers dwindle," Eros continues, "my powers do, too, like a fire burning low. It will not die out—it will never die out—but while the flame is starved, it burns lower." He looks at me. "But as you see, there is every hope of my recovery."

"If people change their minds," I say slowly. *If people cease to fear Aphrodite. If they stop doing what she tells them.* I think of the oracle's words: *prayer is power, too.* Perhaps her words were truer than she knew.

Or perhaps she knows, and keeps the gods' secret for them.

My mind hums and my thoughts toss and spin. How extraordinary the world is, I think. How many secrets are yet to be known.

He runs a hand over my skin and we lie there, looking up at the green roof above us, the cracks of dark sky outside. Then after a while Eros waves his hand, an idle gesture: moonflowers blossom among the vines, small white orbs glowing in the greenish dark.

"They're like stars," I say, gazing up. To him I suppose it's nothing but a little party trick. To me, a reminder of what power runs through his veins, even now.

He stands, reaching out to pluck one for me, but I shake my head.

"Let it live," I say. "It belongs where it is."

He looks down at me, that dazzling stare of his. He rarely smiles, I am coming to learn. And when he does, it is no more than a half-smile, a ghost of a smile.

We have so much to fear. And yet, I cannot help but feel elated, when I see his face.

He flicks instead at the canopy of vines, making the leaves and flowers tremble. They let fall a shower of stored raindrops, cascading down on my bare skin. I protest, but the sensation is delightful.

Eros kneels beside me, dips his thumb in the pool of rainwater on my breastbone, and begins to trace a pattern.

"I hope I will not exhaust you," he says, his mouth quirking a little. "You are used to the appetites of men. I am the god of desire itself; I am not so easily satisfied. You will have to let me know, if I demand too much."

Heat runs through me. This is how it is with him—he sates the hunger and whets it again. But I arch an eyebrow at him.

"You will have to tell me, if I exhaust *you*."

He laughs gently into my ear.

"Very well, wife."

Wife. For once the term sounds neither alien nor mocking on his lips.

"Am I really your wife?" I say. "Even if it is not recognized by the gods?"

"They will recognize what it suits them to recognize," he says. "But you will come to know this about my people, Psyche:

the gods are nothing if not inconsistent. They sway like the wind."

"Even you?" I say, and he looks at me.

"You doubt me?"

I shift a little, turn my gaze back to the vined ceiling. He may be a god, but he fell for me the same way mortal men do—by watching me from afar, and liking the sight of me.

"You of all people should understand," I say. "Beauty is only a shell, a skin. It means nothing. And I am mortal—whatever beauty I have will fade."

I've lived all my life overshadowed by my own reflection. People see what shimmers on the surface, and all that swims beneath might as well be dead. It's hard for me to believe that *he*—this being of divine beauty, of wild power—could actually see me as I wish to be seen. That what he feels is more than some passing infatuation, the desire to conquer and move on.

"I am familiar with desire, Psyche," he says quietly. "There is none who knows its ways better than I. I *am* desire." He swallows. "So when I tell you that what I feel for you is something else besides, trust me to know of what I speak."

And I remember, then, that he is also a god of love.

He raises himself on an elbow.

"In fact, if either of us is to doubt the other, it's I who should doubt you. Didn't you spurn me, before you saw my face? Wasn't it the sight of me that converted you?" He gives me a sharp look. "Or was it the knowledge that I was a god?"

I flush, but hold his gaze.

"What I felt took hold before then," I say. "The difference is, I had every reason to fight it. I had no reason to trust you…"

"You had every reason to trust me," he interrupts, but his voice is quiet, not angry. Neither of us speaks for a little while, then. He studies me, his eyes on my face as though trying to memorize it.

"I've *seen* a mortal lose his senses, Psyche. I knew what my face had the power to do, among your kind. I believed myself to be a walking curse among you. And yet *you*, you are completely unharmed. Your only madness was to come back to save me."

I blink; my eyes threaten to betray me.

"But did I? Save you, I mean? Your brother…everything that happened." We are refugees, branded as traitors. "I feel as though perhaps I…ruined you."

He roves over me with those eyes.

"Oh, you've ruined me," he says, his voice hoarse as he bends to kiss me. "You've ruined me all right, daughter of Sikyon."

A few more hours of this, I think. A few more hours, to bask in the magic of each other's bodies. And then, when morning breaks, our real journey will begin.

I reach for him, but as he takes my hand I drop it with a cry.

Pain like a white-hot flash stings my arm.

"What is it?"

I'm cradling my arm, the pain like a bright cord running the length of it.

"Psyche! What is it?"

That's when I see it: a scorpion, white as pearl, scuttling away into the dark.

Forty

P*earl-white.* The color of no other scorpion in this land. It means something, but I can't hold onto the thought. The pain is too much.

And the scorpion is gone now.

Into the vines.

Into the dark.

But Eros lets out a sound of fury, like nothing I've heard before.

Or not fury: pain. Because that's what's in his eyes now, as I slide back to the ground—the world is grey, I'm too dizzy to sit.

"Psyche..."

His voice hitches, my vision swims. But I can still see his look of despair. As though everything is over.

Before it had even begun.

"Psyche..."

All this effort. All this pain. For what? The visions I saw in his eyes...maybe it wasn't anything fore-ordained. Maybe it wasn't anything but imagination. Maybe the future I thought we would have belonged to some other universe, but not this one...

"I can't move it," I whisper. "I can't feel my arm."

The pain has given way to something worse now, a terrible numbness from my fingers to my shoulder, just a flare of pain on its perimeter.

She did this. I remember now: the white deer, the white scorpion. The knowledge sings clear in my head. And I know Eros knows it too. But none of that matters now. There's a blue flush all down my arm, as if I've been held under in a barrel of ice.

His golden eyes lock on me as though to claim me all over

again.

"The poison. We can't let it get to your heart." He takes my arm in his hands, looks for the scorpion bite, puts his mouth to it. He's trying to suck the venom out, and I don't have the heart to tell him it's too late. As I watch it, the blue tint of my arm deepens. I can see the ice creeping past my shoulder now, toward my collarbone, a terrible, cold fire. And where the feeling creeps, the blue flush follows.

Is this death?

The look in his eyes tells me I must be. The scorpion was such a little thing, smaller than my hand. And yet it has poison enough, no doubt, for many mortals.

"I don't think it's any use," I say at last, knowing he must know the same. I want him to be looking at my face when I go.

"Psyche…"

He bunches his fingers in my hair.

This is what it means to be mortal, I want to say to him. *This is what it is to grieve.*

Once more I think of those visions that swam in my head, when I first looked into his golden eyes. I thought they were a promise. I was so sure—so sure we'd have time.

He's staring at me. I stare back, until eventually his eyes move to the blue flush that's been crawling along my collarbone. And then he stares some more.

His hand grazes my neck. The grip of the ice must not be too bad yet, because I still feel his touch.

"Psyche, look."

His hand shakes. I turn my head, blinking through the dizziness. My shoulder swims in and out of focus. I think I see what he's staring at, though. The blue color isn't advancing any more. A little past my collarbone, it seems to have stopped. But perhaps that's just how this poison works. Perhaps its color fades once it has done its job. I suppose by now it's working its way to my heart. I want to tell him not to hope too much. The eyes are tricksters, experts in false hope.

But the strangest thing…even as I stare at it, I see a pink flush blooming at the top of my collarbone, pushing back the blue. The pink is warm, healthy. I can feel it, a glow inside me.

What's happening?

Eros's eyes shift to my face, but he has no words either. Slowly, very slowly, the pink spreads: from my neck along the top of my chest; my collarbone; the ridge of my shoulder…

Can it be real?

"Are you doing this?" I say, and Eros shakes his head.

"I do not have that power."

The blue has receded down to my arm now, just a little above my elbow. But now the advancing pink slows, seems to hesitate. It is as though two forces have reached a standstill, a battle neither side can win.

"You can do it," Eros whispers.

"I'm not doing it," I say, but then, if I'm not doing it, who is? I can feel the glow of it, the surge struggling through my body, life trying to push through. Maybe I *am* doing this.

I close my eyes. The pain is back, worse than before. The numbness was shielding me from it but now it's like a thousand tiny stings, like picks of ice darting in and out of my flesh. Perhaps there's no point fighting it. What can I hope to win back, when a goddess herself wants me dead? If she doesn't kill me today, she'll kill me tomorrow. I open my eyes again, and for a moment the blue patch quivers and spreads, regaining ground. I grit my teeth and close my eyes again.

I am doing this, I think to myself.

I *will* do this.

"Fight, Psyche."

His voice sounds like a stranger's.

When I open my eyes again, the blue glow has faded further. And as I watch, it fades further still. It shrinks—slowly, painfully—until it's the size of a handprint, then just a thumbprint, a vivid blue circle, glowing and throbbing. At the center of the circle I see the mark of the scorpion, a small dark wound in the flesh. Around it, the blue glows brightly, as though all the poison has been concentrated in that one spot. I close my eyes; I'm bathed in sweat.

"Fight it," Eros murmurs.

I screw my eyes tight and push with whatever energy is left in me. But I can't force the poison out of me. I open my eyes.

"I can't get it out," I pant.

He grabs my hand, and puts his mouth to the wound again. And this time I feel it, the warmth of his mouth on me, and a dark thing, dense as lead, black as tar, whispering with evil as it leaves my body.

He spits onto the ground and wipes his mouth.

And when I look at my arm again…

There's a tiny puncture wound, barely visible against the skin, and my forearm is flushed a little pink. But that's the only sign of what just happened. Eros crouches over me. He cradles my arm, turns it this way and that, staring, wondering. Then he lays it back gently over my stomach. When I look into his eyes, they're searching mine for answers. Answers I don't have.

We sit and stare at each other. I feel the cold sweat drying on my bare skin.

"Psyche," he says. "What you just did—what your body did. That is no mortal gift."

I shake my head.

"I felt it," I tell him. "It was like a hand trying to close around my heart. And I felt something in my own body fight back." I don't tell him that at its worst, I thought I heard voices. That it seemed to me the poison itself was speaking, in a voice that said *kill her, kill the mortal, kill.*

"Psyche, did you hear me?" He's staring at me. "What you did," he says. "That is not something an ordinary mortal can do."

I wipe my face. I feel like he's accusing me of something.

"Well, maybe I'm not an ordinary mortal."

"You're far from ordinary. And now I think..." He's staring at me as though he's trying to make me understand. "Psyche, I think perhaps you are not fully mortal, either. I think you're part mortal. Part mortal, and part something else."

I close my eyes again. This is all too much. All these words. All this confusion. What just happened doesn't make sense, but his words don't make sense either. I suppose it's the shock, but tears are forming under my eyelids, and now they're sliding down my face. We lie in silence a little while. Slowly I let his words sink in, and the more I do, the more I have to admit it. What just happened was impossible.

I open my eyes and stare into his amber gaze.

"How can I be anything *but* mortal? I have no powers. No special gifts." I shake my head. "My parents were mortals."

He narrows his eyes, and sits back from me.

"Your leg—when Ajax trod on it, it healed overnight when it should have been broken. Your hair grew back in one night, when it should have stayed shorn. You did not go mad when you saw my face, as a mortal is supposed to. It is not about powers, Psyche, but your life force. It is stronger than an ordinary mortal's. Your body—it resists injury. It is not easily broken."

I stare at him.

I have been used to explaining things away. But the truth is, there have been occurrences before this one, just as strange, if not so miraculous. There are the ones he mentions: my hair, my quick-healing leg. The winter night on Mount Olympus: the harpies swore I would die of the cold, that they'd pluck my body from the icy ground, yet I lived through it. But there were other things too.

Every childhood scrape and scratch that disappeared overnight; every ailment the other children had, or that Father and Dimitra contracted but I escaped.

They said I was healthy. They said I was lucky. They said I had my mother's strong constitution.

But others in Sikyon said my mother was a witch.

That my mother brewed potions and cast spells.

That she was something for mortals to fear.

What if they were right?

She owned a blade of adamantine.

I screw my eyes tight, trying to make sense of it all.

"My mother died giving birth to me," I say. "My father saw it. The midwife saw it. She was mortal."

My father put the coins upon her eyes himself; he adorned her with her funeral wreath and led her procession to the tomb.

Didn't he?

Could he have lied?

I shake my head. Old Lydia was the woman who tended to my mother in her birthing-bed; Lydia was there the day my mother died. She was the one who chased Dimitra from the doorway; who comforted my sister at the sight of my mother's corpse. My mother *died*.

I cannot figure it out.

Eros's words go round in my mind. *Something more than mortal.*

"I don't understand. It doesn't make sense." I look at him. "I'm alive, Eros. Isn't that enough?"

He moves toward me, and takes my head in his hands.

"It is everything," he says.

But how long can such a reprieve last? I stare into his eyes, still wide and dazed, as though part of him even now still sees me dying.

"How did she find us?" I say. It's cold, now, in the treehouse. The white moonflowers have closed up, as though they have already seen too much. The golden glow of the place has dimmed. I pull at the Shroud around my neck. "I thought this was supposed to hide me."

Eros shakes his head.

"My mother has many spies in this realm to do her bidding, animal and human. Think, Psyche. Who did you see at the market today? Might there have been someone there who knew you?"

I shake my head, then stop.

No one at the market recognized *me*, but the stallholder recognized Ajax. I don't think he knew the full truth, but he knew enough, I suspect now, to see that I rode a horse of the gods.

And asked for a fugitive's cape.

I close my eyes again. Even if we are careful, terribly careful…can we really hope to make it to Atlantis? And if we do, what then?

"She will try it again," I say.

I feel Eros slide close to me. There is a long silence.

"I blame myself for endangering you, Psyche. Name me a place and I will take you there. I will leave you safe, and ride on alone. I will draw my mother's wrath onto myself."

I open my eyes again.

"You will *not*. You will not leave me behind, not now."

He smiles at that, just a little. And then he lets me rest. And then, when the night is thickest, he carries me to where Ajax stands waiting, and settles me on his back.

Forty-one

"It will be all right," he whispers in my hair, as he climbs up behind me. I don't know whether to believe him. But I'm choosing to.

"Remember, while my mother believes you dead, we have the advantage."

I shiver. *While my mother believes you dead.* Still, Eros is right. She thinks her work is done. She will not tell her followers to look for me now. It is to our advantage. But just in case, Eros holds the adamantine dagger in his hand, ready for any other creature that may come this way.

The enormity of what we're doing is not lost on me. Looking up at the pitch-black night only makes it clearer.

"They will never let you back into Olympus, while you are with me. Will they?"

He takes the reins and gives them a brisk shake. His voice is brisk too.

"So I will live in the mortal realm, as you do. We will make our home here."

I try to imagine that. To live alongside a god—a fallen god—among my own people.

"And how will we live?" I say. "I have my father's ring to sell, at least." I glance toward the saddlebags. "I suppose that may get us as far as Atlantis."

Eros laughs low behind me—the sound is the last thing I expected, but it warms me.

"I may be a weakened god, wife, but I am still a god. Have a little faith."

And I do. I am learning to live in a world of uncertainty, a world stranger, darker, and more miraculous than any I could have imagined. And I ride with a god by my side.

"You should sleep, Psyche," he says, as the sun starts to wake over the horizon line. "You have not rested at all tonight—nor for many days, I think."

"It's no use," I tell him. "My mind turns too fast." I would dearly like to rest, but sleep eludes me.

"If you wish to sleep, I can command it." From behind me, he brushes a hair back from my face.

I remember the first night I met him. I settle back into his broad chest. I stare around us at the dark plains, the blue glow of the sky over the forests.

"Bewitch me, then," I say, and I think I hear the smile in his voice as he speaks the word. *Skotos*: Darkness. The murmur of his voice is soft, like a blindfold made of silk.

And this time, sleep comes as a friend.

*

The villages rise up and fall away, stony outcroppings on shallow hills, wooden shanties in shadowed valleys. I doze and wake, and doze and wake, and whenever I wake I feel Eros's strong arms around me, girding me at the waist, holding me steady and safe. We don't talk much, but sometimes he sings, and when he does, he sings the music of the stars. I feel the blood in my body sing back to him, resonating to his pitch like a struck chime.

Two travelers, one an earthbound god, and one…What am I?

I thought I knew, but now I cannot say. I would like to think that in Atlantis, we may find some answers. It is my mother's homeland, and the home of the mysteries she has left me with.

We cross rivers and follow mountain passes, and look down at the world from a great height, at forests like green blankets or the wide sweep of ocean. Once we see a fleet of battleships in the distance and I can't help but wonder, *are they going to Atlantis too?*

With every village we pass, I think about the changed world we're traveling through, the one that is weakening him. We pass small shrines in his name that are bare of offerings; I wonder if even the icons sold in the markets here have been put away for lack of trade.

Mostly we camp in the forests, but sometimes a village is safer than bare, open plains. When we stop to ask for shelter, it's Eros who does the asking. Tonight he dismounts and leads us to the door of a little house on the outskirts of a village. There is a hay-barn, and a chicken pecking out front.

My husband knocks, and the door opens on a man of my father's age, but leather-skinned and whiskered. I hear Eros ask humbly for a night's lodging, and for some food for his wife. *Wife:* the word still shimmers in my ears.

I see the man's eyes take me in, and how his gaze narrows. He is wondering at such a beautiful horse, at my torn but once-elegant clothes. Why is it, he's wondering, that a couple such as these should be beggars?

"You are welcome here," the man says at last, though he sounds less than pleased. "Tie up the horse, and you may eat at my table."

I walk inside their small home while Eros attends to Ajax. I feel the gap of cold air behind me where he stood. How quickly my body has grown used to his; without it, there's an absence.

The man's wife greets me with the same wary courtesy.

"Sit, please." The house is small but clean, one large room where this couple must eat, sleep, work, and rest.

"You will eat with us."

In Sikyon mostly the men and women eat separately, but here there is only one room, one table. Eros enters noiselessly through the front door, the cool night air flowing from the folds of his cloak, and the woman of the house looks up, alarmed. The sight of him does not seem to reassure her much, but her husband gives her a small nod.

"There was a festival in our village today," he says. "A goat was sacrificed. So you will eat meat with us tonight. Your visit is well-timed."

It is only a small bit of meat, but they offer it to us first, along with a dish of emmer wheat and some bread.

"You are gracious," Eros says. He eats carefully, from beneath his hood. He takes only a small amount. Human food is neither here nor there for him, but it is important not to offend our hosts, nor to draw too much attention. But tonight, that is not enough.

"Traveler," our host says. "Why do you wear your cloak, still? It is customary, here, to show one's face to one's hosts."

Eros lifts his glass, takes a sip of the wine they have poured. He answers smoothly, with just the briefest hesitation.

"My family, sir, has been involved in a great feud. As a result, there are those from my hometown that would do me harm. I do not wish for others to become involved in our troubled tale. And so I keep my face hidden."

The woman sits back in alarm.

"I assure you," Eros continues, "no one will come knocking for me here. No one who wishes me harm knows where I am. Let us keep it that way."

The man nods slowly, but I see the glance that passes between him and his wife.

"Whither do you travel?" the wife says finally, addressing her question to me this time. Her voice is strained, her hand moves nervously as she speaks, and I feel guilty, witnessing this discomfort at our presence. We should have tried another house.

"To Atlantis," I say, and see her expression change. Eros's boot nudges mine beneath the table.

The husband and wife share another glance, and this one piques my curiosity. What have they heard? Something they're not telling us?

"You are not the first," the man says eventually, "to come

this way, seeking shelter on the road to Atlantis."

"Indeed?" Eros says.

"It's true," the wife chimes in, her curiosity seeming to trump her suspicion for a moment. "There were two others, back when the summer was young. *Ostraka,*" she adds, in confidential tones. "A father and a daughter."

I stare.

A father and a daughter.

But that could be anyone. There may be many such, on the roads between here and Atlantis. This strange feeling in my chest is nothing more than my wishful heart.

And yet…

Atlantis is not only my mother's ancestral home, it is the land where my father fought. He was a leader of troops there; he helped the Atlanteans win their war and won himself some acclaim on the battlefield. They said even the king had shown him some favor.

It would be a logical place, would it not, to try his welcome?

I swallow.

"What did they look like?" I say. "The father and daughter."

Eros's hood turns toward me. I feel him wanting to caution me. The eagerness in my voice must be too sharp to miss.

"The girl was young, like you, miss," the woman says. "But dark of hair. The man had an old soldier's build, and walked with a limp. Grey, but with a little red left in his beard."

I stifle the gasp in my throat, but if I fool our hosts, I don't fool Eros. He understands. He knows.

My family. Alive.

"Excuse me," I stand from the table, so abruptly that I almost overturn the meager meal. "I—I am very tired. Is there a place I might lie down?"

Another glance passes between our hosts, and the woman glances down at my barely touched plate with some resentment.

"I will show you." She stands, and Eros stands too, and bows deeply.

"Good hosts, I will accompany my wife. I fear she is feeling faint after our journey. We are most grateful for your kindness. We will leave at first light, once she is rested—I will bid you our thanks now; we will be gone before you wake."

"Very well," the husband says, but his eyes have narrowed again at such abruptness. We file out after the wife, who takes us to the barn. It is dry in here, warm enough and sweet with hay.

"Rest well," she says, but with some doubt in her voice, and casts a last, lingering look at Eros's cloaked face. When she has gone he lowers the hood. I feel his stare, and he takes my chin in his hand then, gently moving my gaze to his.

"You believe it is your father and sister?"

I nod. *Early in the summer*, the woman said. It is autumn now.

"My father had ties to Atlantis," I explain. "It would be a logical place for an outcast to try."

Eros hesitates, looking at me.

"Psyche…even if it was them, even if they are alive: you remember, don't you, what the oracle said?"

His words bring me unpleasantly back to earth. I remember all too well. She said that though they lived, I would not see them again in this life.

And then I start; a tremor goes through me.

That's not what she said.

She said I would not see them again *as a mortal.*

As a mortal. What if she meant…

"Damn the woman for talking in riddles!" I burst out. "Eros"—I turn to him—"you said, before, remember? You said I was no ordinary mortal. That I was 'something more than mortal.'"

What if the oracle wasn't talking about death? What if she

meant a different sort of transition; if my days *as a mortal* are now behind me?

The thought sends shivers through me. Could I really be such a creature as Eros has described? It seems likelier that this is some wishful fantasy.

And yet.

And yet.

Eros looks at me gravely. He has understood.

"I take your meaning," he says. "And it's true: trickery is the nature of an oracle's speech. But…we cannot know, Psyche."

He gestures toward the hay, and uses some small power of his to transform it into a bed of feathers. These little tricks cost him nothing. Even in his weakened state he can perform them without strain.

"Come. Lie down. If what she has said is true, there may be cause for rejoicing, but you must rest either way."

He sounds almost stern. There's something he's not saying. I look into his eyes—even now, that shock of being able to see him, the whole of him, uncovered, sends a bolt through me—but he turns away.

"What is it?" I say. "You do not trust our hosts? They have no reason to lie."

I wonder for a moment if it could be jealousy. Does he want me all to himself? Does he not *want* me to find my family?

Eros says nothing, just removes his cloak and takes the fastening from his robe. It falls from his body and despite myself, I flush. Is he trying to distract me? He spreads his *chiton* out over the feathers, until it stretches wide enough to accommodate the two of us.

"It's not that," he says.

"Then what?"

He sighs, and meets my gaze.

"I fear for you, Psyche," he says. "I fear for your hope; I see it in your eyes. Even if you are reunited…your family has abandoned you once before. Who is to say they won't do so again? Perhaps they will not welcome your return in the way you expect."

I feel as though I've been slapped. He knows where my most vulnerable places are. He knows it in my body, and he knows it in my soul. It hurts, to be so transparent to someone else. I can't hide my hopes, any more than I can hide my desire. I lie down, and pull my own *chiton* over us as a cover.

"Hope is no bad thing," I say.

He sighs, settles a warm hand on my hip.

"It's late in the night to argue." He pulls me in close to him. "Psyche..." His hand caresses the length of my spine, and the touch makes me shiver, that heady rush that blocks out thought. Tonight, though, my thoughts are persistent. But then he whispers my name again—my god-husband, my demon lover—and this time I yield to it. I forget the future, and the past. I let the world shrink until it's just the two of us, and nothing more.

*

A little while later I find myself awake. I hover for a moment at the threshold of consciousness, my mind still soft with dreaming, and at first, I cannot recall where I am. But there are gaps in the thatch roof above us, where starlight shivers through the crannies, giving just enough grey light to make out the outlines of things, and remember. And then a noise comes, and I realize I did not wake by accident.

I hold my breath, noiselessly turning my head toward the door. Beside me, Eros lies enveloped in the sheet as if it were a shroud. By the door, something moves again.

Some*one*. The husband—our host. I see the shape of him as he takes another step toward the bed. He is only a few paces from us now. The sheet has pooled below my breasts; I dare not move it to cover myself.

Is that what he is here for? Some voyeurism?

I do not think so. My heart palpitates furiously. I remind myself my husband is a god; that nothing short of the adamantine dagger he keeps under his pillow could slit his throat. *But any sharp blade could still slit mine.*

A small light flares, and I hover my eyelids low to feign sleep. The man holds the oil lamp high over his head, and takes a final silent step to the bed. But it's not me he's looking at: his eyes are on the shrouded figure beside me. His hand reaches out and closes over a fold of the fabric, ready to pull it back, and uncover my husband's face.

I shake off the paralysis.

"No!" I shout, but Eros's hand has already darted out from under the sheet, clenching around the man's throat with a movement so sudden I gasp. Our host calls out in horror and drops his oil lamp to the floor, wheezing for air.

I gather the sheet around me as I leap from the bed. Eros stands tall, holding the man aloft; the man's bare feet pedal the empty air, looking for purchase. His eyes are closed, screwed up as he fights for breath.

At least there's that.

And then his wife bursts into the room—roused, presumably, by all the shouting.

"Close your eyes!" I scream. "Woman, look away!"

I see the flash of her terrified gaze, but something in my voice must get through. She shuts her eyes, though she's trembling.

"What witchcraft is this?" she whimpers.

Then Eros tosses the man toward the floor, where he lies for a moment, panting and wheezing. And in that instant Eros has pulled his cloak from where it lies on the ground, and covered himself.

"You are safe now," he says, his voice low with spent anger, and I realize then that the fury I saw was not really about our host or his insolence. It was about having to live like this;

about the curse he carries with him, and having to guard against it, night and day. About having to live a concealed life.

The man climbs slowly to his feet, staring in the half-dark. The woman's closed eyelids tremble.

"Michalis?" she whispers. "Are you all right?"

"You can open your eyes," I say. "You will find your husband much as he was." *Just a little shaken up,* I add silently, which is no more than he deserves.

"Sir, I—we meant no harm." The man speaks hoarsely. "I…my wife made me come in here. You would not show your face, and she feared we had a murderer sleeping among us, or a monster. I tried to disabuse her of her foolishness, sir…"

He rattles on, but I am somewhat relieved. Not spies of Aphrodite's, then—just human nosiness and fear.

"Do not blame your wife for your own actions," Eros says. "And be thankful you did not see what is under this hood. We mean you no harm, but will take our leave of you now. You may return to your beds."

But the two seem frozen to the floor.

"I told you," Eros says, "I mean you no harm. Whatever pain I caused you, believe me, it was to your benefit, rather than achieve what you intended."

They are unconvinced, still, but nervousness has got the better of them, and the wife backs toward the door.

"We'll go, then, and ask no questions. Whoever you may be, sir, it's nothing to us."

"Wait!"

The word bursts from me suddenly, as unexpected to me as it is to any one of them. Now is the time for us to leave quietly—and any other night, I would. But tonight…call it courage or foolishness. Call it an impulsive streak I thought I'd buried, but suddenly I want justice. Why should my lover hide in the shadows? Why *should* he be thought a murderer and a fugitive? Why should he be denied his name as well as his power?

"There is a reason why my husband hid from you," I say. "But it is not the reason you think."

Beneath his hood I feel Eros look my way; I can sense his surprise, his wariness, but it seems I've shocked him into silence.

I look our hosts in the eye.

"He is no criminal," I say. "He is a god. That is why he cloaks himself like this from you."

At that, their eyes truly boggle. What a wild claim they must think this! They stare, jaws agape, and for a moment I wonder if one will laugh. But the moment passes.

"Did you say, miss..."

"Mortals may not look upon his face, for to do so drives them to madness. To spare you such a fate, he shields himself when he walks among mortal folk."

"Psyche..." Eros murmurs, but it's too late now.

"Turn around," I beg him. "Show them your wings."

He hesitates. Then finally he turns and loosens the robe from his shoulders, spreading two majestic wings. The sable-black expanse of them seems almost to fill the room, and his skin radiates light in this dim place, as if from somewhere in the core of him. Our two hosts stare, mouths agape. The room is silent as a stone. Then the wings retract, and he pulls the cloak back across them. When my husband turns, his face is veiled again.

The man drops to his knees, and pulls his wife down beside him.

"What god are you, Great One?"

"He is the lord Eros," I say. "Son of Aphrodite, and of Ares the Destroyer."

"Lord Eros," our host murmurs. "We have insulted you. Yet you have been merciful."

I sense Eros's discomfort.

"Rise, both of you, rise," he says. All of this has embarrassed him, I think, but it does not embarrass me. Let them see him for who he is. He is a true god, truer than those parasites on Mount Olympus who do nothing for their followers except drink our world dry. And yet his following has been stolen from him, his power shrunken while Aphrodite's power grows.

Well, followings can be rebuilt.

I watch the couple as they shuffle to their feet.

"What you say is true. This god *is* merciful: for the benefit of mortals he hides his glory, though it would please him more to walk in the light as you do." I clear my throat; I don't dare look at Eros. I don't know that he will approve of what I'm doing.

"If you haven't heard the rumor, no doubt you will soon: that Aphrodite, his divine mother, no longer wishes our people to worship him. But let me ask you this—has Aphrodite ever walked among you? Does she break bread with her followers? Does she visit them and share their table? Aphrodite," I continue, "believes mortals are here only to serve her, and have no value of their own. That is how most of your gods think. They do not trouble themselves to descend from Olympus to know you. But my husband is different. He does not disdain the mortal race. Remember this, when you next visit your temples. Tell your friends that the god Eros walks among you, and consider who is deserving of your prayers."

Their faces are ashen by now. I suspect they have heard of Aphrodite's demands already. They're wondering exactly how hard she'll punish them if they leave offerings at a temple that's forbidden.

"Your acts need not be public for all to see," I say. "Grand offerings at the temple are just one form of prayer. Even Aphrodite cannot see the silent offerings made in the heart. These too count."

The silence seems to pulse while I wait for someone else to move or speak. Though all I see of Eros is his dark hood, I know every motion of his now, and I know that beneath the hood he's staring at me. Surprised? Amused?

Concerned?

"We shall do so," the woman says finally, and bows. Then she hesitates, and looks at me.

"And will you tell us your name, goddess, so we may do the same for you?"

Now I'm the speechless one.

"Oh." I clear my throat. "No, I…"

"She is Psyche, my wife and consort," Eros speaks. "Whatever you offer in my name, you may offer to us both."

As one, the grey-haired couple bow, and I'm the one left staring.

*

Outside, as I'm untying Ajax from the post, I see Eros press his hand against the barn wall. It's a deliberate gesture, the kind a man might make to test the stone's warmth. I glance curiously at him, then go to the barn wall and peer inside a crack. Now where before it housed only bales of hay, it is full of grain, and barrels of wine.

"You *are* a merciful god," I say, and take his hand in mine.

He gives me one of his impenetrable looks, and lifts me high onto Ajax's back. Then he swings himself up behind me and grips the reins. Ajax breaks into a trot, then a canter, and soon a gallop. Behind me, Eros's warm body barely shifts with the motion. I lean against him, then feel his hand brush my jaw; he runs a finger slowly down my neck.

"I am merciful," he says. "To those who deserve it. And for those who injure what I most treasure: Psyche, you will learn, I am something else altogether."

Ajax's sleek black mane thrusts ahead. The village is far behind us.

We gallop through the last, soft hours of the night, through fields and woods, until the sea is in view at last.

And we wait on the clifftop, Eros and Ajax and I. We watch the light creep pink across the horizon. We smell dawn on the air.

There, out over the water, our sun is rising.

Dear Readers,

I so hope you enjoyed *The Ruin of Eros*! I loved writing it. I have been a fan of the Greek myths ever since my dad came home with a musty ten-volume "Children's Encyclopedia" from my grandmother's house; it dated from around the 1940s, I think, and to me it felt quite antique! Each volume had sections on science, nature, geography and history, but I happily skipped through all these to find the segments on Greek mythology. I loved those stories—the big, sweeping emotions and high drama, the sense of Fate at work and all the human ingenuity that went into trying to escape said Fate (almost always unsuccessfully). I loved the huge cast of characters, and the quirky explanations these myths provided for the natural world (who knew that the narcissus flower was named after someone who fell in love with his own reflection!).

Reading those stories from a dusty old tome, the world of the Ancient Greeks felt impossibly far away and distant to me. But now, many years later, these "ancient" people somehow don't feel quite so foreign, or so distant in time. So many of our fears, our joys, our human mistakes, are still so similar. It's not surprising that the myth of Eros and Psyche bears a lot of resemblance to another story that many of us grew up with: *Beauty and the Beast*. The first written record of the story of Eros and Psyche comes from a 2nd-century book, Apuleius's *Metamorphoses*, which was "rediscovered" during the Renaissance and became very popular, so there's every reason to imagine that the myth of Eros and Psyche was quite familiar to readers in 1740, by the time the first written version of *Beauty and the Beast* was published.

Probably, both *Eros and Psyche* and *Beauty and the Beast* both come from even older myths, ones that are now forgotten in our modern culture. Myth scholars (what a great job!) say that the "animal bridegroom" myth is found across many cultures—usually the story of a woman (though sometimes a man) encountering a non-human or monstrous groom (or bride), whose true form is revealed later, often through love or a breaking of enchantment. Isn't that fascinating? You have to wonder how so many cultures find themselves exploring the same sort of myth across time and space! Some people would say the Beauty and the Beast story is about our shared hope for transformation and redemption—that we all want to know that our inner beauty will be recognized, even though we might be misunderstood at first (or need to learn some lessons before our best selves can truly shine). Some people say the "beast" represents a more primal version of ourselves, and the myths about the paradox of being drawn to this freer, more animal version of ourselves, and at the same time wanting to "tame" it. Other scholars say the popularity of these myths is connected to the role marriage historically played for women (or, throughout much of history, young girls): often an arranged marriage to a near-stranger, an event that might have inspired many fears, anxieties, and uncertainties.

For whatever reason, I can only say that the myth of Eros and Psyche has always fascinated me, and I loved having the opportunity to revisit it and make it my own! If you know the original myth, you'll probably notice that there are big differences here. The plot goes in a lot of directions that are my own invention, for one thing. For another, in traditional "Beauty and the Beast" tales, the young woman tends to play quite a passive role, but I really enjoyed imagining a somewhat feistier Psyche for my own story, one who is not afraid to speak up for herself. She is imperfect, too—she may judge harshly, or jump to conclusions, or hold grudges. But hey!—it's an imperfect world, and I like imperfect heroes. I hope you do, too. Another thing I always liked about the original Eros and Psyche myth was how Psyche ends up going on a quest to win her lover back, even though in the Greek myths, it's usually only men—like Hercules, or Theseus—who go on quests. Again, the quest story here is pretty different from the original, but having a courageous, adventurous female hero was definitely important to me.

If you're wondering how Eros and Psyche's relationship continues, or what's going to happen with Eros's angry brothers, what the deal is with the adamantine blade, or whether Psyche's family really made it out alive (so many questions!)… I hope you'll pick up the next book in the trilogy, *The Bride of Atlantis*. I loved continuing this story, and I'm crossing my fingers that you'll want to keep being part of the journey!

I'm excited, and a little bit nervous, to share this story with the world. I really hope you like it, and I would love to hear what you think! Please feel free to reach out—it's a wonderful thing to hear from readers—and if you have the time, it would mean the world if you were able to post a review on Amazon or Goodreads. I'm sure as an avid reader you'll know how much power a review has over the choices we make over what to pick up next! I so hope that other readers out there will get a chance to meet Psyche and hear her story—especially since I have two more in the trilogy still to come!

Again, thank you: I really appreciate the time you have given to reading this book—I know you have a *lot* to choose from—and I want to make sure you know how grateful I am!

Maya Gryffin

Acknowledgments

A lot of work goes into indie publishing, and although I pay amazing professionals for most of the help I need, I also rely on some incredible people who are very generous with their free time to help me iron out some wrinkles, test-drive the first reads, and give my work some of that early love and support it needs to grow in a crowded marketplace with millions of other books competing for a little bit of limelight. Most of all, this help comes from a wonderful group of friends (you know who you are and *thank you*!), but also some dedicated and brilliant readers I've found out there on advance reader programs. (If you'd like to join my ARC team, please reach out and let me know!)

Maya Gryffin is actually a pen name: I picked it to honor my grandmothers, May (O'Neill) and (Margaret) Griffin. I also loved that Maya is a Greek (and Roman) goddess, and the gryffins are mythological beasts also found in the ancient myths (they pulled Apollo's chariot, among other things!). So it felt very fitting in the mythological sense. Honoring family also felt very fitting: although my grandparents are no longer around, I have a wonderful tribe of aunts, uncles and cousins who have also been incredibly supportive on my writing journey, and I'm so grateful to them for cheering me on and celebrating my successes like they were their own (oh, and buying my books!). My mum and dad, and stepdads Manuel Dudli Bertran and Frank Lowe, are the heart of all that support and love. The fact that I have this Dream Job of being able to write for a living is thanks to my parents, without whose support, encouragement, and wild faith, none of this would ever be happening. Finally, this book is dedicated to my husband, Pavol, who may not be a god, but is surely as divine as mortals get.

Thanks to you all, from the bottom of my heart!

Printed in the USA
CPSIA information can be obtained
at www.ICGtesting.com
CBHW022250271124
18131CB00010B/44